CUERNAVACA

A NOVEL

RICHARD PERHACS

Copyright 2014 by Richard W. Perhacs
Published in the United States of America
by Juridico Press

Designed by Mallory Rock.

Cuernavaca

Library of Congress Control Number: 201392203
ISBN-13: 978-1493785261
ISBN-10: 1493785265

For Fran, to whom I owe everything...

A WORD ABOUT XOCHICALCO...

Throughout, the reader will encounter the word Xochicalco, the name of a prominent archaeological site in southwestern Mexico, located near the modern city of Cuernavaca. Once a vibrant crossroads where indigenous peoples met to conduct commerce and affairs of state, Xochicalco was a city which sat astride major Mesoamerican trade routes. Its ruins now beautifully restored by the Mexican government, the city was home to more than 20,000 inhabitants, and flourished between 700 and 900 AD. The entirety of United States history spans barely fifty years more than the period of Xochicalco's dominance. Physical evidence suggests that much of the site was destroyed suddenly, in a single, great cataclysmic event. No one knows how, or why.

The origin of the name is Nahuatl, the language of the Aztecs, and the most dominant of Mexico's indigenous languages. Lest the reader be frustrated with the sometimes odd pronunciations common to Nahuatl, it's pronounced "so-she-kal-ko."

RP

PRIMERA PARTE

CHAPTER ONE

By 11:40 a.m. Scott Flores had swallowed his third aspirin of the morning, washing it down with the club soda he kept in his office mini-fridge for mornings after. Like opposing pieces on a chessboard, stacks of papers waiting for grades faced him across a cold metal desk. He'd have to think before he could deal with them, something out of the question in Scott's present condition. He pushed them back, closed his eyes, and lowered his forehead to the desk.

Jesus. You can't drink like you're twenty years old anymore.

Sitting up after a moment, Scott rubbed his face and turned toward the small faculty office window overlooking the quad at the State University of New York at Albany. The slate gray late November morning outside suited his mood just fine. He opened the window a crack, letting the cold air flow over him. It felt good, the only thing that had so far that day.

Another day in paradise.

Settling back into his chair, his head throbbing and his mind a blank, Scott stared at the window. Although he wanted to go home, crawl under a blanket, and go

1

back to sleep, he forced himself to pick up the phone and dial.

"I'm not sure about today."

Struggling to get the words into the cold handset, his halting voice barely enough to connect with the person on the other end, it had taken everything he had to make the call. He wanted it to end right there, with "sure, no problem, click." Then home. Instead, Jerry Dwyer answered.

"Up too late again?"

Scott understood the code, and he'd anticipated the lack of sympathy.

"You know better," said the voice on the other end. "Give me a half hour. I've got something you need to see."

Jerry's raspy voice was suddenly its own unique source of discomfort as it continued its intrusion of Scott's difficult morning.

"I just got another email from Arturo. He wants me to come to Xochicalco this summer."

I don't care about Xochicalco. We can talk about Xochicalco tomorrow. The hell with Xochicalco.

Scott struggled to clear his head, managing enough focus to toss a remark back. "You won't give up a summer off."

"This is a seriously good opportunity, kind that can get you published someplace meaningful," Jerry replied.

"You don't need another publication at your age," Scott said before covering the phone and turning toward the wastebasket next to his desk, just in case.

In a year, Jerry would turn down more chances to make a name for himself than Scott would see in ten as an assistant professor of anthropology. Jerry's connections in

2

Central America landed him dozens of offers each year to do significant field work, and he carefully cherry picked them when sufficiently motivated, which wasn't very often. Jerry enjoyed summers at his Jersey beach house, and, at 68 with a long, distinguished career behind him, he'd earned them. He had nothing to prove.

"We'll talk about that. See you in a half hour," Jerry said before Scott heard the click signaling Jerry had decided the call was over.

Son of a bitch. He never gave me a chance.

Headed to a lunch meeting he knew wouldn't involve him eating anything, Scott's head cleared just enough to consider that Jerry didn't get excited often. He'd have to find out over Jello and black coffee what made this different.

With a secure position and a relaxed schedule allowing a full life away from the classroom, Scott loved the academy. The inheritance and sizable trust fund his father had left meant the low pay of an assistant professor didn't matter. His father had given him more than money. Quite by accident, he'd also left him his life's work.

Young Scott Flores had an intellectual spark that set him apart. Curious about everything, when his father sponsored a grant so the anthropology department at his dad's alma mater could conduct an archaeological project in Mexico, it didn't surprise anyone when Scott asked to spend the summer after his college freshman year tagging along. The youthful adventure ended up setting his life's course.

Scott loved his summer sifting through the dirt of the Mexican State of Morelos — the meticulous discipline of the team he worked with, the deep sense of history that pervaded the work, the sheer beauty of the place. He also learned that even otherwise boring anthropologists and archaeologists can be quite interesting after several shots of mescal. Returning from Mexico, to his father's temporary dismay, Scott changed his major from finance to anthropology and never looked back.

Seven years and an Ivy League doctorate later, he landed a position in the anthropology department at the State University of New York at Albany, an institution that bragged on its website about being home to the "largest collection of Mesoamericanists north of Mexico." His father's generous donation to the university didn't hurt his application, and neither did Scott's newly minted Harvard Ph.D. SUNY Albany's Institute of Mesoamerican Studies was the place to be, and Scott settled into the quiet life of an academic.

A fixture at the university, Jerry Dwyer had taken an instant liking to the young assistant professor. Despite their age difference, and with Jerry nearing the end of a career, and Scott just beginning his, the sometimes gruff Dwyer had become Scott's mentor and closest friend.

Bundled against the early winter wind biting into his face, Scott's regret over the prior night's extra glasses of scotch grew with each difficult step he took as he trudged through the cold toward Dwyer and the university dining hall. As he entered, his head felt like he'd walked through the doorway without noticing the door was closed. Scott found Jerry sitting in a far corner of the hall, face buried in the New York Times.

God, it smells like roast beef and mashed potatoes in here.

Scott forced himself forward toward Jerry's table. "Why do you read that rag, Jer? It lost its integrity years ago," Scott muttered before settling into a hard, plastic chair, still wearing his coat. His stomach knotted, and still

4

shivering, he sat with his hands jammed into its pockets. His nose was running.

Scott and Jerry had an easy, tension-free relationship that allowed for disagreement on many things, including, notably, politics, which they often discussed. Jerry was a liberal; Scott a conservative. Yin and yang, they had chemistry, and shared genuine affection. The politics didn't matter, and they loved to spar.

"Bullshit," Jerry replied, without looking up, his lips curling into the slightest smile, invisible behind the newspaper. "I suppose you think I ought to be reading the Wall Street Journal or the Washington Times."

"Better," Scott managed in a barely audible voice, a grin struggling to cross his face.

Jerry's brow furrowed as he looked up from the paper and took the full measure of Scott's distressed appearance.

"You trying to make me feel as lousy as you look?"

Jerry's look spoke of something deeper than a clever retort, and, for a moment, Scott thought he saw worry in the older man's eyes.

"Truce?" Scott asked.

"Junior, put your white flag and your barf bag away and take a look at this," he said, moving the newspaper aside and handing Scott a sheet of paper drawn from his shirt pocket. "By the way, you look like hell. Take your coat off. You're embarrassing me. And wipe your face."

From Arturo Lopez, an anthropologist with the Mexican government's antiquities department, the INAH, the copy of an email Jerry handed Scott described a layer of ruin at a place called Xochicalco, near Cuernavaca, Mexico. Xochicalco had been excavated and restored years ago, and no one expected to find much new there,

5

yet Arturo thought the recent discovery extraordinary. Rather than deteriorating gradually over a thousand years, it looked as if the newly discovered pyramidal structure had collapsed very suddenly, perhaps in a cataclysmic event. In the message Arturo speculated it may have been an earthquake, or a military event, and he supposed it had the potential of producing a host of artifacts of great value. A serious player in the field of anthropological research in Mexico, Arturo's opinions mattered, and Scott knew Jerry thought the world of him. The message went on to ask Jerry to join him in Mexico after school let out in May, but the tone was curiously pleading.

"What does he mean 'I need you here more than I can say'?" Scott asked, his mind suddenly focused. "You guys got something going? That's sort of an odd way to put it, don't you think?"

"Stop it. And that's exactly what I thought," Jerry said. "It doesn't sound like him. Arturo's a confident guy, very professional. I can see where he'd like having me around on the dig, but..."

"You're going to take him up on it?" Scott interrupted, handing the email back to Jerry.

Jerry looked at the paper for a moment, then at Scott.

"Actually, I thought this would be something you might want to do with me." When Scott didn't react for a few moments, he added, "I could make that happen."

You don't know what you're asking.

"I'd love to go, but it's a whole summer." He thought of his wife. "I can't leave Lisa here while I go adventuring."

He struggled with his response, realizing that using his wife as an excuse for not jumping at Jerry's offer sounded unconvincing. Jerry's expression confirmed that

6

was exactly how it sounded. Despite their close relationship, Scott had never shared with him the few, but real, problems that existed in his marriage.

Scott and Lisa adored each other, and angry words seldom passed between them. When they did, they always involved Scott's drinking. Scott surely wouldn't admit to being an alcoholic, but he damn well enjoyed drinking, if not the day after. Never belligerent, he rarely lost control, and that enabled him to deny that the issue existed. He could be quite charming with a few drinks in him, but he did it a lot, and it troubled her.

Scott had inherited the problem from his father, and felt little investment in it when he thought about it at all. His father's drinking had led to arguments, separation, and eventually divorce. Scott blocked all of that out, refusing to see any pattern that might be of concern to him.

The couple also shared heartache. Desperate to have a family, despite the best medical intervention Scott's considerable money could buy, the young couple couldn't conceive. The problem rested with Lisa, they'd learned, and the pain it caused her broke Scott's heart. When the disappointment became too much for them to bear, as it had lately, Scott's helplessness often led him to commiserate with his old friend Jack Daniels. He couldn't imagine leaving her now to go adventuring in Mexico for three months.

"Come on, Scott," Jerry said with a scowl. "She married an anthropology professor, for God's sake, so what the hell does she expect you to do? This is your work. You want to be an assistant professor for the rest of your life or do you want to make something of yourself? You haven't done decent field work since graduate school, and it's past time to publish. Please don't tell me she doesn't understand."

Scott wouldn't share Lisa's personal struggle with anyone, not even his best friend, and after an awkward silence, Jerry gave Scott a reprieve.

"Besides, this summer will be a particularly interesting time to be in Mexico, especially for a politically minded guy like you."

Scott had no idea why the summer would be interesting in Mexico, and, when his expression registered as much, Jerry rolled his eyes and said, "You really need to get out more. Haven't you read anything about RENO?"

Scott knew all the nuances of politics in the United States, but little about events in Mexico.

"RENO? What's RENO?" Scott replied.

"Good lord." Jerry buried his face in his hands, rubbed his eyes, then looked at Scott with a pained expression. "Not what. *Who*. Rodrigo Ernesto Neron Oro. R-E-N-O. The man with many names. It's what the media calls him. Pretty sexy name for a politician, don't you think? Maybe we ought to use acronyms for our politicians. Spice things up a bit, wouldn't it now? I can think of some funny ones," Jerry said, laughing at his own joke, as he often did.

"Oro is going to be the presidential candidate of the leftist coalition that's making a big run at displacing the conservative PAN party in the July presidential election. Oro is really hard left, thinks the Castro brothers are great guys, and worshiped Hugo Chavez, bless his soul. He even borrows Chavez' lines and promotes 'Mexico for the Mexicans' and all that. The election is going to be a fight to the death, hell, maybe literally. You *did* know there was an election down there this summer, didn't you?"

Actually, Scott knew about the election, but very little else about the political situation in Mexico, something he'd never admit to Jerry.

"Of course I did Jer. Give me a little credit."

"Well, if you've never been in Mexico when a full blown national political campaign is going on, it's worth seeing. They take their politics very seriously. It's incredibly entertaining, and, in this particular case, it just might mean something besides settling the question of which crooks get to steal for the next six years. At least promise me that you'll talk to Lis about Xochicalco. She may surprise you. She's more interested in your career than you give her credit for."

She probably is, but I'm not leaving her. Not now.

Chapter Two

Scott knew he was in trouble as soon as he walked through the door of the condo. Neither of them could hide feelings very well, and they rarely tried. Their relationship was close cut, and honest. He hoped to avoid what he knew he almost certainly couldn't.

"Hi babe. Your day go okay?" he asked, trying to sound cheerful as he dropped his coat on a chair.

"It was alright," she said.

Her abrupt and unwelcoming response confirmed to Scott that there would be an unpleasant exchange. He just wanted to get it over with and do his penance, as he had many times before, hating the stress he knew came next.

They rarely argued with raised voices, instead going after each other with controlled, sharp edged honesty, usually delivered in measured amounts, calculated to have the desired corrective effect, but not much more. There was never anything gratuitous about it. It had intensity and could hurt, as truth sometimes does, but it had its boundaries. Lately, coming Scott's way, it was almost always justified.

"How could you work this morning? After last night, I don't see how. You had to be worthless."

Scott considered trying to downplay the extent of the previous night's drinking, but quickly abandoned the thought, instead choosing admission, and contrition.

"I overdid it last night. I know. Made for a tough day, but I got through it."

"You don't get paid to get through it. Don't you think your students can tell something's not right? And it's not fair to put me through this, Scott. If we ever have this baby he'll need a dad who's serious. I need a husband who's serious. You're not."

"Not serious? What does that mean?" Scott asked, trying half-heartedly to rally a defense.

"It means that you're acting like you're not responsible for anything but yourself. And you're not taking very good care of that. You act like you're still in college. I need to know I can count on you, Scott. I'm not sure I can."

"I'm sorry Lis. I don't want you thinking that. I don't."

"Scotty, how many times have you told me that now? How many times do we have to talk about this?"

Scott didn't answer. He only stood, looking pathetic, unsteady and vulnerable.

The tension drained away and when Lisa saw her husband's surrender, she took him into her arms. Their angry talk always ended this way.

"Baby, you're just so difficult sometimes. Damn you." She pounded on his back with her hands. "If I didn't love you so much..."

"You'd what?" he asked when her voice trailed off.

"If I didn't love you so much, I'd be so damned unhappy.

***

The test results, always disappointing, normally came during a phone call. Lisa had grown accustomed to the conversation. She should be patient, they told her, not anxious. It can take years for any of the procedures to work, and she and Scott were fortunate to be able to afford to keep trying. No guarantees, they said, only a chance.

Patience and money had accomplished nothing, and Scott and Lisa had reached the end of the long list of options. They'd started with the fertility medications, one after another causing Lisa to become so ill she actually joked about being in worse shape than her husband after one of his nights out. When Dr. Reilly thought minor surgery might improve their chances of conceiving, Lisa didn't hesitate. For the last six months they'd struggled unsuccessfully with in vitro, their last real chance. The talk had turned to adoption, but they refused to stop trying.

The caller from Dr. Reilly's office, this time, asked her to make an appointment as soon as possible. When Lisa asked why, the nurse told her she couldn't discuss it on the phone. Lisa would have to speak to the doctor.

She'd been waiting in the examination room for over 15 minutes, occupying herself with the wall charts depicting various parts of the female anatomy, and grateful to be sitting in a normal chair and not the examination unit that robbed patients of their dignity. When Dr. Reilly entered carrying a thin manila folder, she managed a weak, worried smile.

"How are you feeling, Lisa?" he asked as he laid the file on the exam room table, his expression telling her nothing. "Notice anything different the last week or so?"

Lisa searched his face for some sign of the point of his question.

"Different? No. Nothing I've noticed."

"Well, you'd best get used to some changes," he said, as his smile gave away the precious words he was about to share. "You're pregnant."

Dr. Reilly's words stunned her.

"You're sure?" she asked, her voice starting to break, not believing what she'd heard.

"Positive," he replied. "After all you've been through, I didn't think a phone call was the right way. I wanted to tell you in person. You and Scott deserve this as much as anyone could. Congratulations."

In an instant, Lisa's world transformed. She'd struggled so long for this, against nature and long odds and her own unrelenting biology. Suddenly triumphant, she wore a smile as wide as her face could hold.

Chapter Three

Lisa planned the evening in great detail, running through the conversation, what she'd say, how she'd act, what she'd wear. All that remained was a gift, something she normally needed little help with. Buying things for her husband had never been difficult, but this was different. Out of ideas, an afternoon at the mall didn't help any more than a quick check on the Internet had.

Inspiration came in the form of the cover photo on *The Aztecs, Maya, and Their Predecessors, Fourth Edition*, a text Scott used in his classes. Sitting on the kitchen counter, the face on the curious looking artifact staring at her from the cover caught her attention. An antiquity like the one in the photo would be perfect. The problem would be finding it. She had no idea if it was even possible, or what it would cost, but she knew who to ask.

Lisa hurried into the building housing the offices of the Department of Anthropology, hoping to avoid seeing her husband. She hurried up the narrow flight of stairs to Jerry Dwyer's small second floor office and knocked.

"Yes, come," said the voice behind the door.

CUERNAVACA

Expecting a student, Jerry rose from behind his desk with a puzzled look which quickly turned into a smile when he saw her.

"Lis. Come in. What brings you down here, of all people?" he asked as she hugged him.

Lisa chose one of the chairs waiting in front of Jerry's desk for the next student.

"I need you to help me, Jerry. It's important."

"Of course, Lis. Something wrong?" Jerry asked, concern crossing his face.

Tossing her long blonde hair back and laughing, Lisa said, "God no. Relax. I'm sorry. I don't mean to sound mysterious. I could've called you, but I thought it might be better if I explained in person. And I just don't want Scotty to know about this, so I kinda sneaked in here."

"You don't have to worry about that." He glanced at his watch. "He's in class for another hour or so. You're sure there's nothing wrong?"

Jerry's special interest in Scott Flores meant he had a special interest in Lisa Flores, as well. A frequent guest at their home, he knew her almost as well as he knew Scott. She'd brightened every room he'd ever shared with her, including his office this day.

"Positive. I want to get him a gift, something special. And I need you to get it for me. I don't know much about Mesoamerican archeology, so I wouldn't have any idea even where to look, but I want something from his work that'll knock him over when he sees it. I want something recovered from an excavation. It has to be authentic, not a reproduction, if that's possible. I figure if anyone could help me with something like that it would be you."

"Authentic?" he asked. "As in actually recovered from a historic site?"

"Yeah," she answered. "The real thing."

"That's a tall order. Very little is held privately. At least not legitimately," he added. "What's the occasion?"

Lisa waited before answering.

"This is important, Jerry. It really is."

She hesitated again, then, deflecting his question, said, "And I want it to relate to a child, to children, in some way. Maybe a child's toy, or a small figure."

Jerry's lips curled up, ever so slightly, into an almost imperceptible grin.

"Children?"

"Yes. Children," she replied.

"I can think of a few things." He looked down at his desk, trying to hide his reaction. "There are a few original artifacts that might work that are legitimately on the market. Those are beyond special, though, and rare. I may be able to find something, but, if I can, there's probably going to be a pretty stiff cost involved, considering that you're looking for something legally exported. How much are we talking about spending?"

"I don't care."

"You don't care?" Jerry asked, his voice rising. "Good lord, Lisa. For something of quality, an authenticated artifact can cost thousands of dollars. And you're looking for a specific type of relic, which will make it more expensive. I'll need at least some idea what you can spend."

"This has to be something that Scott will keep forever. Just see what you can find for me. Please. Then we'll talk about the cost."

Jerry was already thinking of who he would call.

"I see," he said. "Give me a few days, then. I'll see what I can do."

"Oh, and Jerry? As soon as you can, okay?"

As Lisa got up to leave, Jerry walked with her the few feet to the door. She turned and hugged him. "That's the nicest thing that's likely to happen to me all day," Jerry said.

"I knew you could help me," she said. "You're precious. It'll mean so much to him. I love you for doing this," she said, kissing his cheek.

After Lisa left his office Jerry stood at the window, finally free to break out in a broad grin as he watched her walk to her car. Although the scene through the window was a barren, winter landscape, Jerry saw only life outside.

It looks as though Scott will be staying in Albany this summer, no matter what I say to him.

CHAPTER FOUR

After tossing his car keys on the kitchen table, Scott walked directly to the bathroom and found his wife with a towel wrapped around wet hair, preoccupied with applying make-up. With Lisa wearing nothing but a short, thin robe which hung loosely, untied at its front, Scott saw the gentle curves of her body, and beyond in the mirror the half-round shapes of her partially exposed breasts.

She smiled as she felt him press into her back and wrap his arms around her, pulling her close. She felt his hands reach under her robe and come to rest on her hips, then join just below her waist. She thought for a moment about changing her plan and just taking Scott to bed.

His hands feel so good.

"Missed you," he whispered.

"Missed you, too."

She turned and kissed him.

"What's the occasion?" Scott asked when she pulled away and turned back toward the mirror. "You're putting on make-up at the end of the afternoon?"

"I've decided to let you take me out to dinner," she said, surrendering him for a hair dryer. "How did your day go, hon?" she asked, trying to concentrate on finishing her hair and not on her husband.

She smiled again when she felt his eyes undressing her. She knew her robe was invisible to him, and she thought again about canceling dinner.

Damn this man. No, we're going to dinner.

"Nothing exciting," Scott said. "But Jerry keeps talking about an invitation he has to go to Mexico this summer to work on a dig. Apparently it's a very big deal. He's all worked up about it. He never gets this excited about anything."

"Good for him. But I can't believe he wouldn't go to the shore for the summer. Where's the project?" she asked.

"Place called Xochicalco, near a city called Cuernavaca, southwest of Mexico City toward the Pacific. Not quite halfway to Acapulco. I spent time there when I was in college. You mind telling me where we're going tonight, or is it a surprise?"

"Anyplace you want. Just make it expensive."

"You really ought to have more respect for my father's money, Lis. He worked hard for it, you know."

Scott picked a small, pricey Italian place on a quiet side street, out of the way, with a maitre'd named Enrique.

"Professor and Mrs. Flores, good to see you again," Enrique said, looking up from his desk near the door of La Bella Bistro.

The tiny restaurant had only a bar and a dozen tables, all but three in the main dining room. Quiet and romantic, Scott and Lisa often came here when they wanted a special evening. On a weekday night there were few customers this early. Enrique showed them to a spot in the corner of the small, private room. The only light in the room came from the single candle on the table.

"Will this be satisfactory, Dr. Flores?"

"Perfect. Thank you," Scott said, holding Lisa's chair.

As Lisa read the menu she glanced at Scott several times, each time the corners of her lips turning up slightly into a subtle, mischievous smile. She always looked at him this way when she wanted him. She enjoyed the subtle tease that she knew he could sense.

"How about a bottle of ridiculously expensive wine?"

"If you want, Scotty. I'll pass."

During dinner they talked about the day's events at the hospital and the university, and the excellent meal. Lisa loved time like this with Scott. No distractions. No stress. Just her husband.

After the waiter cleared the dishes she became quiet, staring down at her coffee cup, saying nothing and playing with her spoon. The change in her mood obvious, after a few minutes, Scott asked, "What's wrong, Lis? Something's on your mind, I can tell. I know you had another appointment with Reilly. Is something wrong?"

"No baby, nothing's wrong."

Nothing at all, love.

Lisa rested the spoon on the table and looked up at Scott, the mischief returning to the corners of her mouth.

"I have something for you. Something special."

Lisa reached into her purse and pulled out a small box wrapped in plain white tissue and bound with a thin red bow. She handed it to him and waited.

Scott held the box in his hand for a moment, then, with a puzzled look, asked, "Why the present?"

"Just open it," she said. "It's because I love you."

CUERNAVACA

Scott unwrapped the box, placed it on the table, and inspected it for a moment before lifting the lid. Inside, under several layers of tissue, a small red clay figure of a child, perhaps three inches long and barely more than an inch and a half wide, rested on a bed of cotton. The legs of the figure were folded, as if it was intended to sit in an upright position. Its details crisp, it looked as though it had been made yesterday. The figure held an object in its hands too tiny and indistinct to identify. Lisa waited as Scott held the figure close to the candle, examining it from each side, turning it as he held it a few inches from his eyes. It fit easily in the palm of his hand.

"Recognize it?" Lisa said, leaning forward.

"I think so," Scott answered. "It's Aztec. And later, around 1400 or so I'd guess. Possibly a child's toy. It's a superb reproduction. And adorable. I can hardly tell it from the real thing, except that the detail is too good for it to be authentic."

"It *is* the real thing. Jerry helped me get it," she said, amused by the alarmed look on Scott's face.

"Don't worry, it's perfectly legal, one of the few that is, apparently. I've got the documentation at home to prove it. It was released with the official permission of the Mexican government. How do they say it? 'con permiso'?"

"Lisa, honey, I don't know what to say. It had to cost way too much. You're crazy to get me something like this! For no reason? You should at least have waited until I won the Nobel."

"There *is* a reason, baby."

She paused.

"I have something else to give you. But you'll have to wait a while to hold it in your hands."

As their eyes met across the candle light, she couldn't hold it in any longer.

"I'm pregnant. We're going to have a baby."

Lisa's first gift was expensive, her second priceless. Scott looked across the table at his wife, unable to speak, her words the last thing he'd expected to hear. Seconds later, the dam broke.

"Jesus, baby! Are you sure?"

"It's true," she said, her voice quivering as she struggled to keep control.

Scott jumped out of his chair, barely giving Lisa time to stand and face him before he wrapped his arms around her and held her so tightly she could hardly breathe. His head alongside hers as they embraced, she could feel Scott's warm tears run down her cheek and onto her neck. Finally able to speak again, Scott pulled away just far enough to look into her eyes, even the small distance too far. Their eyes filled with tears.

"Lis...." It was all he could say before he broke again. "Baby. I love you so much. Are you sure? Are they sure?"

He looked so vulnerable, as though she held him in the palm of her hand. She had never seen him like this, or loved him more. She pulled him close.

"It's for real, Scotty. You're gonna be a daddy," she whispered in his ear. "I love you."

The ride home from the restaurant was thirty minutes of disorganized euphoria. Between telling Lisa every few minutes how much he loved her, Scott wanted to know... would they need a bigger home? Had she thought of baby names? When would they know if it was a boy or a girl? Did the doctors think there was risk with the pregnancy? How did she feel? Should she keep working? Lisa called a halt to the interrogation.

"We have time for all that. This time's for us, baby. Just you and me. Right now I just need you."

As Lisa made love to Scott that night, their world seemed perfect. Everything was where it needed to be, and they could see the future so clearly.

Chapter Five

Jerry opened Scott's office door without knocking, as usual, and found his protege buried under a stack of long overdue first semester final exams.

"Congratulations, dad." Jerry looked at Scott with a mock frown, extending his hand. "Although you don't look nearly old enough to be having babies and you sure as hell can't have the first idea how to raise a kid."

When Scott rose to accept his hand, Jerry embraced him.

"I'm so happy for you. And for Lis."

"Thanks, Jer. I'm still getting used to the idea."

A childless bachelor with little family, Jerry's life had been rich and full in many ways. But as he neared what he knew would be the final decades of his life, Scott had become the son he never had, and he couldn't resist giving advice.

"I hope you thought to send her flowers. Lots of them. Preferably white daisies, not roses. Flowers would be a good thing to do right now and those would be perfect."

"I didn't realize you had experience with pregnant women."

"Pregnant women, fortunately no, but women in general, I've had quite a lot. I was a young buck once, hard as that may be for you to realize. As soon as I'm gone, be sure to send the flowers."

Jerry pulled a handful of photographs out of the small portfolio he was carrying and handed them to Scott. The photographs were of small, personal objects recovered by archaeologists in Mexico — a statuette, two perfectly preserved pieces of pottery, and what appeared to be a small mace or club.

"Take a look at these, Scott. I got them from Arturo this morning. They're from the first level at Xochicalco."

Scott studied the four photographs.

"Son impresionantes," Scott said, never lifting his eyes from the photographs. "Magníficas."

Like many anthropologists who specialized in Mesoamerican studies, Scott had acquired a passable conversational proficiency in Spanish and had worked hard to maintain it even though he had only limited opportunities in Albany to use the language. Jerry was fluent, and they often conversed in Spanish, drifting in and out of it. Jerry encouraged him, reminding Scott about the need to surrender his ego and ignore the fear of sounding awkward and foreign. It was how the language became yours, Jerry would lecture him, and how children learn to speak their native tongue with no concern about making mistakes. Jerry tended to use Spanish aggressively with Scott, pushing him. After Scott's invitation, their conversation continued in Spanish.

"They're extraordinary," Jerry said, his voice filled with excitement. "The preservation is outstanding. Take a look at the mace in particular. Amazing. At a ceremonial site it probably had an interesting purpose, don't you think? God, it's even got some faint red coloration on the head," he said, running his fingertip along the head of the mace in the photo, as though he could feel the object. "See? Here? It has to be blood."

Scott focused on the photograph of the mace, and thought of what might lie at the deeper levels of the excavation that would be exposed in another few months. Intrigued, he thought of the purpose of the mace at a site like this. Structures with religious significance, as this one likely had, were places where the indígenas often sacrificed captives and slaves, and he could picture the mace being used to assure the cooperation of human sacrifices who lacked enthusiasm for the ritual.

A forlorn look crossed Scott's face as he handed the photos back to Jerry. He wanted to go out into the field so badly and going with Jerry would be a perfect opportunity. The timing, however, couldn't be worse.

"Sounds like you're going to spend the summer in Mexico," Scott said.

"I think so. If you want to go I can still make it happen, but with the baby, I can understand why you can't. That makes sense even to an old bachelor like me."

"No Jer, I could never leave for that long now," Scott said. "The pregnancy is still early, and if anything happened I wouldn't want to be two thousand miles away. But it's not even that she needs me. Dads are really kind of excess baggage at this point — it's hard to explain, but I need to be close to her now. I just do. It's as much for me that I have to stay."

"It's hard to understand if you haven't gone through it," he added, immediately regretting his words. "I didn't mean it that way. I'm sorry."

Jerry let the remark pass. "Forget it. And you're right about that anyhow. But you're going to be a father, and that's all that matters."

CHAPTER SIX

Scott smiled as he read the note on the kitchen table.

> *Hi baby. There's some Chinese in the fridge if you're hungry. Won't be home for dinner. Gone shopping for some baby stuff. Get used to it. Should it be pink or blue?*
>
> *Lis*
>
> *Blue would be nice.*

He stuck a fork in the cold rice and turned on the television in time to hear the evening weather report announce the first big storm of the winter.

He glanced at the Christmas tree Lisa had talked him into buying, and considered the profound change about to remake his life. Before the baby, they simply exchanged gifts, never bothering with a tree. Even though Lisa was barely seven weeks into her pregnancy, the baby had already started to reshape their lives.

Finished eating, Scott stood at the large picture window of the condo's living room and looked over the green commons two floors below. Although he hated the long, unforgiving Albany winters, tonight he drew comfort from the sight of oversized snowflakes dropping slowly out of the dark sky and then down through the lights of the parking lot below. There was no wind, and the big, wet flakes floated straight to the ground, quickly turning the last of autumn's lawn to white. The quiet of the condo and the stillness of the scene outside made perfect companions.

Scott usually preferred to remain where he found warmth, and, often, a glass of better than decent scotch. Tonight, though, the serenity he saw through the window drew him outside. A spectator, bundled against the cold, he stood and watched as flakes so large he could almost hear them fall quickly covered the ground around him. He let out a long breath, closed his eyes and saw her face. He'd never felt so close to her as he did now.

I hope she's not too late.

Back inside, he headed to the bedroom to change. As Scott passed the two dozen fresh cut daisies on the dining room table he stopped to read the small card lying at the base of the vase.

"Always and forever... Scotty."

Jerry had been right about the flowers.

A ringing phone invaded his solitude as he finished dressing.

"I got another email from Mexico."

The man is obsessed with this. God love him, doesn't he have anything better to do?

"They've uncovered another layer of really fabulous stuff there. Wait till you see these photos. This is fantastic. I'm definitely going this summer. This has more potential than anything I've seen in ages. They're recovering jewelry, weapons, all kinds of religious items. Hell, I'm surprised they haven't found any bones yet."

Scott just didn't want to talk about it. Ordinarily he'd be anxious to talk to Jerry about something that excited his friend so, but not on this particular evening. Not now. He did his best to act interested, but his distance must have been obvious.

"You still have your old Indiana Jones hat and your whip?" Scott joked, trying to contribute something to what had become an awkwardly one sided conversation.

Jerry laughed.

"I think I can find them. Sorry to bother you, but I got all excited. Give an old hand a little room."

"It's good to see you this way. It really is. I'm happy for you."

Despite his annoyance at the call that invaded his private time, Scott couldn't help but love Jerry for his excitement.

"And you're not old. You're experienced. Lis is gonna be home any minute and I have something to do before she gets here. We can talk tomorrow. I want to know all about it. I just wish I could go with you."

"So do I amigo. So do I."

After he hung up, Scott walked past the guest bedroom, soon to be a nursery. He opened the liquor cabinet in the hallway, and looked longingly at his friends. They lined up like soldiers, waiting to be called to action. "Pick me," they all but spoke to him. His eyes focused first on the Patrón tequila at $50 a bottle. There were two of them. Scott's liquor cabinet wasn't just a collection of liquor bottles. It was the collector's edition. The assembly of scotch, his favorite, included at least one of every bottle that cost over $40 in any of the local liquor stores, and a few priced at less. The prize was a bottle of Dalmore King Alexander III that had drained him of $250 in New York City.

Good stuff. Damn.

Scott picked up a bottle of Chivas Regal and carefully examined the label as he felt an urge to pour a long drink.

Twelve years old. Treasure.

From the moment Lisa told him she was pregnant, Scott knew he would have to do this. He hadn't touched a drink since that night almost three weeks before, and, until just now, he hadn't even been tempted. The comment he made to Jerry about expectant fathers being excess baggage had a lot of truth to it, he'd decided. But solidarity demanded he do something to show her that he was as committed as she.

He held the bottle of Chivas in his hand, slowly tilting its open mouth toward the sink. As the precious honey brown liquid slowly poured into the basin, Scott had another moment of doubt, hesitated, then kept pouring. Every bottle followed, a crying shame of top shelf liquor slowly working its way into the Albany sewer system. Finally, only a few bottles of Lisa's favorite wine remained. It felt liberating, like growing up and discarding the toys of childhood.

Adios, mis amigos.

After he'd finished, Scott placed all of the empty bottles on the kitchen table where Lisa would see them as soon as she came through the door. Pleased with himself, he dropped onto the sofa and flipped through the channels. In a moment, he drifted into a dreamless sleep.

Scott heard the doorbell faintly at first, through a drowsy fog. After a while, when it didn't stop, he woke enough to look at his watch. He looked around for some sign that Lisa was home.

"Lis?"

He waited.

Nothing.

Who the hell's at the door this late?

He prepared to tear into whoever had come to sell him something or to ask him to sign a petition. The condo association had a rule about that sort of thing.

It took only a fraction of a second for Scott to feel sick when a serious looking New York state trooper faced him in the doorway. In the instant before the trooper spoke, Scott's mind had already considered that he had no overdue speeding tickets and hadn't had a conversation with a cop in years. The neighborhood was totally crime free. There was no reason for him to be here.

"Are you Scott Flores?" the trooper asked.

Scott nodded.

A few words later, his world broke into a million pieces.

CHAPTER SEVEN

He liked the place. Out of the way, Scott could count on not seeing anyone from the university here. Especially not students. Mostly, he liked it because it wasn't home. Tommy's Place was a short distance from the condo, and he and Tommy had a deal. When Scott didn't drive, Tommy let him drink more than the bar's insurance company would approve of.

With Scott such a frequent flyer, Tommy had become a friend of sorts, and, on slow nights, they'd talk until one of them tired of replaying the disaster Scott's life had become. The conversation repeated itself, night after night, with the parts occasionally rearranged. Scott told him everything, all about Lisa, the baby, the accident, about the problems he was having at the university since she died. All of it, over and over. The bartender and the Harvard Ph. D., best of friends.

"Usual?" Tommy asked as Scott slid onto the same stool he always took, tucked away at the end of the bar where he could hide.

"Yeah."

"Things gettin' any better for you, professor? I mean, personally," Tommy asked as he poured a triple shot of scotch, neatly over a few ice cubes.

"Not really." Scott drank almost half of the glass as soon as Tommy put it down. Hands wrapped around the drink, nodding toward it, he said, "Now, that's the best thing that's happened all day."

"Sorry to hear you say that, professor. You know, I've been thinkin' bout you."

"Me? Why?" Scott asked.

He really didn't care why.

"I've held a lot of hands, but, to be honest, you're different."

"I imagined drunks are pretty much all alike."

"Naw. Most of the guys who come in here with a story aren't like you. They're losers, one way or another. You know what I mean? They don't have stuff goin' for them the way you do."

"Stuff? What stuff?"

"We don't get too many Harvard Ph.D.'s in here on your average Friday night," Tommy said, pausing. "Professor, you ever thought maybe you should take a look at what you still got, instead of what you don't? Might help."

In no mood for bright lights and encouragement Scott was used to being down low and had become comfortable there.

"None of that means a damn thing. Zero. Money, the job, the degrees, they don't mean anything now. I'd fucking give it all up," Scott replied.

"I don't want to argue with you, professor, but you got dealt a bad hand, you know? When that happens, there's nothin' you can do, even if it ain't fair. You throw the cards in but you don't have to quit."

"It wasn't poker, Tommy," Scott said, downing another inch of scotch from the glass. "It was my life. You can't just throw cards down and wait for the next hand. It's not that simple."

"Didn't you ask the university for time off? Hell, they had to give it to you, didn't they? I mean, somethin' like this."

"They offered it right off," Scott said. "But I thought it would be better if I kept working. I had no idea what to do then, so I said I'd stay with it. I figured the distraction would help."

"Maybe you were wrong about that, I'm thinkin'?" Tommy said.

"Sure as hell seems so. Nothing but trouble since."

"What kinda trouble?"

"You name it," Scott replied. "I just can't concentrate on things. Like on most of what I'm supposed to do. Universities have schedules for everything — classes, exams, reports, office hours, all that. When you can't keep up with it, they come down on you. Especially someone like me, who's young and doesn't have tenure. I'm expected to follow the program."

Scott finished the drink and slid the glass across the bar toward Tommy, silently asking for another.

"And there's another problem. My department chair hates me. Always has. I have no idea why, but he's never liked me. Since Lis died it's worse. You should see the stack of memos he's sent me in the last two months."

"Excuse me, Professor," Tommy said when the phone behind the bar rang.

34

CUERNAVACA

Good. I really didn't want to talk about how promising my life is.

***

Scott had managed to get punched in the face on a Friday night in a Cambridge tavern, and when his turn came in the Massachusetts General emergency room, his head hurt so badly that he'd paid no attention to the nurse assigned the job of cleaning him up.

"You don't look like the type who's in the habit of getting into bar fights, Mr. Flores," the nurse said as she wiped away the dried blood around the cuts on his face. The fog of too many drinks lifted just enough for Scott to appreciate his attendant. She was almost as tall as him, and had long golden hair that cascaded over her shoulders, framing sparkling, metallic blue eyes. Despite his impairment, Scott noticed the trim, athletic build he favored on women. His head clearing with the moment, he hoped the reference to "Mr. Flores" was either protocol or sarcasm, since he couldn't be more than a year or two older than she.

"Well, I'd like to tell you that it's never happened before, but I'd be lying. You believe me if I told you that I got this defending a woman's honor?"

The antiseptic rinse stung his face as she carefully swabbed it over the cuts. "Damn that hurts," he said.

"No, I wouldn't. And I'm sorry. About the pain, I mean," she said with a laugh, her eyes still focused on her work. "But we have to get this cleaned properly. Go on. Please. I enjoy a good story."

"Actually, I was just trying to help out a couple of guys who weren't getting along well and I didn't move fast enough. Not so noble, I'm afraid."

35

"No, it wasn't. But much more believable. What do you do? You a student?" she asked, still concentrating on the cuts. "You look like one."

"How do students look?" he asked before crying out again, wincing from the sting of the antiseptic. "Yeah. I'm in the doctoral program in anthropology at Harvard. Most women think that's boring."

"Not at all," she said. "We get Harvard anthropologists injured in bar fights all the time in the ER. They're usually the life of the party."

She fussed with some bandages, and, when she spoke again, Scott noticed a change in her tone. She spoke quietly now and he found himself leaning forward, toward her, to hear.

"Does it hurt very badly? Looks like it might," she said, wiping the wounds a bit more carefully than Scott suspected the hospital required her to do. "You must have gotten pounded pretty good."

Scott glanced down at her hospital ID badge.

Lisa.

He took a small chance.

"No. Better now. It's fine, Lisa," Scott said, wondering if he'd made a mistake. Ignoring his familiarity, she leaned close to finish her work. Her eyes found his for a moment, then darted away, nervous. She put the antiseptic swab down, picked up a soft cloth, warmed it with hot water, and turned back to him. Resting one hand along the side of his face, she ran the cloth along his wounds with the other. Scott now felt certain that this wasn't standard procedure. Her eyes returned to his, and this time they stayed, the nervous look gone. Their faces barely a foot apart, he fought the urge to lean forward and kiss her. It made no sense,

36

would certainly ruin the moment, and probably get him into more trouble than he needed. But it would have been so easy.

She told him he really ought to be more careful around strangers.

A year later they married.

***

"Last one, professor, I'm gonna make it small. It's on me. Then you ought to be heading home. You're walkin', right?" Tommy asked.

Tommy's words tugged Scott out of the memory where he'd been hiding.

When Scott didn't answer, Tommy asked, "You want me to call a cab?"

"No. No. I'm alright. I was just...I was somewhere else for a minute is all."

"I don't mean to sound preachy, but you really ought to think about what we were talkin' about, doc, about how you still have a lot goin' for you. You're a young guy. I hate to see you like this."

Like this? Well, so do I.

CHAPTER EIGHT

The alarm rang and rang before Scott groped for it on the nightstand. When he found it, eyes still closed, he threw it across the room. Still plugged in, it didn't travel far before slamming into the wall and leaving a gouge before the sound stopped.

Scott pulled a pillow over his head.

On Saturday he wouldn't have to share the time with students and faculty and college employees, all going about their lives. He lived in a profoundly dark place, and he preferred living in it alone as much as he could.

Nothing had prepared him to deal with this. The grief was like a shadow, always there, moving with him through his day, following wherever he went. As relentless as the upstate New York winter that refused to yield to spring, there wasn't a moment of escape. The only relief he found was sleep, and that didn't always work. There were the ghosts and the dreams. His heart was gone, torn out and left behind.

Scott struggled to get out of bed, finally throwing off the blanket's protective warmth. It was so much easier to lay there than to get up and try to manage, but after 10 minutes, he yielded to the light that filtered through the shade of the bedroom window. Still barely awake after he turned on the coffee maker, he noticed the message icon on his cell phone's screen. It was the real estate agent, letting him know about a showing of the condo that afternoon. Her message reminded him to pick the place up before he went out and told him how much she hoped the day went well for him. Since learning why Scott wanted to move, she had never worked so hard to sell a home.

In the two months since Lisa's death, Scott's life had unraveled. He'd lost 15 pounds off of a solid 190 pound frame that had carried a football for almost a thousand yards in his senior year in college. He sometimes went all day without eating. The fatigue that comes with grief left him with barely enough energy to get through most days. The university had become a disaster. Scott's department chair, George Hoffman, received regular complaints from students about unprepared lessons, missed classes, unreturned papers and exams, and office hours not kept. George wanted his head, and, with George's encouragement, the complaints had reached the dean. Other faculty members talked openly about his disengagement. He'd completely withdrawn from his colleagues and the friends he and Lisa had enjoyed. It had been months since Lisa's death, and the automatic understanding from friends that comes with such a tragic loss had passed, people now expecting him to be more or less as he had been before. An expendable, untenured assistant professor, Scott's career began slipping away. He knew it, and he didn't care.

Jerry Dwyer, however, did.

Jerry rarely worked on Saturdays, but he'd seen enough, and on this Saturday, he came to the university looking for his wounded friend. He found Scott sitting in his office at 2:30 in the afternoon with a glass of scotch on his desk.

"That shit will kill you if you let it," Jerry said entering the room unannounced.

"Jerry, I don't want to fight. But I really don't need the lecture, thanks," Scott said, not looking up from his work.

"I think you do. I think you need a helluva lecture..."

Before Jerry had finished his sentence, Scott put down the test booklet he'd been reading and turned toward Jerry, anger flashing in his eyes. Jerry saw the indignant look and cut Scott off.

"Scott. Listen, please. I don't pretend to know how you feel. I couldn't. But I can see what's happening. It's bad. This'll destroy you."

Scott lashed out like a man who'd been cut.

"Don't tell me about how fucking bad it is." He spat out the words. "You want to know what bad is? Try looking in the closet in the morning to find a shirt to wear and seeing your dead wife's clothes hanging there. Try starting your day that way, then tell me how God damned bad it is. I'm living in a haunted house, for Christ's sake."

Jerry took a deep breath.

"Scott. Just listen. Give me a chance, then I'll leave you alone. I promise."

Scott slowly moved his hand away from the glass and looked back down at his desk. When he lifted his face again, pain had replaced anger, and streaks of tears covered his cheeks. He started to cry, quietly at first, then uncontrollably.

Jerry rested his hand on Scott's shoulder. Scott turned in his chair and looked up at Jerry, who dropped to his knees.

"We need to do something. I can't lose you like this." Jerry waited for the words to come to him. "I won't let that happen."

"Look in the mirror, Scott, for Christ's sake. Look at what you're doing to yourself."

Jerry wiped his face in his sleeve. Scott had never seen Jerry broken.

"You have to trust me. You're going to make it. I need you to believe that. Don't you dare give up on me," Jerry pleaded. "One goddamned tragedy is enough."

CHAPTER NINE

Two blasts of the car's horn brought Scott to the apartment window, where he saw an impatient looking Jerry Dwyer sitting in a new Corvette. It was something not many men nearing 70 could pull off without looking at least slightly out of place, but Jerry got away with it, and a lot more, refusing to give in to the expectations others had for how he should act. He hated the accumulating years, but he liked fast cars, and that was the end of it.

"You ever think of getting something a little more age appropriate to drive?" Scott asked as he slid into the passenger's seat. "Like a sedan."

"Hell, no," Jerry answered as he pressed on the accelerator a bit harder than necessary. "Wouldn't be caught dead in one. At my age, every minute counts."

Weeks earlier Jerry had imposed himself on Scott's world, trying to bring some order back into it. He'd had only modest success. As Scott's self-appointed nanny, he stopped at Scott's home unannounced, had what passed for lunch with him most days at the university, and, when he could, tried to see that Scott got to his classes on time and kept his office hours. Jerry ran interference with the department chair and the dean, constantly reminding them that Scott needed understanding. As best he could, Jerry struggled to protect Scott's increasingly tenuous grip on his career. But he couldn't do Scott's job for him, and he worried about the fading prospects for Scott's survival.

He tried to keep Scott where he could see him, fearing most the time Scott spent alone. He'd even tried accompanying Scott to bars at night, worried about the risks his friend ran drinking alone, and trying, mostly unsuccessfully, to put some limit on the consumption. Unable to keep Scott consistently sober in the evenings, at least Jerry could keep his charge from killing himself driving home.

Just as preoccupied with Xochicalco, Jerry exchanged daily emails with Arturo. As the emails went back and forth, Jerry's interest had turned to concern, and, over a quiet dinner, they talked about it.

"Have you heard from Arturo lately?" Scott asked.

"Almost every day. By June he thinks they'll be down to something very rich. It's obvious now that this structure of theirs collapsed all of a sudden. They're speculating it may have been an earthquake, or a military event, and it must have been a monster to take it down. Whatever was going on at the time is probably all still buried under there, like a damned time capsule. They're finding small cavities that have been sealed off for seven hundred years. They dig like maniacs, and not always like archaeologists, I'm afraid."

"Archaeological projects are supposed to be boring. No one's supposed to do anything in a hurry," Scott said, knowing an archaeologist of the stature of Arturo Lopez wouldn't rush anything in the field.

"They're supposed to be that way," Jerry said. "And my friend's not happy about what's going on. He just can't do much about it. Part of it's the nature of what he's working with at the site and part of it's the way the government people are behaving."

"What's wrong with the site?" Scott asked.

"Well, he's basically dealing with a really big, disorganized pile of large rocks and stones. So he has to disturb a lot of the area before he can sift through everything. He's actually using backhoes and bulldozers, for God's sake. It's nasty business for someone used to sifting every little piece of soil through tiny screens in neat little one meter squares."

"What did you mean about the government people?"

"That's what's puzzling. Arturo says they're pushing him to dig up the site quickly. Normally they just sit back and watch the academics work their asses off, if they show up at all. He wants to take his time the way you'd expect, and make sure everything is properly cataloged and recorded before going deeper, but they've taken over the processing of the recovered items and they keep pushing him."

"The folks at the INAH are probably just all worked up about it," Scott said. "Xochicalco hasn't been the hottest location for new work, so this must be a novelty for them."

"Perhaps," Jerry continued. "But the site is already yielding an extraordinary number of items and the authorities are all over, asking questions and frantically grabbing everything when normally all they want to do is sign off on paperwork. Something's troubling Arturo. I can sense it in his messages. He ought to be thrilled, but instead, he's worried, and I don't think he's telling me everything in the emails, either. I'm sure he's uncomfortable with the government people he's dealing with."

"Well, you have to expect that. Artifact recovery in this kind of volume attracts a lot of attention, especially with the problems they've had with the black market. They're probably just a little jumpy about that."

"This is more than the usual concern, I think," Jerry said.

Jerry looked down at the table and hesitated. He'd given a lot of thought to the next part of the conversation.

"Scott, we need to talk about something else."

This had to work, or Jerry knew his friend was finished.

"The dean called me yesterday. About the National Science Foundation grant. He's pissed, and you're in trouble. A lot of trouble."

***

Jerry had been running interference for weeks, convincing Dean Charles Watson that Scott needed understanding. The dean's long friendship with Dwyer had caused him to leave Scott's problems for Jerry to handle, despite the complaints that reached the dean's desk with increasing frequency. The problem that had landed on the dean's desk this morning couldn't be handled so simply.

By overseeing the administration of a grant from the NSF worth hundreds of thousands of dollars to the university, Scott had taken on a major responsibility for his department. The letter from the foundation that arrived in the dean's morning mail couldn't be ignored.

Money made the university run, and Scott hadn't responded to multiple requests for information from the foundation about the progress of the grant. He'd canceled two meetings with foundation representatives without explanation, had overdue reports on hiring and expenditures, and didn't return phone calls or emails.

Watson dialed Jerry's extension.

"Jerry. It's Charlie. I should be calling Scott Flores about this, but since you seem to have assumed responsibility for this young man, I thought it best to start with you.

"I received a letter from the National Science Foundation today about our research grant for the project in Guatemala. I put Flores in charge of this, at your suggestion. The NSF says he's ignoring them. They want to know how the money's being spent, and they say they're going to pull the grant. I gave this to him because you told me he could handle it. You recommended him. Now this. I know you have a special thing about this Flores, and that he's had a difficult time personally, but this has to be dealt with.

"And you probably know his department chair wants his head anyhow," the dean continued. "He's off track for tenure. He's overdue for publication and never goes into the field to do the research he needs to do to get something worthy on paper. On top of that I'm getting students trying to make appointments with me to complain about him. I've no time for that, Jerry. He's a damned disaster."

"I understand, Charlie. Please give me a chance to talk to him."

"That's fine, you go right ahead and talk to him all you want, but haven't you been talking to him all along?

There's a lot of money involved with this NSF issue. This is more serious than getting exams back late and not keeping office hours. The university's reputation is implicated, not to mention my personal standing. You realize how bad it will look for me if the way this grant has been handled becomes common knowledge? And what if we lose it, for God's sake?"

Suddenly angry at himself for not checking on Scott's handling of the grant, Jerry realized he hadn't given the NSF project a thought in months. Instead of making sure Scott's disengagement didn't jeopardize hundreds of thousands of dollars in university funding, he'd been worrying about whether Scott made it to class on time.

Jerry's mind raced ahead.

"Certainly I do. Just give me a day or two before you call him in," Jerry said. "I have a thought about what we should do with Scott and I need to work through this a little with him. Is it alright if I come when you talk to him?" In fact, Jerry had no idea what to do with Scott.

"Of course. We've been friends for a long time. I don't know Scott very well, but his credentials were outstanding, and I know you like him. That means something to me, because I trust your judgment. I just hope you knew what the hell you were doing by backing this kid."

"Understood. Scott's worth saving. I'm positive of that. Just give me another chance."

"That's what you asked me to do when the complaints started coming in, but this has gotten too big to ignore. This has gone too far now, Jerry. I hope you understand that."

"I do. Just give me a little more time."

After Jerry had hung up the phone, he rubbed his temples and tried to relax, to think things through.

Yes, it's clear enough. It's time to get out of town. If they let him.

***

After telling Scott about Watson's call, Jerry poured himself a cup of coffee from the carafe the waiter had left.

"You can't be drunk or hung over when you're supposed to be taking care of business. I can get you cut some slack for the small stuff, but this NSF grant is a much bigger deal. You're going to get hauled in front of Watson over it, and when you do, all the other problems you've caused are going to come up, too. They all land on the department chair's desk and he's ready to let you go anyhow. Hoffman has never liked you and you're just giving him a reason to fire your sorry ass."

"I hate to cause you all this trouble, Jerry. This is my problem, not yours."

Jerry had expected Scott's attitude.

"Bullshit," Jerry barked. "I've made you my problem. You know what you need? You need your ass kicked. You need to stop feeling sorry for yourself and start listening. Who's your damned friend? You tell me."

Scott retreated.

"You are, Jerry. You're the only one I have."

Jerry leaned forward, invading the space between them.

"Then it's about time you listened to me. I'm going to Mexico this summer, to Xochicalco, and you have to come with me. And I don't mean you should come with me. I mean you have to come with me."

"I'd be a drag on you. I don't think I'd be any good down there the way I am."

Scott had crawled back inside of himself, where he felt comfortable. Not about to let him hide there, Jerry dragged him back out into the harsh light. Jerry couldn't abide self-pity, and he knew it was destroying Scott.

"Don't give me that. That's exactly what you shouldn't think. You can help me. And if I left you here you wouldn't last a month the way you're behaving. I'd worry about you every day. I need you where I can see you, and you need to get to someplace where you don't see a ghost every time you turn around."

Jerry pressed.

"Scott, your career here may be over, and you have to face that. I didn't like the tone of Watson's call at all. I've worked with Charlie a long time and I can usually read him. He may have been telling me to prepare you. But even if that's what happens, your whole life isn't over. Unless you give up on it. Let me lay it out for you," he continued. "If you stay here you'd be lucky to survive the summer, and that's going to be true whether they let you go or not."

"You sure you want that much baggage on your trip?"

"Damn you. You're maddening. Why do you think I've been telling you all this?"

Chapter Ten

Fidgeting in his chair as he waited outside of Dean Watson's office, Jerry glanced at the over-sized clock that seemed to fill half of the wall opposite them. In the quiet of the small waiting room its loud ticking seemed intrusive, as though the clock had been placed there so visitors would be sure to record the time that had passed since their appointment became overdue.

The only other sound was the soft clacking of the keyboard as the dean's prim secretary typed. With her hair pulled back tightly into a bun and her ramrod straight posture, she looked like she'd been sent there from central casting to play the part.

Gatekeeper. That's what she looks like. A damned gatekeeper. Like no one gets in without her saying it's okay.

They had reason to be nervous aside from Scott's obvious troubles. George Hoffman, the dour, strictly business, chairman of the Department of Anthropology had been in with the dean for 30 minutes before them.

"What the hell could they be talking about for this long?" Jerry whispered, shifting in his seat.

"They're probably debating whether to boil me in oil or hang me," Scott whispered back.

The secretary's phone made a soft buzzing sound. She picked it up, listening silently before replying, "Yes, sir." She looked at Jerry and Scott and said, "The dean can see you now."

Jerry wondered if she knew why they were there and had made some unspoken judgment about it.

He could have seen us a half hour ago if that windbag Hoffman wasn't in there.

A burly, overweight, affable looking man with a full head of thick, bushy, gray hair and a deep voice worthy of his stature, Dean Watson had a reputation as a thoughtful man who played the academic political game with skill. Despite a rule prohibiting smoking in university buildings, his still warm pipe lay in the ashtray on his desk and a pleasant aroma filled the room.

George Hoffman sat off in a corner, looking as he usually did, like his lunch disagreed with him. He did not rise to greet them.

After shaking hands, the dean settled into his overstuffed chair and folded his hands on the desk. He looked directly at Scott.

"Scott, I want to tell you again how sorry I am about the loss of your wife. I'm sure these last few months have been difficult."

"Thank you. Most everyone here at the university has been very supportive and it's meant the world to me." Scott glanced in Hoffman's direction before adding, "Professor Dwyer, especially, has been a great help."

"Jerry, yes. Jerry and I've been together a long time," the dean said, a slight smile crossing his face. "I go to him for advice probably more than I should. I understand he's made you something of a personal project."

The dean picked his pipe out of the ashtray and re-lit it.

"Scott, when your wife passed you were offered an extended leave. Quite understandable. But you declined it. That appears to have been a mistake for you. I have to be honest, you've become a significant problem now."

"I'm sorry, dean. I thought it would be good to try to stay occupied. Back then, I couldn't imagine just sitting around with nothing to do. I know I haven't been the best member of the department."

"I'm afraid that's an understatement. Frankly, your behavior has been a disaster. Students waiting on exams and papers that should have been graded long ago, complaining that you don't keep your office hours, and that you're not showing for class. Repeatedly. Missed faculty meetings. And now this," Watson said as he handed Scott and Jerry copies of the letter from the National Science Foundation.

"According to this, you're unresponsive to the point that they're talking about pulling the grant from the university. You understand the amount of money involved and what it means to your department? And to me personally?"

"Yes I do."

"Then why did I receive this letter, Scott? I expect better from my faculty, especially on something this important"

"I have no excuse except my personal circumstances. It's difficult to explain."

"Let me be clear," the dean said. "Regardless of your personal circumstances, the business of this university goes on. We do what we can to help you, but our jobs all need to be done, including yours. If you can't do what we need you to do, then we'll have to come to some other solution. You agreed to oversee this grant and we trusted you, never giving it another thought. If you couldn't handle this, your responsibility was to tell us before things got to this point."

Jerry rose to his friend's defense.

"Charlie, we need to recognize that right now it's impossible for Scott to perform the way we need him to. None of that's his fault. But let's not forget why we hired him in the first place. We thought there was potential and, up until just a few months ago, most of us were convinced that we were right."

It was Jerry's turn to glance at Hoffman, who sat in the far corner of the large office, looking anxious to say something. The way the light fell in the room, Hoffman's seat was in shadow, far from the only window. Sitting there in the dark, with his sharp, angular features, Hoffman reminded Jerry of a predator waiting to fall on a helpless victim.

"It would be a mistake to give up on that now," Jerry continued.

"I don't agree that he's completely blameless for this," the dean said. "Apart from his unfortunate loss, I don't know what other life style issues he may have, but whatever they are, he could have come to us before things got to this point. He chose not to. He's only one faculty member, and a junior one at that. I can't accept this type of behavior and hold everyone else to something higher."

"So what do you suggest we do? We can't just excuse this," Watson added, pointing toward the letter lying on his desk.

"It would be best for the university, and Scott, if he took time away," Jerry replied. He's got an opportunity to work with me in Mexico this summer on an extraordinary project, and I think time away from Albany now would benefit him and the department."

At the mention of the department, George Hoffman finally spoke, his shrill voice violating the room from his corner seat.

"That's out of the question. Giving him a pass, which he isn't entitled to, simply avoids responsibility for the grant issue and all of the other problems he's caused. I have a department to run, Jerry. Scott's behavior is being talked about, and everyone's waiting to see how we handle this, and how much we'll tolerate."

"George has a point. You've put us in a difficult position," Watson said, puffing on his pipe and turning to Scott for some response.

"I understand. If I may," Scott said.

"Certainly," the dean replied. "This is about you."

The meeting had taken a turn Jerry had feared but anticipated, and they had talked about how to handle it. To have any chance at all, Scott had to say something compelling. Anxious, Jerry listened, hoping Scott wouldn't overdo it.

"When I was an undergraduate I spent a summer in Morelos at an excavation not far from where Jerry wants to take me this summer. The experience changed my life. It's why I chose the field. I learned the importance that patrimony has in the present, most of all to the people who own it. In Mexico, our discipline is incredibly meaningful."

As Scott paused, Jerry searched the Dean's face in vain for some sign that Scott was making an impact. Watson looked attentive, but Jerry couldn't read him.

"Working there is like being a missionary," Scott continued. "We teach students about anthropology and archeology as dry academic subjects but when you have a chance to go in the field and work alongside the people who actually own the patrimony, when you can recover their history, touch it and then give it back to them and tell them what it all means..."

"I understand all of that, Scott," the dean said, interrupting, his face impassive. "I was a young teacher once. I think all of us felt like that at some point. But you could have felt this epiphany before you made your commitments and none of that appreciation for our work here is an excuse for how you've neglected your responsibility to your students, or this fiasco with the NSF grant."

He wasn't impressed. We should have taken a different approach.

Jerry knew that Watson's direct and brutally honest comments made sense. He felt Scott's chances of survival slipping away.

"Charlie, let me be very candid with you," Jerry interrupted.

The dean smiled, and said, "That's a switch now, isn't it?"

"What's happened to Scott is tragic. Worse than tragic, it's heartbreaking. But we have a chance to turn it into something positive and shame on us if we don't. Scott needs to get away from Albany, away from home, from the university, from everything. He needs to bury himself in something meaningful. And I can't imagine anything better for him or the university right now than this chance."

Watson turned to Hoffman.

"George? Anything further?"

"It's all well and good," Hoffman sniffed, "and Jerry and Professor Flores give nice speeches, but there's no justification for having different rules for him than we have for everyone else."

Before Jerry or Scott could say anything further, Watson held up his hands, signaling a decision and the end of the discussion.

"Scott, I'm afraid this has reached the point where we can't tolerate it any longer," the dean said. "You've abandoned and shortchanged your students, who deserve better, and you've burdened your department, and George and me personally, beyond what's reasonable. Our expectations for you can't be different than they are for all of your colleagues. I'm going to ask that your appointment be terminated at the end of the semester. I'm sorry about this, especially considering your personal situation, but you accepted the responsibility to continue after your personal loss, and we trusted you. Quite frankly, if I handle this any differently I'll lose the respect of my faculty, and we may lose the NSF grant. We can't afford to risk that."

"I prefer that this be done in a way that gives you the opportunity to survive professionally," the dean continued. "I can arrange for the university to accept your voluntary resignation from your position at the end of the semester, for personal reasons, and I can see that your record reflects that. If you can straighten yourself out, with your credentials you should be able to find another position. You can even tell the truth when they ask why you left. You can tell them you can't function in Albany any longer, in these surroundings. I've no doubt that you have the ability to be a fine anthropologist, Scott. Whether you succeed as an academic is up to you. But it won't be here."

CHAPTER ELEVEN

By 6:45 the next morning he'd be gone, and, by evening, thousands of miles away and wrestling with demons he knew would follow him there.

Driving through the stone pillars at the entrance to St. Agnes Cemetery at sundown, he searched for other visitors. As far as he could see, he had the cemetery to himself. He preferred it this way when he visited her. He'd been here on many evenings since December, but this time was different. He'd be gone for a long time.

Scott stopped his car at the familiar spot, and lifted the flowers off of the passenger seat. He took a deep breath and braced himself before he walked the few hundred feet to the grave.

He hesitated before looking down at the bare earth, and the gray granite. Seeing her name there always hurt. She'd been buried in the winter, and like a wound that hadn't healed, even with late spring the grass hadn't had time to grow over the grave.

I miss you so much, baby.

No one could hear him crying.

On his knees, he rested the bouquet of white daisies on the ground.

Te amo. Ahora y para siempre, amor mía.

SEGUNDA PARTE

Chapter Twelve

Jerry had managed to sleep for almost an hour in the cramped tourist class airline seat, and Scott took full advantage of it.

After Jerry dozed off, a $50 bill slipped discreetly to the steward had secured as many of the miniature bottles of Jose Cuervo tequila reposado as Scott wanted. Scott had just finished number three when the pilot announced they would be in Mexico City in 45 minutes.

Cute. When we flew, that's what Lisa used to say about these little bottles. She thought they were cute.

Three of the small drinks was one more than Scott usually needed before slipping into a kind of soft melancholy that was a hell of a lot easier on him than the mood he usually had when completely sober. After finishing number three, he didn't care about much of anything except number four.

Scott glanced through the window, past Jerry's body slumped against the side of the cabin. Cotton ball clouds floated by, but the view held no interest for him. He used to plaster his face against airplane windows like a kid on his first plane ride whenever he flew, but he'd handed Jerry the window seat this time without a thought.

She used to tease me about always wanting the window seat. She said I was like a little boy.

Scott reached into his pocket and closed his hand around the small figure of the Aztec child, squeezing it hard. Even the alcohol didn't help now. He closed his eyes and tried to keep control.

God I miss her.

As the Aeromexico jet approached the edge of Mexico's capital, Scott leaned toward the window, his head still clear enough to wonder about what he saw below. The sunlight glinting off of the flimsy looking corrugated metal roofs caught his attention. Impossible not to notice, they covered mile after mile of the land passing by. As the plane descended and he got a clearer look, Scott realized that underneath those roofs were homes, thousands upon thousands of them, with hundreds of thousands of people living in them.

These were the barrios pobres, where people lived in quiet, suffocating poverty, many cooking over open fires and hanging clothes out to dry in the sun. They were places where sanitary facilities might consist of a community cesspool and water had to be hauled a long distance, sometimes on the backs of children. Scott wondered if there was energy down there, some way to do something about this. In a typically North American way, he wondered what had caused it, what needed to be done to change it, and how that might be accomplished. But he also knew that the poverty here had existed forever, and so he let his thoughts turn to what lay ahead.

After the attendant rattled off the landing instructions in English and Spanish, Scott tucked the empty tequila bottles under his seat so Jerry wouldn't see them. He poked Jerry in the ribs, and waited for a response. Jerry grunted and rolled onto his side in the narrow space. Scott poked harder, impatient, until Jerry finally stirred.

"We there, are we?" Jerry asked, drowsy and rubbing his eyes.

"Sí, estamos aquí, finalmente."

Jerry ignored the Spanish invitation. "Long ass trip from New York," he grumped in English, unflappable, even half-asleep.

Cuernavaca was a 40 minute bus ride from Aeropuerto Benito Juarez, up and over a mountain and down the backside of it on ruta 95, the "autopista del sol," which switched back and forth as it wound down toward the city. The autopista was the escape used by residents of Mexico City to get away for the weekend to Acapulco on the Pacific coast, and it passed Cuernavaca on its way. The highway was bordered by a mix of pine, cactus and scrubby trees, broken here and there by rocky outcroppings. The autopista inclined steeply and offered a striking view of the city below at almost every turn. They'd crested the mountain while it was still light enough to see the rocky terrain clearly, but dark enough for the lights of the city to reveal its size and depth against the pastel sunset. Shining like a jewel, Cuernavaca nestled in the darkening valley below. For a moment, Scott felt excitement and anticipation, the distraction bringing brief freedom from the sorrow that had followed him here like a bounty hunter sitting in the back of the bus, ready to take him down.

Looking through the window, Scott thought of his summer in Morelos as an undergraduate. Although he was hardly over 30 now, it might as well have been a lifetime ago. So much had happened to him, certainly enough pain for one life. As he watched the lights of the city, Scott felt as though he was placing his finger at the corner of a book's page, ready to turn it, yet hesitating.

Darkness had blanketed the city as the Pullman de Morelos tour bus pulled into the station near the casino in Cuernavaca. Anxious to meet the norteamericanos, Arturo Lopez had arrived a half hour before the bus.

As Jerry and Scott walked down the bus stairway and turned toward the platform, Arturo spotted Jerry and extended his open arms. The two old friends embraced.

"It's been too long, my friend," Arturo said in halting English.

"Sí. Ha sido demasiado tiempo, amigo. It's been way too long."

Listening to the two friends talk, exchanging Spanish and English like gifts, Scott realized he'd need to jettison English quickly. He'd not considered how profound an adjustment that would be.

"Arturo, this is Scott Flores, the young man I told you about," Jerry said. "He's the very best young person we have at the university."

Jerry and Scott had decided to maintain appearances by introducing Scott as a professor at SUNY Albany, even though Scott's relationship with the university had officially ended the moment he turned in his final grades for the spring semester.

"He worked in Morelos as an undergraduate," Jerry continued. "Let me warn you, though, to lock up your expensive tequila. Scott's an aficionado."

"I'll keep that in mind," Arturo laughed. "You speak the language?"

"I do my best. I think I can get by," Scott answered in Spanish.

"Bueno. Entonces, bienvenido a Cuernavaca, otra vez, Scott. Can't tell you how happy I am to have you two here. We're in great need of discipline at the moment and I hope you and Jerry can provide some of it. Jerito's good at that sort of thing," he said, smiling at his friend. "We're up to our necks in a tremendous location, but some of the people working with us, you'll see, have created some....how shall I put this...issues? And..."

Arturo hesitated before continuing.

"...some things are...let's say, out of place."

Scott struggled, trying to think in Spanish. In his mind, he tried to throw a switch. Tired, and still shaking off the last of the Jose Cuervo from the plane, he struggled with the change of language.

This is going to take time. Este va a tomar el tiempo.

"Out of place?" he asked.

"It's late, mi amigo, and you're tired. I don't mean to be mysterious, but I can explain all that in the morning over a decent meal. Let's get you settled now. My car's been in the drop off lane too long and I don't need to deal with the policía."

Arturo had made arrangements to have them housed in separate private homes within walking distance of each other in a gated community in the Colonia Acapantzingo, an area typical of Cuernavaca's middle class. Scott's home until August would be a small, one room apartment the Mexicans called a bungalow, separated from the main dwelling of a cooking instructor who worked with one of Cuernavaca's Spanish language schools. It was simple and comfortable, and Scott would assuredly eat well.

Jerry billeted around the corner in the home of a retired government employee and his wife.

The next morning, Arturo drove them to the center of town to have breakfast at Cafe Colibri, an open air restaurant that fronted one end of the two block long wooded town square that dominated the center of downtown Cuernavaca. The zócalo was the heart of the center city, el centro, where many people ate, listened to music, protested the government, argued about politics, and met lovers.

Looking into the zócalo from their table, Scott could see at the near end an enormous statue of a man on horseback, with a rifle in his outstretched hand. The base of the statue was covered in papers and posters, but the distance made it impossible to read them.

"Arturo," he asked, motioning toward the square with his fork. "Who's the man on horseback? I apologize for not knowing the history."

"Zapata. Emiliano Zapata Salazar, the local hero of the Mexican Revolution. He ran the rebel army in this part of the country."

"And those signs and papers all over it?" Scott asked.

Arturo laughed. "That, amigo, is the poor man's political advertisement. Señor Zapata still does service as a revolutionary. People with strong political opinions seem to think it helps their cause to make posters and hang them under the statue. It happens whenever there's an election. I don't think many people pay attention to them, except maybe those who already agree."

"And that large building at the far end? It looks very official," Scott asked.

"The central offices of the state government. So, you see, we have the establishment on one end, and the revolutionary at the other. A miniature version of Mexican history." Arturo smiled before adding, "You'll have to make a point of coming at night. At night the women are much more interesting than the statues. You're not married?"

Scott hadn't been asked the question since Lisa's death. It seemed a strange notion that anyone would ask.

"I'm a widower. My wife died last year in an auto accident."

The animation drained from Arturo's face as he said, "Dios mío. I'm so sorry, Scott. I didn't know. You're so young to have experienced such a thing."

"It's alright. I'm getting on and being here will help," Scott said, not believing it.

"With God's help, yes," Arturo said.

As they finished breakfast, Scott remembered Arturo's comment the night before, and the promise to explain it.

"Arturo, last night you said some of the people at the excavation were creating issues and that things were 'out of place.'"

Arturo paused before answering.

"The recovery of Mexico's patrimony is one of the priorities of our government, and, of course, the results of our work at sites like Xochicalco are a source of great pride here. Unfortunately, many of the items we recover also have great value to collectors who've created an active black market in Pre-Columbian artifacts. You've read all about this, I'm sure."

"Of course," Jerry interjected. "But this problem has been with us for a long time."

"It has. But it's far worse now than you may think. The amount of money that's changing hands is great and the items that we're recovering here on an almost daily basis have significant value. It's not unlike the drug trade. There's a market, mostly in your country, and where there's a market willing to pay a high price, someone will find a way to make money on it. ¿Es capitalismo, no?"

"I understand all that," Jerry agreed, "but how is your situation here a particular problem? I mean at Xochicalco?"

"It's simple. Artifacts are much easier to divert into the black market if they're never cataloged, or perhaps if the records are altered or conveniently lost. The best place to divert them to collectors is at the source. Once the government has them identified and marked, and they've been shipped to Mexico City, it becomes much harder, almost impossible to traffic them. To put it plainly, things are disappearing here in Cuernavaca."

CHAPTER THIRTEEN

Raul took care to park his car several blocks from his destination.

Even though darkness had descended on Cuernavaca, he didn't want to risk curious eyes noticing his visit to this particular address, and his ride was likely the only fire engine red BMW convertible in the city. At least he'd never seen another one. With a fedora pulled down to the middle of his forehead, Raul walked as quickly as he felt he could without attracting attention. Only one car had gone by as he walked, and he turned his face away from the narrow street as it passed.

From the street, his destination resembled many upper class properties in Cuernavaca, the residence invisible and securely embedded behind a high, solid wall topped with a spiraling loop of razor wire. A large steel double door allowed vehicles to enter only with permission, and the entire enclosure was painted black. Raul knew the home hidden behind the high wall must be substantial because the wall stretched for several hundred feet along the curb — far longer than the enclosures of any of the other properties he'd passed. Affluence in

Cuernavaca often could be measured by the amount of frontage of a razor wire topped wall.

He pressed the call button next to a man door and waited. After a few seconds, a scratchy, barely understandable voice asked his name through the intercom.

"Raul Cathedra."

Raul sensed eyes on him, through a security camera, he guessed. Uneasy, he waited on the walk, turning his face away from the street when a car passed. He'd waited long enough to grow impatient before he heard "adelante," followed by a sharp metallic click as the lock on the heavy door disengaged. He pushed the door open and stepped in, finally shielded from the street.

His first look at the residence inside confirmed his assessment. Toward the rear of the lot, a large, elegant two story home and a smaller outbuilding he thought to be a guest house, or quarters for a servant, rested on the far side of a lush lawn. The whole scene was bathed in soft accent lighting that showed off meticulous landscaping, the grassy areas and flower beds all neatly edged. Bright lights shone through the windows and open doors of the residence as a hissing automatic sprinkling system tossed gentle streams of water onto the lawn in front of it.

The black, unwelcoming security wall that had greeted him on the outside enclosed the entire property, providing a comfortable sense of privacy. From the inside, surrounding the manicured grounds, the razor wire seemed out of place.

After a few minutes, a short, slight man emerged from the house and walked toward him.

"Bienvenido, Señor Cathedra. I'm Felipe Bencivenga. From Oro's staff. Thank you for coming. Most of the people you'll be meeting are already here. There were preliminary discussions earlier in the evening with some of the others and I apologize for having to ask you to park outside, but, as you can see, the drive is already quite full."

He gestured toward the cars that filled the drive leading to the front of the residence. Raul noticed the makes of the parked vehicles. BMW, Audi, Lexus, Mercedes. The idea that he hadn't been invited to attend the entire evening with their owners troubled him.

What was it that I wasn't privileged to hear? Am I not important enough?

Bencivenga escorted Raul into the living room of the residence, where two dozen people talked in subdued voices. Everyone had a drink, and several smoked, able to avoid offending the others because the warm Cuernavaca night allowed for the opening of the room's oversized sliding doors. A light, refreshing breeze flowed through the space. Raul recognized several of Cuernavaca's important business and community figures, the presence of some a surprise at a meeting like this. A few he'd done business with nodded in his direction when their eyes met, and he assumed they were here searching for opportunity, the same as he. He guessed others were simply curious or enjoyed the excitement of attending a meeting with a controversial national figure. The mood of the room felt like a party where one knew all of the other guests, but still had to be mindful of where the conversation led.

Being seen here is probably as much risk as most of these people ever take.

Raul spotted Rodrigo Oro, whom he recognized from television, and whose visit to Cuernavaca was the purpose of the meeting. Wasting no time, Raul walked straight toward him.

"It's an honor to meet you, Señor Oro," Raul said extending his hand to the tall, immaculately groomed Oro. "I'm Raul Cathedra."

With a slow, deliberate motion, Oro placed his drink on a small table before turning to face Raul and accepting his hand.

"Please, it's Rodrigo," he said with a soft spoken manner that surprised Raul, who'd expected a more sharply cut demeanor, and appearance. Oro was dressed in a neatly tailored tan linen sport coat that framed an open collar French blue shirt.

"Just don't call me RENO, like the newspapers," Oro said, smiling. "The acronym serves its purpose, but the truth is, I hate it. And the honor is mine, Raul."

Rodrigo appeared to study Raul for a fleeting moment before continuing.

"My friends in Cuernavaca speak highly of your political skill."

Raul wondered, and worried, about just how much Rodrigo knew about him. The presence of so many wealthy people in the room suggested to Raul that Rodrigo probably knew his bank balance, and perhaps where the money had come from as well.

"You know, we take a bit of a chance inviting you here," Rodrigo said, his eyes searching Raul's face. "But then, life is full of risks as well as opportunities, isn't it?"

A chance? I wonder what he knows?

"Indeed it is, Rodrigo. But you take no risk with me," he said. "I doubt we disagree on very much."

He liked the idea of calling Oro by his first name.

"That's good to hear. We're facing a difficult challenge in the next few months and we'll need committed people who have Mexico's future in their hearts, as I hope you do."

Rodrigo paused for a moment, his ice blue eyes locked on Raul.

"Tell me, Raul," Rodrigo asked. "What would you expect to accomplish if I'm successful? Personally, I mean."

"Like you, I believe in Mexico," Raul said.

He wanted to make an impression, and had given a lot of thought about what to say when he met Oro.

"My work is devoted to preserving our patrimony and so it isn't much of a leap to devote myself to her future as well," he added, particularly proud that he'd come up with that phrase. "I've no desire to be a hero, but if I believe that I have a place in the future of Mexico, then I'll fight with you for Mexico. And for myself at the same time. If there's risk, well, then there's risk."

He'd come on strong with a national political figure he'd barely met, and hoped it wasn't a mistake.

Rodrigo Ernesto Neron Oro was the undisputed head of the left wing Partido de Revolucionario Acción and would be the PRA candidate in the national election for president in July. The 58-year-old Oro looked almost 10 years younger, and his charismatic personality commanded a devoted, and at times, fanatical, following.

Rodrigo was a committed populist who'd grown up in the barrios outside of Mexico City. He'd fought his way through the rough Mexican political culture and eventually rose to become mayor of Mexico City, and then governor of the state of Hidalgo, adjacent to the capital. His admiration for the Castros and Venezuela's Hugo Chavez pretty well summed up his world view. He despised the norteamericanos, whom he viewed as exploiters of his country, much as the Spaniards had been when they arrived over 500 years ago.

Despite his rough-hewn past and his sometimes harsh views, Rodrigo was as polished as a gemstone. His handsome, silver haired bearing and soft spoken conversation charmed women, who often found him irresistible. Rodrigo could draw people to him and make them want to believe in him. A dynamic orator, his effect on a crowd could be as intoxicating as a drug. Privately, his staff sometimes referred to him as "la droga Oro."

Raul had presented himself to Rodrigo as a man who could be counted on as long as there was something significant in it for him, which was, in fact, an accurate assessment.

"You're refreshingly honest, my friend," Rodrigo said. "Not many are willing to admit they need to be invested personally in our success. There's nothing wrong with that, as long as you don't lose sight of the purpose you serve. Never lose sight of that, my friend."

After talking with Raul, Rodrigo paused to spend time with several other guests, working the room. Some had been invited because they had wealth that could be of use to him. Others had influence in the state government, or in the civic and commercial institutions of the capital city of the state of Morelos. In common, all belonged to one of Mexico's other two political parties, the PRI and the PAN, and, to succeed, he needed support from many like them. After he finished his rounds, Rodrigo moved to the center of the salon, surrounded by his guests.

"Damas y caballeros.....I want to talk to you of Mexico... and her future."

Unlike the quiet, conversational tone he'd shared with each of them a few minutes earlier, his voice now carried a resonance and depth that filled the small space. With a few brief words, spoken barely loud enough for everyone to hear over the subdued background conversation, he'd commanded the room to fall silent. He waited a few seconds for the room to settle completely.

"In a few months the course of our country's history will change."

He paused as his eyes moved about the room, taking care to make contact with most of the guests.

"The future of our beloved Mexico will change," he repeated, his voice now rising slightly. "Permit me to explain. Our history, sadly, has been one of choices between groups of corrupt thieves who govern for themselves and who turn their backs on the people. Every six years, after the sexenio has run its course, our people get to choose...but what exactly have they had to choose between? They get to choose only which group of thieves will steal for the next six years, and nothing more. With your help, this is the year it will end. Mexico is a great and abundant country, mis amigos, but she needs leaders who will rule for all of los Mexicanos, not only for the privileged. Mexico must be for los Mexicanos. For all of them. And it falls on us as leaders to make it so."

Rodrigo's words electrified Raul. He'd seen Rodrigo speak on television many times, but the way his presence dominated the room went beyond anything Raul had expected. Clearly, the salon was too small a stage for him. Raul looked around as the rapt guests all stared at Rodrigo, but, here and there, as he surveyed the faces of people he knew well, Raul thought he saw judgment being withheld.

"The Mexico of the future will not be for the norteamericanos to exploit. They think they are the new conquistadores. The gringos make deals with our corrupt government so that they can build their factories here, and then what do the gringos do? They use our people as cheap labor to make their products while they pay three or four times as much to workers in their own country. And for a price, our government lets them get away with it."

No one moved or made a sound.

"And when our people try to join their families in the north, to find work at a decent wage, what then?" he asked. "What then? The gringos build fences to keep them out. They treat our people like criminals. The gringos have conveniently forgotten that their own patrimony was made of immigrants who spoke no English and came with nothing but hunger in their bellies. Our corrupt government does business with these people, when it should have stood with Chavez. This must change too, mis amigos."

"You were invited here because others listen to you and will follow you. You are all leaders in Morelos but most of you, for reasons I well understand, are not members of my party. That is precisely why you were invited here this evening. I respect the realities you have to deal with, and the risks you have personally accepted by coming here to speak to me, but I must ask now if you share my vision for Mexico. If you do, party will not matter to you. Mexico will matter more."

Raul had made his decision before he'd arrived at the meeting.

"I feel as you do, Rodrigo. I stand with Mexico," he shouted.

"Muchísimas gracias, Raul. I'm in your debt. You serve our country and honor your patrimony."

Around the room it went, most of the others voicing support, some more enthusiastically than others as each calculated how his own interests might be affected if this impressive man eventually succeeded and they hadn't been invested in him.

"Let me speak of something else, mis amigos. If we're unsuccessful in the election, I fully expect it will be because the government bought the votes it needed, or simply miscounted them. It's happened before, and they'll do it again if they must. If we let them get away with that, then what good have we done? What is the point of pretending to have a democracy? If we simply permit them to dictate the outcome there is no democracy."

"We must not let that happen. Not this time. It has to be different, and we must do whatever is necessary to assure the proper result. If we have to take to the streets to vindicate the will of the people, and take the government from their hands and return it to the people by whatever means we can, then so be it."

The audience which had been entertained by Rodrigo's speech now stood in stunned silence. "Take to the streets?" their expressions asked. Raul was as unprepared as the rest, yet understood Rodrigo perfectly. He found the prospects both frightening and exhilarating. He sensed the opportunity to be in on something monumental, to be an insider.

As he had in so many other places, Rodrigo had tried to plant another seed of revolution.

CHAPTER FOURTEEN

Sitting atop a high, dry plain south of Cuernavaca, baking under a fierce tropical sun, even from a distance Xochicalco made Scott's heart race. He hadn't seen it since the summer before his sophomore year in college. Once a city of 20,000, much of it had been restored or rebuilt in a dozen magnificent stone structures. Watching a mile away from the narrow road that wound upward through the green hills below the ruins, Scott imagined that if you added smoke from cooking fires, and some thatched roofs above the smaller buildings, people could be living in it still.

They passed the tourist stop and small museum that the Mexican government had built at the base of the high plain, then drove another 2000 dusty yards up the hill to the road head which ended at the area reconstructed for visitors. Continuing on foot through the restoration, they crested a small hill on a path that led to the restricted working face where tourists couldn't go. Scott got his first look at where he'd spend the next three and a half months.

The dig at Xochicalco looked something like a small quarry. It sat a bit lower than the surrounding terrain, only 20 meters lower in all, and consisted of narrow dirt passages coursing through piles of stones and earth. The activity covered an area of perhaps a quarter mile square, including the tents, trailers and equipment. Here and there, Scott saw small pieces of earth moving equipment he hadn't expected at an archaeological site.

"We're late?" Scott asked, counting more than 25 people working in the distance, some bent over, others moving about purposefully.

"A little," Arturo replied. "But you needed the extra rest."

A large tent canopy in an open field served as headquarters and gathering place for the professional crew and the laborers. Arturo grew serious as they drew close.

"There's going to be some reaction to the two of you that you might have to deal with."

"Oh?" Jerry asked.

"Many of the people you'll meet are simply workers engaged to help with the physical labor. They're good men and they're friendly enough. They'll do what's asked and shouldn't be a problem for you. But the government has many functionarios here that get in the way, and you won't like them any better than I do. I don't fully understand why so many are here or what they're doing, but this site is infested with people from the National Institute of Anthropology and History looking over our shoulders. To be honest, it makes everyone nervous."

"Why would they be a problem for us?" Jerry asked. "My dealings with the INAH have always been fine. I've worked with them before."

"It's only a sense," Arturo said, "but the government people that came here are different from what I'm used to, as well. To me at least, they don't seem right. I doubt they're going to like having gringos watching them."

Jerry laughed at Arturo's comment.

"Watching them? We aren't your average gringos, for God's sake. We're here to help, not watch people."

"I know that, but everyone here won't necessarily see it that way. And, as I've said, something's wrong. Just don't expect to be welcomed with open arms by everyone, and let it go at that. Even I'm made to feel uncomfortable sometimes."

Scott's morning consisted of introductions and a re-acquaintance with the hard, painstaking work of archeology. His job as an anthropologist involved understanding and interpreting what the excavation revealed about the people who'd lived here. Scott wanted to create a rapport with the Mexican archaeologists who sifted through the ruins enabling his work, and he began to appreciate Jerry's efforts back in Albany to get him to speak their language. He would struggle, but the immersion could only help.

Over a lunch of quesadillas at picnic tables under the canopy, as Scott and Jerry talked about their morning, Arturo interrupted with a tall, thin man in tow. Arturo's expressionless companion wore closely trimmed, dark hair, a straw hat, and a small, neat mustache.

"Jerry, Scott. I want you to meet Raul Cathedra. Raul is with the National Institute of Anthropology and History and is in overall charge of the project from the government's point of view. Raul, this is Jerry Dwyer and Scott Flores, the professors from New York I told you about."

As the two rose to shake Raul's hand, Raul smiled down at them, and said, "Por favor, professors, continue with your meal. You probably need the break after this morning. The sun is intense this time of year, especially up here on the high ground. Arturo's told me all about you. Your expertise should be a great help to us and we're fortunate to have you with us, even if only for a very short time. You will only be here for a few months, no?"

"Well, three and a half months, if everything goes as planned," Jerry replied.

"And tell me, what exactly will your contribution be?" Raul asked.

Something about Cathedra's tone made Scott uneasy.

"This is our first day, Raul," Jerry replied, "so Arturo and I haven't had much time to get organized, but Scott and I specialize in the broader study of anthropology, and we probably won't have much to do with the physical operation. Our expertise is more in the analysis of what's found. We may be able to help you better understand the value of what you've recovered. In historical and cultural terms."

"The government certainly appreciates the generosity of your university in sending you here to help us understand our own history, but I doubt we need much help in that regard."

Scott and Jerry exchanged a glance.

Our own history?

"We'll try to make the most of our time here, Raul," Jerry said. "And we'll give you the very best that we have."

"I'm sure that you will, Professor Dwyer. Welcome to Mexico. Now, if you and Professor Flores will excuse me, I have some matters to attend to."

After Raul left, Scott turned to Arturo. "Welcome to Mexico he says? Is he always that charming, or was that something special just for us?"

"I'm sorry for the tone," Arturo replied. "I don't like the man."

"He's not exactly warm and cuddly, is he?" Scott added.

"His arrogance is the least of the problems he causes. He constantly comes and goes from the excavation. I never know when he'll show up, and when he's here, he pulls his government men aside and talks to them about I don't know what. He's very secretive, and insists on having all of the records given to him as soon as they're prepared. What bothers me the most, though, is that he doesn't talk to me. I don't know what he's thinking, or what he's doing. And he scares my people."

"What's his training?" Scott asked

Arturo laughed.

"Undergraduate degree in some social science, as I understand."

"You mean he's in charge of this project and has no training in the field?" Scott asked.

"None. His position has to be from political connections, or perhaps he just paid for it. That's sometimes how it happens. He appears to be quite wealthy, at least judging from the car he drives. You won't see any other new BMW's in the lot here."

"Lovely man," Jerry said, as he finished a quesadilla and wiped the corner of his mouth with a paper napkin. "We'll try to avoid him. Have you tried the chicken? It's excellent."

Arturo asked Scott to spend the afternoon examining artifacts awaiting shipment to the government's offices in Mexico City. The small trailer where they were stored had a flimsy door with a cheap lock, and, when he arrived, Scott saw no sign of the security he'd expected. He turned the door handle and pushed slightly, surprised when the door opened freely.

Unbelievable. It's not even locked.

Inside, Scott found several large folding tables strewn with artifacts of various sizes, partially filled out government inventory forms, and a large supply of small plastic bags. The walls were lined with storage racks containing bagged items, some with labels, many without. From one of the tables he picked up a narrow silver bracelet inlaid with bits of turquoise and what appeared to be small emeralds. Held up to the light that streamed through the trailer's windows, the bracelet caught the light and threw it back into his eyes, so bright it caused him to turn away.

How beautiful. It's magnificent. And not even a lock on the door that works.

One after another, Scott examined objects of a kind he'd only seen in collections. Jewelry inlaid with gemstones, knives, pottery of all sizes and dozens of small statues, some depicting deities and others with significance he could only guess at without spending hours on his computer. To his anthropologist's eye, it was all priceless. It would be priceless to collectors, too. He remembered Arturo's comment about things "disappearing."

Someone could make a lot of money off of this place.

He looked around for the paperwork that would surely have been done on what he'd seen, detailing when and where each artifact was found, its orientation to the site and to other artifacts, its physical description — size, weight, color. Scott found nothing but scraps of paper with fragments of incomprehensible information.

How long have these things been here? Are they just going to toss them in a trailer and wait until someone gets around to figuring out exactly what they have? Where are the notes? Where's the research? It should all be here, with the artifacts.

Although Scott was far more interested in what the site and the artifacts could tell him about who lived here and what their lives were like than he was in the physical evidence itself, he thought the chaos tragic. He'd found a job for himself straightening out this mess.

"Are you authorized to be in here?" said a loud voice penetrating the small trailer from the direction of the doorway.

Startled, Scott turned and faced a tall, dark complexioned man wearing a tan field coat. From the man's facial expression, Scott guessed that he didn't have much of a sense of humor.

"As far as I know I am. Arturo Lopez asked me to take a look at the artifacts in here and make recommendations on how they're being handled. My name is Scott Flores. I'm one of the professors visiting from the United States." He extended his hand.

The man looked down at Scott's outstretched hand, hesitated, then accepted it with no enthusiasm.

"My name is Jorge. From the National Institute of Anthropology and History, Señor Cathedra's agency. This trailer is an area you must have specific permission to enter, and I haven't been told that you're permitted here. Señor Lopez doesn't have the final say over that. Someone will have to talk to Señor Cathedra about your being in here."

Scott began to wonder whether being rude had become a requirement for employment with the INAH.

"I'll do that, Jorge. I was just leaving."

CHAPTER FIFTEEN

The virgin stood guard in front of almost all of the shops their bus passed, and many of the homes.

Scott had expected to be well out into the countryside in a matter of minutes after leaving Cuernavaca. Instead, the bus passed miles of small shops and makeshift storefronts selling everything from car parts to lunch, and endless numbers of simple homes with those corrugated metal roofs he'd seen from the air. She stood in front of them like a department store greeter.

What is it with these statues?

Scott had no use for religion and couldn't fathom the constant presence of La Virgen de Guadalupe. He saw her everywhere. In each of the four homes he'd visited he'd seen a large image of La Virgen prominently displayed. In his billet home the picture was a full five feet long and so large he wondered how they managed to mount it. The farther they got into the countryside, the more of her he saw through the bus window. Unable to contain his curiosity, he turned to Arturo in the next seat.

"What's behind all of this devotion to La Virgen?"

"Ah, La Virgen. La Virgen de Guadalupe is revered here by many. The legend's a very old story, but basically she's the image of the Virgin Mary who's supposed to have appeared to a native during la conquista. She told the man to go to the local bishop and instruct him to build a church at the spot where she appeared. Of course the bishop didn't believe him, so she appeared again and gave him roses to show the bishop. Since at that time no roses grew in Mexico, the bishop had to believe that he was telling the truth, and the church was built. Or so the story goes."

"And people accept this?"

"Many, yes. And likely, most of the people who put these statues out along the road."

Scott thought of the family he'd been staying with and couldn't picture them accepting such a fantastic story.

"You believe any of this, Arturo? The legend, I mean."

Arturo laughed.

"Any of it? Well, who can say what's true and what isn't when it comes to matters of faith, Scottsito? I'm a scientist, and I tend to believe in what I can prove or hold in my hands, but I'm not so arrogant as to suppose that things I can't explain aren't possible."

"But such a tale," Scott protested. "I don't want to insult your countrymen, but why is that any easier to accept than what the Aztecs believed? If you can accept that a woman appeared out of thin air after thousands of years and handed someone a bouquet of roses, why can't you believe that the Aztecs' god told them to build their capital where they found an eagle sitting on a cactus eating a snake? Or that God required human sacrifices before crops would grow? Why believe one and not the other?

Arturo held up his hands.

"Please, I'm an archaeologist, not a theologian. As far as the Catholic church and what it believes, I have many issues. But I also realize that there's a lot I don't understand. Perhaps some things are just matters of faith. Leave it at that."

"And let me give you some advice while we're speaking of this," he continued. "If you're going to get along, you need to remember that many here take matters of faith very seriously. Perhaps more so than in your country. You should be careful not to offend, particularly if it's someone important to you and you don't know what their view is of such things. The culture here's different in many ways."

The trip from Cuernavaca, with all of its stops, had lasted forty minutes, and as he stepped out of the bus, Scott immediately sensed a place very different from Cuernavaca. With barely 15,000 inhabitants, the village of Tepoztlán had a quaint, charming appearance that alone would have made it an interesting destination. Scott quickly spotted the town's true attraction as his eyes were drawn upward to El Tepozteco, the craggy 2000 foot high mountain ridge towering over the pueblo. The top of Tepozteco held what Arturo had brought him to see.

Pointing at the mountain, Arturo asked, "Scottsito, look there, between the two high points of the saddle, in the middle, then to the right. Do you see it?"

Scott could barely make it out, but even in miniature, its unmistakable man-made shape stood out from the natural terrain surrounding it in the notch between the two craggy peaks of Tepozteco. It was an archaeological curiosity that most students of Pre-Columbian culture had visited at least once.

"How the hell did they ever build it up there?" Scott asked, now unable to take his eyes off of the low space between the two mountain tops.

"It had to be a chore," Arturo said. "The stones surely came from the top of the mountain, although we aren't positive exactly how they managed to move it all around in such a difficult location. Wait till you see how tight it is up there."

A 50 foot high remnant of a pyramid built by the Aztecs, the temple of Tepozteco sat astride a narrow, jagged mountain ridge, almost a half mile above the town. The site was so narrow and vertical that a fall down the backside of the pyramid would be fatal. No one was quite sure how the Aztecs had managed to build it, although why they put it there was clear enough.

"There's speculation that the Aztecs thought these mountains might contain an entrance to heaven, or perhaps hell, and that the spirits of the gods could pass through portals here," Arturo said. "So it was a logical enough place for a temple, although no doubt their engineers would have preferred a different location. You won't find any statues of La Virgen up there," Arturo said laughing as they walked through the town and toward the path that led to the top of the mountain.

Scott spotted something that drew him into one of the curio shops lining the town's narrow cobblestone main street.

"How odd," Scott said as he picked up a foot tall plaster figure. "It looks like what we call the grim reaper in the US."

"Santa Muerte. It's Santa Muerte," Arturo said. "You know about her?"

"Saint Death? Never heard of her," Scott replied as held the curious looking statue, examining it more closely. Santa Muerte was a skeletal figure clad in a black cape and holding a scythe in her left hand and a world globe in her right. A golden bag with an owl perched atop rested under her outstretched left arm. Her long black hooded robe was cut in the style of the Benedictine monks.

"She'd make a good Halloween ornament back in the states."

"She's worshiped in a few parts of the country as a legitimate saint. The cult is popular where the drug trade is strong. She's thought to bring favors to the faithful, just like the saints the Catholic church officially promotes. She's supposed to protect the narcos, in particular."

"That's sick," Scott said. "A saint for the narcos?"

"Something like that," Arturo explained. "But it's complex. Here, the drug trade isn't just black and white, good guys against bad guys, which is how it's viewed in your country."

Arturo's comment held Scott's attention as they turned back into the cobblestone street and continued toward the base of Tepozteco.

"You see, to the narcos, the drug trade is just business," Arturo continued. "And the violence happens when the business runs into competition, or when the police, or the army interferes. The narcos don't view their business as evil. To them, it's just business. They think all they do is move the stuff from Columbia through Central America and up to the US. As they see it, they're in the transportation business, and they don't see Mexicans as getting hurt by it. It's myopic, but it allows many of the traffickers to lead respectable lives when they're not working in the shadows. Many live out in the open and give a lot of money to charity, even to the church."

"People actually have faith in this drug saint?" Scott asked.

"In some places. Not so much here in Morelos. More in Guerrero next door. But, yes."

Scott took a last look up at the craggy peak before they ducked under the canopy of trees at the base of the mountain and started up the path.

The steep climb to the top took over an hour, winding through barely discernable trails and often requiring a scramble over boulders and fallen trees. It was damned hard work, and Scott marveled at the number of tourists he passed on his way up, many of whom looked out of shape and struggling. At the end, a breathtaking view of the Tepoztlán valley below rewarded them. The long climb left them tired, and they sat for a long time, legs dangling over the edge of the pyramid, hundreds of feet above the rocks below. The top of the temple at Tepozteco seemed a good place to talk confidentially.

"Now that I have you captive, I have to ask about what's troubling you," Scott said. "At the excavation. You told us that things are disappearing. And it's plain you're worried, but you haven't told me what you think is going on."

"I was thinking of Señor Cathedra's men," Arturo replied. "The rumors are that errors in cataloging and inventory happen and that everything that goes into the cataloging trailer does not necessarily find its way to Mexico City. There's no proof, of course. Just talk."

"But you think it's more than talk. I could tell from the emails you sent to Jerry all spring. He showed all of them to me. Over and over, actually," Scott added, remembering his friend's obsession with the Xochicalco project.

Arturo sighed. "Yes, I'm fairly sure. But even if I had the proof, what could I do about it?"

"Isn't there anyone you can report it to?"

A smile crossed Arturo's face as he said, "Scottsito, you have a lot to learn. Raul was forced on us, which means he has friends and influence. You don't report people like that."

"There has to be something you can do," Scott said.

"Then tell me what it is I can do. I'm just happy to have you and Jerito here for the summer to force things to be done properly. Perhaps it will help."

Scott decided to change the subject.

"Arturo, do you pay much attention to politics?"

"More and more I do, yes. I didn't used to have much time for it, but with all that my country has been through, now I do. Why do you ask?"

"Tell me what you think about the election. And what you think of this Rodrigo Oro who's running for president."

"Oro. Yes, he's causing quite a lot of excitement. Rodrigo Oro is a very provocative man. He's what I'd call a demagogue. He gives fiery speeches and gets people excited with lots of talk about how the common man has been made a victim of corrupt politicians. He uses a lot of slogans about 'Mexico for the Mexicans' and such. He hates your country."

"You don't agree with him?"

"It's all overblown. He says things that he believes will make him popular, but I don't think he really understands the people. Many are drawn in by his personality, and there are surely some who agree with him, but I don't think he'll win. Most Mexicans know better, I think. But still, I worry."

"About what?"

"Oro is different. There's something about him that's troubling. I don't trust him to play by the rules. It's just a feeling I have."

"He'll have to accept the results of the election if he loses, so he has to play by the rules. What choice does he have?"

Arturo laughed.

"You need to study Mexican history, amigo. This is not the United States. We haven't had two hundred years of stable democracy here. We've really had only a little more than 15 years of it, and things are still unsettled. We've had many years of stability, but not necessarily democracy. Until three elections ago, the same political party claimed to have won every election for 70 years. You think that was a coincidence, or that everyone loved them for almost a century?"

"I suppose not," Scott said.

"So, would it be so surprising for one of our elections now to produce, how shall I say it — an inconclusive result? Things aren't so certain here. Don't be deceived because you don't see mobs in the streets and because Mexico looks like home when you go out in the evening. This is a different country in many ways."

Scott reached into the pocket of his hiking vest and pulled out a small pewter flask. The smooth tequila felt good going down, and he took a second, longer drink. Arturo watched as Scott tipped the flask.

"Scottsito, if you want to understand Mexico, you don't have to look any farther than the people around you. Just ask them what they care about. We're an open book. There's nothing subtle about us."

"And what do you care about?"

"A fair question after my speech. Simple things. I want what most people want. To be left alone to do my work and to be able take care of my family. It's not much, and I have that now. I want to keep it that way."

Scott noticed Arturo eyeing the flask.

"I'm sorry. I should have offered."

He handed the flask to Arturo, who drank fully half of its contents.

"You know, Scottsito, this temple we're sitting on was named for the god Tepoztecatl? You know what, exactly, he was the god of?"

Scott laughed as he remembered that gods had assignments in those days.

"Of course I know," Scott replied. "The god devoted to pulque. A local alcoholic drink, isn't it? It's a bit of a joke among my colleagues. To think they went to all the trouble to build this place up here to honor a god who represents devotion to a drink."

"Ever tried it? The pulque?" Arturo asked.

"No, never have."

"Pobrecito, you deserve it after climbing all the way up here and listening to my philosophy. They sell it in the town. When we get back down, I'll buy you a drink. You may end up with an entirely new appreciation of Tepoztecatl."

Chapter Sixteen

The sign outside read "El Rincón" and it looked like as good a place as any. The little hole-in-the-wall met his need.

From his seat in the darkness, Scott could barely make out the hand lettered poster on the wall behind the bartender advertising cheap drinks. At the end of the bar, he saw a dirty, pathetic man with a three day beard and matted black hair staring into a glass of beer.

God knows what his problems are.

A few stools away from Scott, a thin, elderly woman with skin resembling worn brown leather nursed a glass of whisky. She looked up, glassy eyed, and smiled at him with a toothless grin.

"A large glass of Cuervo, por favor, with a little ice?" Scott asked when the bartender nodded in his direction.

"Sí Señor," the bartender replied, eyeing Scott. Few gringos visited El Rincón.

"The Cuervo isn't a problem, but the ice is. And straight is okay?"

"Sure," Scott replied.

"Where are you from, Señor, if you don't mind me asking?" the bartender said as he poured Scott's drink. "You're not Mexicano."

CUERNAVACA

"New York."

"New York? And what brings you to Cuernavaca?"

"My work. I'm helping with archaeological work at Xochicalco. I'm an anthropologist."

"Are you now? I'm certain you're the very first anthropologist we've had the pleasure of serving here," the bartender said with a grin, proud that he'd managed to pronounce the word "antropólogo" correctly. He'd never heard the word, and had no idea what an anthropologist was.

"Did you hear that, Rosa? The gringo is an antropólogo," he said to the elderly woman.

She said nothing, and kept looking at Scott with her empty headed half smile.

"She doesn't hear so well," the bartender laughed. "And this time of night, she doesn't understand so well, either. I'm curious, Señor, what is it, exactly, that an antropólogo does, and why would you come all the way from New York to do it here?"

"Well, there are places in New York where anthropology is important, but my specialty is Central America, Mexico in particular. You know, los indígenas, the Aztecs and the Maya? So I came here."

Scott paused as he took another long drink and looked at the bartender, wondering if he understood.

"An anthropologist is someone who studies cultures and how people live, or lived, in this case, what they believed, their religions, how they fought wars, that sort of thing. Basically, everything about them. In Mexico you refer to it as el patrimonio, and it's very rich. Very rich. My country has nothing to compare to it."

"Does that little statue you have in your hand have

95

something to do with your work here?" the bartender asked, nodding toward the small figure Scott held.

Lisa's gift never left him. Scott had taken it out of his pants pocket without thinking. Small enough to be concealed in a closed fist, the bartender, an acute observer of everything that went on in his domain, had noticed it.

"In a way, yes," Scott replied, holding it up to the light so the bartender could get a good look. "It's a figure of a small child, made by your ancestors, a very long time ago."

A look of surprise crossed the bartender's face.

"It's real?" the bartender asked. "I didn't think you were allowed to possess such things. Isn't something like that supposed to be in a museum?"

"It's real," Scott said, handing it to him. "Go ahead. Take a look. It's your history, not mine."

"Most *are* in museums, but there are ways to obtain them," Scott continued. "They're hard to get and very expensive."

As the bartender examined the tiny relic, Scott said, "I always carry it with me. It reminds me of what's important."

"So, you've come here to help our Mexican...what did you call them...antropólogos?" the bartender asked, handing the tiny figure back to Scott.

"Exactamente," Scott replied. "And to study what they find so I can share it with my students. I'm a teacher. Or at least I was," Scott added, not expecting the bartender to understand.

"You're a teacher? I have great respect for teachers. My son is a teacher. The next drink is on me, Señor, and I'll break my rule and have one with you. We can drink to — what did you call it? — el patrimonio?"

As they shared a drink, Scott noticed a sign behind the bar that read "Oro para Presidente."

"Do you mind if I ask you something — what's your name by the way? I didn't catch it."

"Eduardo. You can call me Eddie."

Scott extended his hand.

"Well, Eddie, nice to meet you. Scott Flores. I see the political sign there behind the bar, that you're supporting Señor Oro. What is it about this Oro you like so much that you put his sign here?"

"Oro cares about the common people, not the rich and the politicians. And that's what we are here. Common people. So we support him. See? It's simple."

"That's as far as it goes?"

"Yes. As far as it goes. What more is there? It's simple."

"Have you ever thought that this Oro might be using you, people like you, and that he might not really care so much about common people as about himself? After all, he's a politician and you can't know what he really thinks."

"You're right, I have no way of knowing, but you have to believe in something, and he's the best we have."

Scott noticed a small image of La Virgen de Guadalupe a few feet to the side of Oro's poster.

"I suppose you do. Can I have another Cuervo, por favor?"

After his fourth drink Scott considered calling a taxi, but with the familiar, comforting, mellow feeling running through him, he stayed. Going home meant sleep, sleep meant dreams, and sometimes being awake was better. He closed his eyes...

***

His nights out with his friends had become more

common, and lasted longer. On many evenings at home he never put much distance between himself and a drink. As he knelt on the cold bathroom floor with his head in the commode at 1:30 in the morning on a weeknight Lisa had snapped.

"Where have you been? You have class at eight. Look at you. You won't be in any shape to teach tomorrow."

"I'm alright," he said. "Just go back to bed and don't worry about it. I just don't feel well."

"Don't tell me not to worry and send me back to bed. I can see what's happening. Scott, I'm afraid."

Scott managed to pull himself up on his feet to face her.

"What are you scared of? There's nothing wrong with me. I just lost track of the time."

"Oh yes there *is* something wrong. Damn you Scott, you do this two or three nights every week and it's getting worse. I'm afraid of what's happening to you. And us."

"Us?" he asked. "Having a drink once in a while isn't going to do anything to us unless you make a big deal out of it."

"Scott, this isn't just once in a while. And it's not just 'having a drink.' I'm scared you won't be able to stop. I'm a nurse for God's sake. You think I don't know what's happening?"

"You're worrying about nothing," he said. He brushed past her and headed to their bedroom.

She followed him into the room.

"Don't you treat me like this Scott."

He turned to face her, ready to reply with something sharp and angry, but the tears streaking down her face stopped him before he could speak. She'd been crying all the while, he realized. Through the haze that he'd been

98

pretending for the last few minutes didn't exist, he saw how much she hurt.

They stood silently for a moment, looking at each other, Lisa starting to sob. Scott wrapped his arms around her and let her rest her head on his shoulder.

"I'm so sorry baby," he said in a soft voice, stroking her hair. "I didn't mean to treat you like this. Maybe you're right. Sometimes I just don't see things clearly. But I love you. I see that clear enough."

The rest of that night, Lisa had held him tight, hardly sleeping at all.

***

Scott had lost track of time. He'd been looking down at his glass, quiet, for a long while when closing time came. Eddie had left him alone.

"Amigo, I'm afraid it's time for you to go. I have to close up," Eddie said.

Grateful for the interruption, Scott's red eyes looked up at Eddie.

"Sorry I wasn't more sociable," Scott said, his soft voice barely audible.

"Señor, you have nothing to be sorry about. I'm just the bartender. Con permiso...I don't know you, but I've learned a little from being here so long. I've been watching you sitting here since we talked. I know when someone has a weight on his heart, and I think you do. I don't know what troubles you, but I don't think you'll find the answer in the bottom of a glass of the Cuervo, as good as it is."

So far from home, Scott had stumbled onto a big hearted man.

"Well, Scott Flores, antropólogo, whatever the trouble is, if you feel the need, the door to El Rincón is always open."

99

It was 1:00 a.m., and still very warm when Scott left El Rincón, stepped out unsteadily into the evening, and looked for a taxi. The street was narrow, dark and empty, lit only by a few dim street lights spread far apart. It had rained briefly, as it often did in the evening in Cuernavaca, and the lights reflected off of the wet pavement. He should have felt afraid in the darkness, but not much could happen to him that would be worse than the way things already were. There was no traffic of any kind, much less a taxi, and Scott began to walk in the general direction of home. It would take 30 minutes if a cab didn't happen by, and he'd decided that the walk might do him good. The moist night air felt clean and fresh.

The walk cleared his head a little, but not enough to alert him to the presence of the short, swarthy man who was following 50 yards behind him. After Scott had gone a half dozen blocks toward home, the man turned down a side street and keyed a number into his cell phone.

"He was in there about an hour and a half and left at closing time, alone. He talked some to the bartender but I wasn't close enough to hear anything. He just sat there quietly most of the time. He looked pretty drunk by the time he left. To come to a place like this and drink as much as he did, I'd say he has a problem."

The man listened for a moment before continuing.

"Understood. I'll stop in tomorrow and find out what I can about him. Eduardo doesn't know when to stop talking. He'll tell me all about the gringo."

After talking for a minute more, the man ended the call and headed for his car, leaving Scott to his solitary journey home.

CHAPTER SEVENTEEN

The sweat rolled down Arturo's face as he labored under the sun, bent over a boxed screen, sifting dirt, his shirt soaked.

For Arturo, archaeology wasn't anything like the Indiana Jones movies. Hard, painstaking work, it demanded patience. Like all archaeologists, Arturo wanted to take his time, working slowly from the surface downward, centimeter by centimeter. He wanted his workers to sift carefully through the soil, using a grid system of neat one meter square sections to record the precise location and orientation of anything of interest, no matter how small. They called it recording "provenience." Done well, it was tedious.

At Xochicalco, doing it well could be impossible.

A backwater in the world of Mexican archaeology, the area surrounding Cuernavaca had been overshadowed by more recent work at Mayan sites in the Yucatan and spectacular places like Teotihuacan, north of Mexico City. Long ago explored and restored, Xochicalco was on a list for eventual further attention, but the government, with a limited budget, put off working in what seemed an unpromising location. That changed when a group of academics from UNAM, the Universidad Nacional Autónoma de México, uncovered an exciting new field adjacent to the long restored ruins at Xochicalco. The following year brought Arturo from the university to Cuernavaca, with a government provided budget to spend.

Scott descended the 20 vertical feet to where Arturo worked and handed him a bottle of cold water before taking a seat on a large stone next to where the archaeologist knelt.

"You're going to get heat stroke if you're not careful," Scott said.

"I know my limits." Arturo smiled as he stood and wiped his forehead with a bandanna. "I've been doing this for a long time."

He took a welcome drink and wiped his forehead again, this time with his shirt sleeve. He looked up at the blinding sun, then at Scott.

"Gracias. I struggle with this place. I wish we could go about this differently."

"Meaning?"

"I don't like having to disturb things so much all at one time. This isn't like excavating an earthen area, where you can be careful and move slowly. Archaeology is a destructive science, after all, and when we excavate we're destroying the site forever. It can never be put back together. All that I've learned taught me to respect that. So, when I pull these stones aside, everything around them and under them is disturbed. I know we're losing information here. It's frustrating."

The working face at Xochicalco was unusual. Hundreds of meters from the restored structures of the original site that the tourists visit, at the start it was little more than a large pile of stones, partially buried, surrounded by shrubs and trees. It looked like rubble with no particular organization. The UNAM people revealed it to be much more than that. The problem for the Mexican archaeologists was that instead of working with small hand trowels, dental tools and brushes, they found themselves using backhoes and construction equipment to dislodge stones that centuries ago were part of something quite large.

"It's the nature of this place," Scott said. "But from what I see in the trailer, the way this came apart is a blessing as well. So many of the cavities hold artifacts that have been sealed away in little time capsules for us. It's much better than having to dig them out of the soil. So much of it's preserved."

"Yes, the quake, if that's what it was, is a blessing for us, but surely was a curse for them," Arturo said. "To take this structure down it must have been incredibly powerful. There wouldn't have been much left standing anywhere close by. Many must have died. And if it was some type of military event, well, they probably all died. War was in some ways more brutal then."

Arturo glanced at his watch.

"Scottsito, you must be hungry by now. It's almost three. I don't suppose you've grown accustomed to the meal schedule here."

"Hardly. I don't know how you can go so long between breakfast and dinner, which is really lunch. Your stomachs must be put together differently than ours."

Arturo laughed as they walked toward the tent. "Let's feed the gringo."

"May I join you, Señor Lopez?" she said.

Barely loud enough to be heard over the background noise of the mealtime conversation, the first feminine voice he'd heard at the project commanded Scott's attention.

"Of course, Anarosa. Please. Sit. Ana, this is Scott Flores. Scott's a professor of anthropology from the State University of New York who'll be spending the summer here. Scott, this is Anarosa Mendes, one of my assistants. And one of my favorites," he added with a smile. "I'd be lost without her."

"Señor Lopez, please," Anarosa said.

Scott extended his hand. Hers felt warm and soft, unlike the dozens of others he'd touched at the site, and curiosity about her stirred as soon as he touched her. Her coal black hair, worn past her shoulders, framed warm, tawny brown eyes, set in a mellow complexion that North American women spend hours in tanning booths trying to manufacture. Tall for a Mexican woman, and fit, for some reason she made Scott feel uneasy.

"Señor Lopez overstates my importance here. How long have you been in Cuernavaca, Scott?" Anarosa asked.

"Just two weeks. It's been an adjustment, but I'm getting along okay."

"Your Spanish is quite good."

"It's getting better quickly, and turning into a survival skill. Do you speak any English?" Scott asked, hoping.

"I do," she responded in English. "Are you more comfortable with this?"

"Either is fine."

He lied.

"But I need the practice. And it's your country," he responded.

"I'm sure you're getting all the practice you need. I studied a year in the states, so I know what it's like to be a foreigner. Sometimes finding a friend who speaks your native language can be a blessing," she continued in flawless English.

"I appreciate that," Scott said, grateful.

"It's Ana. Please. Your name, Flores, it's Hispanic?"

"It is, but it's from way back in the family history."

"I thought maybe you learned the language at home," Ana said.

"My grandfather was born in Cuba, and, no, I came by the language the hard way."

During lunch, Scott marveled at Ana's easy grace, which he supposed spoke of both breeding and a personality filled with self-confidence. Although quite respectful in her tone, particularly with Arturo, she managed to avoid seeming subservient and youthful. He guessed her to be in her late twenties, noticed she didn't wear a ring and wondered why.

"Tell me about Anarosa, Arturo," Scott asked, after she'd gone.

"She's bright. Beyond bright, really. And one of the best in the doctoral program at UNAM. That's why she's here for the summer. She comes from a wealthy and very prominent family in Mexico City and is devout. Her father is influential with the government, and I believe he's a close friend of the president."

"Devout?"

Scott wondered why Arturo would mention her religious conviction.

"Yes. Her family is quite religious. Católicos. You're interested?"

"No. Not at all. Just curious."

"I'd put the curiosity aside and concentrate on the antiquities."

"Why? She's taken?"

"I've no idea. But I can tell you she's focused on her career. She's a very serious young woman and seems to have no time for anything else. I don't ask about her personal life, and she doesn't volunteer anything about it. But I can tell you that Señor Cathedra has paid a lot of attention to her. They've been seen together and when he graces us with his presence here at the excavation he always manages to spend time wherever she's working. It's pretty obvious he's interested in her. How much she's interested in him, I'm not so sure, since I'm not privy to their conversations or their private lives."

Raul?

In the few minutes he'd spent with Anarosa, Scott had already begun to create a place for her in his imagination. Raul didn't fit into that picture at all.

"I doubt you'll have enough time in Mexico to get very far with her, if that's what you're thinking," Arturo continued. "I can't speak for her personal standards, but, as I said, the family is very devout, and to me she seems the old fashioned type who would take up a lot of time."

"What do you think of her, Arturo? I mean personally."

"Well, let me tell you plainly. You won't find a finer young woman in all of Mexico. She's delightful. But then, you're just curious?"

Scott smiled, and Arturo smiled back.

"Yes, Arturo, just curious."

CHAPTER EIGHTEEN

Weary, Rodrigo rubbed his eyes and let his head sink into the comfortable seat of the tour bus. He watched through the window for a few minutes as the countryside passed by. The view in this stretch between Mexico City and Querétaro was all too familiar. Miles and miles of small, primitive homes, shacks really, barely providing shelter. He knew the barrio because he'd lived there. Now he needed the people he'd left behind in places like these. The trick was getting them to vote.

As a small, bespectacled man slipped into the seat next to him without speaking, Rodrigo turned toward him and asked, "How bad is it?"

Felipe Bencivenga handed Rodrigo a sheaf of papers and let Rodrigo read them before answering. Rodrigo pulled his glasses out of his shirt pocket and studied the report.

"Well under 30 percent, I'm afraid, Rodi," Felipe said when Rodrigo had finished. "The problem isn't so much the percentage, although it's not good. It's the trend. Or I should say the lack of a trend. We've barely moved in the last two weeks. We only have seven weeks to go and 26 percent isn't going to be enough. We've gone flat."

Felipe had been with Rodrigo since Rodrigo's days as Mayor of Mexico City. He was the candidate's closest confidante, and the intellectual heart of Rodrigo's campaign. They agreed on most everything, and Felipe's commitment to Rodrigo's plan was total. With Felipe, Rodrigo could speak plainly.

Rodrigo put the papers down on the tray in front of him, folded his glasses and put them back in his pocket. He sat back in his chair, and closed his eyes.

After a moment, he leaned forward, and said, "Felipe, we won't win the election. We never thought we would, did we? The count will be a fraud. It always is. The question is, what comes next?"

"I'd feel a lot better if we were closer to 35 percent." Felipe replied, his voice full of concern. "The PAN is surely going to come third, but the PRI is polling at over 40 percent, Rodi. It's going to be impossible to support a real challenge when we're under 30 percent and they're close to a majority."

Mexico's three party system made Rodrigo's job difficult, and his plan looked increasingly futile. The incumbent conservative Partido Acción Nacional candidate trailed badly, but the moderate Partido Revolucionario Institucional, which had ruled Mexico for most of a century before the last several elections, had a commanding lead, and was closing in on an outright majority. Its candidate, Ricardo Ruiz, the popular governor of the State of San Luis Potosi, had promised that the PRI had shed a legacy of corruption and would govern as a moderate force in Mexican politics. If one added together the support of the PRI and the PAN, Rodrigo's PRA party had support from less than a third of the country. Rodrigo didn't expect to win the election, but he needed a strong showing to continue the fight afterward.

"We have time," Rodrigo said. "A lot can change in seven weeks. I'm more concerned that we'll have all of the right people in place after the votes are counted. We still have a lot of work to do there. No matter what Ruiz says, it's the same old PRI. They won't be able to resist making sure that they win, but this time we'll catch them at it and use it. Most people still think the PRI will rig elections, and they'll believe us."

"I know you look at the PAN as our enemies, but after the election they'll become our allies," Rodrigo continued. "You'll see. It's inevitable. They may be conservatives, but they're politicians first, and they won't be able to resist attacking our mutual enemy. Their biggest fear is that the PRI will re-establish itself for another 70 years. They'll join us, if they must, to stop that from happening."

Patient, and convinced that time was on his side, Rodrigo took a long range view of things. Losing the election would be a temporary setback, but it would provide an opportunity to destabilize the system and shake the country's confidence in it. Eventually, somehow, he would have his chance. But to fully exploit the lost election he had to convince more than half of the country that the election had been stolen, not won. His base of supporters believed most anything he said, but that only gave him whatever percentage he managed to win outright. For every percentage point he didn't win outright, he'd have to convince people who had voted for one of his opponents that the process had been corrupted.

"The entire plan depends on our ability to show that the results are illegitimate. As soon as Ruiz is announced as the winner we have to be ready to claim massive fraud, all over the country," Rodrigo said. "And it has to be everywhere. Our most important job right now is to make sure we have all of the people in place to do that. We need to be ready with announcements and demonstrations in as many municipalities as possible. Right after it's over, we have to create the impression that the entire election was a joke. There will only be a very brief window when that will be effective"

"We're in good shape there, Rodi," Felipe reassured him. "By July we'll have something in place in all of the major cities."

"That's not good enough," Rodrigo said. "We need to work it all the way down to the smaller state capitals. If we're going to lose the election we have to get as much mileage out of it as we can."

"That will take a lot more money than we have at the moment," Felipe said. "We barely have enough to handle the rest of the campaign and then we need to fund the demonstrations in the major cities. Mobilizing the post-election operation is as expensive as the campaign. There are new people to pay off. There will be media people now, and the police officials who control crowds and demonstrations. A lot of new people will have their hands out before we can put on the kind of show we need."

"It will be alright, Felipe," Rodrigo reassured him. "We have access to a source of money that our opponents won't touch. An almost limitless supply of it."

Felipe frowned. "You've decided to take it, then, haven't you?"

"We have no choice."

"God help us," Felipe said quietly. "Isn't there another way?" He shook his head slowly. "To make that deal..."

"There's no point in worrying about the morality of how you raise money to pay bribes, now, is there?" Rodrigo answered.

Rodrigo knew it would take more than a well-turned phrase to overcome Felipe's worry. He put his arm around his confidante's shoulder.

"We've come too far and risked too much. We have to see this through, no matter. It will be worth it all. You'll see."

An hour later the bus arrived in Querétaro where it was immediately swamped by a crowd of supporters chanting, "¡Oro, Oro, Oro!" As he stepped from the bus to work the crowd, Rodrigo felt energized. He never got used to it.

Rodrigo hadn't polled particularly well in Querétaro, and the size of the crowds that met him at his three campaign stops there gratified him. A surprising amount of money had been collected here, he'd learned. If he could manage to pull over 30 percent in places like this, his plan might work.

That night, as he sat in the chartered plane from Querétaro to Oaxaca, exhausted from a 15 hour day, Rodrigo leaned over and turned to Felipe. "We've been together a long time, haven't we?" he said.

"Since Mexico City. You're feeling sentimental?"

Rodrigo laughed. "Hardly. I was just thinking about how incredibly difficult it is to take an entire country and move it to where you want it to go. You realize the odds against us?"

"Of course I do, Rodi. But I can't imagine a better way to spend my life than this," Felipe said. "Can you?"

Rodrigo looked out the window at the lights of the Mexican countryside passing by below him.

"No, Felipe. I can't."

CHAPTER NINETEEN

They use their public spaces so much better than we do.

The project took weekends off, which left Scott time to walk the city. The zócalo was a 20 minute walk from home, and he'd spent parts of his first few Saturdays there. He always found it crowded with what he supposed was a cross section of the town. They were old and young, and from their appearance he concluded that while some struggled, most were just average people. Few, it seemed, were prosperous. Those folks, apparently, congregated elsewhere. Scott felt sure he could learn something of the character of the city here.

He remembered what Arturo had said about the statue of Zapata still working for the modern day revolutionaries. Sitting on a bench not 20 feet from the statue's base, he could read most of the crude signs that hung on its sides. Almost all expressed support for Rodrigo Oro and his PRA party.

Someday an archaeologist will dig up a piece of General Zapata and wonder what it means.

An older man, perhaps 60, caught Scott's attention. Dressed in a simple white tee shirt and a pair of light colored pants that looked like they hadn't been washed in a long time, he wore scuffed work boots and a baseball cap, and had a bushy gray mustache. As Scott watched, the man occupied himself with taping a crude poster to the base of the statue. The sign advocated disarming the entire Mexican army, and Scott couldn't resist asking him why he thought such an odd notion would be a good idea.

"Señor," Scott said, interrupting the man's admiration of his own work. "May I ask you about this?"

The man turned to Scott, eyeing him before responding. "You're norteamericano?" he asked.

When Scott looked surprised at the question, the old man smiled and said, "It's the accent. Hard to hide."

"Of course," Scott replied. "Tell me, why on earth would you want to disarm the entire army? It seems a strange thing to be advocating. Your sign says that it has to be done to assure liberty. But you live in a democratic country. Isn't the army here to protect your country?"

The old man's lips curled into a wry expression suggesting that he thought he'd figured things out better than most.

"Protect us from what? Why do you suppose Mexico has such a large army?" the older man said. "You think it was created just so the government could fight the narcos? It existed for many years before the narcos were a problem, and will still be there when they're gone. Mexico has always had a large army, many times larger than it has any reason to have. What are the chances that Guatemala is going to invade us anytime soon, eh? Or your country? Hell, we'd probably be better off if you did. And that covers it, as far as protecting the country goes."

"No, Señor," he continued. "The army in Mexico has always existed to protect the government from its own people and no other reason. It was the government's army that Zapata fought during the revolution. Except for when your country invaded us 170 years ago, the only people the Mexican army ever killed in the whole history of the country were other Mexicans. Our history is different from yours."

Scott hadn't expected such a clear and sensible sounding explanation for an opinion he'd thought eccentric. He was beginning to appreciate the elemental, straightforward way average Mexicans sometimes looked at things that, to him, seemed nuanced and complex. He remembered his conversation with Arturo about La Virgen, and how Eddie the bartender at El Rincón had explained his support for Oro.

Scott walked the two block length of the zócalo, toward the dour looking state office building at the far end, past the food vendors and the young lovers holding hands sitting on the benches that lined the square. The early evening was warm and sweet, like almost every evening in Cuernavaca. Scott was quickly growing fond of it.

To one side of the main entrance to the central offices of the State of Morelos, Scott confronted a curious collection of posters, candles and flowers, surrounded by a knee high white picket fence. Scattered throughout were photographs, mostly of young people and women. Several were of police officers. It had the character of a shrine. Some of the posters expressed a poignant grief over "desaparecidos" — the disappeared, or the lost — which Scott took to be people who had been kidnapped or killed by the narcos. Mexico, he knew, had a serious problem with organized crime centered around the drug trade, but the narcotrafico involved other forms of criminal activity, notably kidnapping, which often ended up a sideline business of the narcos.

As he studied the photos and handwritten notes, he wondered what it must be like to be touched by such sadness. Or worse, to be one of the victims. He thought of his own melancholy.

Perhaps there's something worse.

"It's all so sad, isn't it?"

The soft feminine voice startled him.

Scott turned and saw Anarosa Mendes standing behind him. She looked past him, at the desaparecidos. "Anarosa. Buenas noches. Sí, es."

"It's Ana."

"Of course. Sorry."

Why the hell does she make me nervous?

"I understand what this is about, Ana," he said, motioning toward the display. "But I can't see how people find any special comfort by displaying their grief to the public square. We have crimes in my country, God knows, but you'd never see this. At home, this is usually a private matter."

"In your country, perhaps," she said. "Not here. Mexicanos feel the same emotions as anyone else, but we aren't embarrassed to show our feelings, and this place is very much in our character. The photos are placed here so that the families' grief can be shared with others who may choose to accept some of the burden, symbolically. It comforts them."

"Then it serves a purpose," he said.

"It does," she replied.

"You want to sit somewhere and talk for a while?" he asked.

"Sure. I'd like that," she replied in English.

Scott worried that his conversation might seem strained, stressed in some way. He imagined that in

Spanish he might sound more like a high school boy, or worse, an immigrant, than he would a 34 year old Harvard Ph.D.

"Thanks," he replied in English, relieved. "It'll be good to speak English for a while."

She tossed her head back and laughed. "I thought so, Scottsito."

Scott smiled at the "ito" suffix Mexicans reserved for those viewed with affection. He'd barely had a conversation with Ana.

They stopped at a small restaurant called La Universal, just off the zócalo. From a sidewalk table, they could watch the people in the square, bathed in the light of the street lamps and the bright vendors' stations. Although after dark now, the center of the city was just waking.

Despite the presidential election, politics had fled the square in the evening. In the afternoons, Scott had grown accustomed to seeing tables distributing political pamphlets, and hearing people speaking on bullhorns advocating some position or another. He'd seen several parades of local candidates around the square. In the evening, people cared more about music, food, drink, and each other, and Scott preferred it.

Under the lights of the zócalo, Scott and Ana talked of their educations, their families, even the national election. He explained about studying at Harvard and teaching at Albany, and she about growing up in Mexico City in a privileged family that counted the president among its friends. Scott worried that Ana would ask about his relationship status and he considered how he should respond if she did. He could simply say he'd been married for a while, but that seemed dishonest, and, he knew it wouldn't be enough. She didn't seem a woman you could easily misdirect, nor did he sense that he should he try. Whether on this evening, or another, he knew he'd have to expose his wounds. He decided to invite a direct approach.

"Ana, can I ask something personal?"

"Depends how personal," she laughed.

"Is there anyone special in your life, a man I mean? I don't want to sound forward, but I'd guess that you have someone," he asked.

She hesitated before answering.

"You asked that so politely. And so carefully. The answer to your question is, no, there isn't anyone special in my life right now. Is that what you were hoping to hear, Scottsito?" Scott saw a familiar mischief in her smile. She never let her eyes break contact as she waited for an answer.

Disarmed, Scott hadn't expected to have his question turned back on him so deftly. When he didn't answer quickly, Ana backed away.

"I'm sorry. I didn't mean to make you feel uncomfortable," she said.

"No, it's alright. It's what I wanted to hear. You're a very interesting person to talk to, Anarosa Mendes."

"At the risk of being even more interesting, let me ask you the same question," she said. It was what he'd expected when he started the conversation.

"No, I don't have anyone either. I'm a widower. My wife died last December in an auto accident."

Whenever he shared what had happened to Lisa the reaction was always the same — sympathy and surprise, followed by the obligatory condolence. He could almost hear the "how young for such an awful thing" that usually followed. It had become a ritual. He hated it.

Ana's expression barely changed, except that she looked at him more intently, he thought. She seemed to invite a connection, her warm, expressive eyes staying focused, yet causing him no discomfort. She just watched him for a moment, as if to say she understood he'd heard too many times how sorry people felt for him.

"Do you have any children, Scott?" she asked.

"No. Lisa was pregnant with our first when she died."

Lisa. He hadn't spoken her name to many people since she died, and the mention of it was something of a line for him to cross. It made things personal, and exposed him, as though a secret had been revealed.

"It must have been unimaginably difficult," she said, looking down at her drink for a moment. "When I was 15 I lost a sister. I remember how awful it was for us. It was a long time before any of us had what I'd call normal lives. Our faith helped."

Scott noticed the crucifix that hung around her neck on a bright silver chain and remembered Arturo's description of her as devout.

"But time does heal us, Scottsito. I know it from my own life. We heal."

Scott marveled at how gracefully Ana had handled learning about his wife's death, and how she had avoided the reflexive expression of sympathy he despised, replacing it with something fresh, something that actually helped.

"Walk with me around the zócalo," she said.

They walked around, and then through, the two block long square, pausing to look over a few of the street vendors, finally stopping at the end of the plaza where the mariachi bands gathered, waiting for commissions to play.

Scott spoke briefly to one of the musicians and passed him a bill.

"For the Señorita," the bandsman announced, nodding in Ana's direction as the trumpet player began to play Besame Mucho. The other three band members joined as the ensemble drew a crowd taking advantage of the free concert.

"Muchísimas gracias, Scottsito," Ana said to him over the music. "It's such an honor to have a song played for you. Especially in front of an audience." She smiled like a schoolgirl.

The band finished to loud applause from the people gathered nearby, and, after Scott's generous tip, to the delight of everyone, played an encore.

"Mariachis are supposed to be commissioned to play for one's novia — your girlfriend," Ana said after the band finished. "Not that I minded the concert. They were wonderful. And it was so sweet of you."

They walked around the zócalo a while longer before Ana said, "I'm afraid it's time for me to go. Finding you tonight wasn't at all what I expected. Tonight was wonderful."

"You're taking a taxi or do you have a car here?" he asked.

"A taxi," she said.

"Let me walk you to the curb."

Scott wanted to extend the evening, even if by a few minutes.

"Can I drop you somewhere?" she asked.

"No. Thanks. I think I'll stay here a while longer."

Scott watched her cab pull away, then turned toward the end of the square and headed down Fray Bartolome de las Casas toward El Rincón.

CHAPTER TWENTY

He left El Rincón earlier than usual, and, instead of heading home, Scott turned up the steep incline of Fray Bartolome de las Casas and back toward the square. Light headed at first, then faint, he stopped halfway up the long block, before the top of the hill, and leaned against the wall, steadying himself.

Is the hill that steep or is it the alcohol?

Gathering himself, Scott finished the walk, pushed his way past an assortment of old men and young couples and sank into a spot on one of the hard metal benches that ringed the zócalo.

Why didn't I just go home? This will only make it worse.

Suddenly weary, his shoulders sagged. He tilted his head back, letting the sound of the busy square roll over him. He heard laughter, music, cars driving by, and bits of conversations.

This place reminds me of the university. Everyone just goes around happy, no clue about me. I'm right here looking just like them. For all they know, I have a normal life, too. Normal. Now there's something to aspire to.

He thought about heading home, but didn't have the energy.

No, better just to stay here a while longer.

Odd. Who knew that this would be so exhausting? I'm always tired. No, not tired. Weary. Odd, too, how some days I want to be alone and other days I can't stand to be. There's no sense to it.

Scott closed his eyes and tried to empty his mind. After a while, he drifted off, his arm falling to the side as his chin came to rest on his chest.

***

"I don't like you this way, Scott. You worry me so."

He turned toward Lisa's voice and saw her sitting on the bench next to him.

"I need to know you're safe, baby," she said. "But I'm afraid. There are bad things here."

He wanted to reach for her but his arms wouldn't move. Neither would his lips. It was always this way. All he could do was listen.

"Look at you. It hurts me to see you like this. What are you doing, Scotty? Please baby. Don't do this."

Scott struggled to say something but no words came.

"Lover," she said. "It was my time, not yours. You need to live, baby. And you're killing yourself."

Chapter Twenty-One

Each Friday afternoon for as long as he could remember Raul had made the same 40 minute trip east from Cuernavaca to the town of Cuautla and the orphanage called Hogar de Esperanza. He always went alone, and he never talked to anyone about it. His regular disappearance from the project had become so predictable that no one expected to see him after 2:00 on Friday.

After he parked the BMW in the visitors' lot, Raul opened the trunk and removed a box of books. Sometimes he brought toys. Other times he brought clothing or sweets. Today, books.

A long walk took him to the building that housed the administration office, and longer still down the hall that lead to the director's office. Raul's heavy footsteps echoed off of the hallway's cold plaster walls and polished tile floor as he struggled with the unwieldy box. He hurried as his arms began to ache.

"Hola, Señor Cathedra," the director's secretary said as he entered the office, anxious to deposit his burden. "Good to see you."

"Hola, Lucinda. The week's been good, I trust?" he asked, resting the heavy box on a chair for a moment as he caught his breath.

"Always is. Go on in," she said, glancing toward the open door to the Director's office. Things were handled informally here, and Raul was a regular visitor.

Inside the Director's office Jaime Contreras worked at his computer keyboard, head down, oblivious to anything around him. Although the simple office arrangement held only a desk, a few chairs and file cabinets, the walls told a more complex story. Photographs of children covered three of them, almost from the floor to the ceiling, with no more than a few inches separating one photo from another.

"Take a break," Raul said.

"It's been a week already? Dios mío," Jaime said, looking up from the screen and turning toward Raul.

"Those are a part of what you asked for," Raul said, pointing through the door toward the box he'd left outside. "I should have the rest of them next week. It took a while to get even these. Some I have to get through the Internet."

Raul could have used a service to send the books, but he enjoyed delivering his gifts personally whenever he could, the gratification somehow amplified by touching them.

"Gracias, as always, Raul," Jaime said to the Hogar's largest financial contributor. "I've told you this a hundred times, but it never seems enough. You've no idea how important you are to us. What you and your business associates give lets us do so many things. I'd love to thank them personally."

"I'll arrange it someday, Jaime. They're very busy and they travel a great deal, but I've thanked them many times over for you."

"I worry about what we'd do if anything happened to

you," Jaime said. "We depend so much."

"There's no need to worry. My investments are all doing very well and as long as that's true I'll see that you get whatever you need. Or were you referring to my health?" he said, laughing.

Jaime grinned, and said, "Both, I imagine."

"You've no need to worry about either," Raul said. "I'd like to stay and talk but I want to see the end of Dario's class."

"I understand. Hurry, then," Jaime said to Raul, who had already turned to leave.

***

The boy looked barely 10 when Father Ramirez, pastor of a small church in Oxaca, found him sleeping in one of the confessionals, wearing clothes hardly more than rags. With his grimy face, the child looked like he hadn't bathed in weeks. Tangled hair hung over his ears and forehead in jagged, unkempt lengths. The boy had curled in a fetal position, tight against a corner of the small, dark space.

Father Ramirez looked at him for a few moments, then knelt down on one knee and said a brief, silent prayer. Finished, he pressed on the boy's shoulder until he stirred. Startled out of his sleep and confronted with the image of the priest hovering over him in the dark space, the boy's eyes opened wide, then shut tight, as if waiting for a blow. Ramirez saw that the boy trembled.

"Calma, mi pequeño, calma," the priest said in a soft voice, trying to settle him. "There's no trouble for you. You're welcome here."

The boy sat up, and, after a moment, began to sob. Without saying a word, he wrapped his boney arms around the priest. Ramirez could feel the boy's ribs through the thin rag of a shirt as he returned the embrace.

"When was the last time you ate?" Ramirez asked.

"Yesterday."

"And when did you have a bath?"

"I don't remember."

"Dios mío. Come with me and let's get you something to fill your stomach and get you cleaned up. I have some clothes that will be better than what you have."

Later, as Ramirez watched the boy devour a second hastily prepared tortilla stuffed with leftover chicken and rice the priest had taken from the rectory refrigerator, he asked how long the boy had been living on the streets.

"A year maybe. Or almost. Seems like it. That's when mamá didn't come home one day."

"No father?"

"No."

"No family you can stay with?" Ramirez asked.

"I have an uncle, but he drinks a lot and when I went there he said I couldn't stay."

"That's it?"

"Uh huh. All I know about."

"I don't suppose you go to school then," the priest asked.

"Not since mamá left. Before that I went, though."

"Did you like school?"

"Yeah. I did pretty good, too."

"I haven't asked your name. I'm Father Ramirez. What's yours?"

"Raul."

***

As Raul entered the classroom of maestra Maria Díaz he smiled at the sight of the 20 scrubbed clean 11 year

125

olds who sat attentively at their desks, finishing up the lesson. He remembered the time, long ago, when he owned one of those desks. The only home he remembered from his youth, the orphanage had given him a chance to make his way.

Dario was seven when Raul asked Jaime to "find me the brightest, most curious boy you have." He told Jaime he wanted a child he could take aside and talk with when he visited, someone he could perhaps help in what he told Jaime would be a "personal way." He also asked Jaime to look for a spark of ambition in the boy he would select for Raul to mentor. As a former resident of the orphanage and now a government official, Raul seemed to Jaime the best of role models, and he eagerly gave Raul what he'd asked for.

Dario expected Raul to visit each Friday and was rarely disappointed. To the rest of his world, Raul was tough, demanding and, powerful. And largely unapproachable. To Dario, he was Tío Raul — Uncle Raul, a kind man who took him places he'd never get to see otherwise, and who taught Dario things he wouldn't learn in class.

Dario's face broke into a broad smile when he spotted Raul from across the classroom, and Raul smiled back as he stepped to one side of the doorway in a vain attempt to be inconspicuous.

"Students," maestra Maria said, noticing Raul, "Say hello to Señor Cathedra."

As the students greeted him in unison, the slightest blush crossed Raul's face as he nodded in their direction.

In a few minutes the class ended, and, with it, the week's schoolwork. Dario and Raul headed for Raul's car and an hour at a small cafe nearby where Raul often took the boy for a meal when he visited.

They talked about the boy's studies, as they always did. Dario knew that Raul was in charge of a place where the government was digging up an old Aztec pyramid and he asked how it was going. Then, for the fifth time, he asked Raul if someday he could go there to see it. Although Raul promised that someday he could, it was a promise he didn't intend to keep. Raul's involvement with the orphanage, and with Dario, would remain his private business.

"Dario," Raul said, changing the subject. "Have you studied anything about the election for president that's happening in July?"

"A little, tío," Dario answered. "The teachers have explained how the election works and how the voting is done. And they taught us about what the president does."

"And what did they teach you the president does?" Raul asked.

"The president's job is to protect the country and to try to take care of people who need help."

"That's so. Have they told you anything about the people who are trying to become president?" Raul asked. "Anything about what they say they will do if they become president?"

"No tío. We aren't taught anything about that," Dario answered between spoonsful of the ice cream he was having for dessert.

Raul wondered how much Dario was ready to understand of life beyond the Hogar.

"That's because most 11 year olds can't understand such things, Dario. But you're smart enough to understand if someone explained it to you."

Raul studied Dario's face, searching for a sign of curiosity in a boy who appeared more interested in ice cream. Raul prodded him.

"Would you like to know about that?"

Dario interrupted his assault on the treat and leaned forward a little in his chair. Raul had worked hard at making the boy feel special, different from the other boys his age. In particular, Raul had tried to convince him that it was good for him to know things the other boys didn't know about.

Dario looked at Raul and asked, "Who do you want to win, tío?"

"Well Dario, it's complicated."

Raul hesitated a moment, thinking about exactly how to explain national politics to an 11 year old.

This conversation may end up testing me as well as the boy.

"There are some people in Mexico who are very rich and have many things, but there are many more people who have very little, sometimes almost nothing. Because you don't have your parents, you're one of the people with very little. If it wasn't for the Hogar, you wouldn't even have a place to sleep at night, Dario. I used to be like you, with no parents and no way to live, until I came here."

"What does that have to do with the election?" Dario asked.

"Well, most of the people who are poor, like you and me, it's not their fault. They can't help it and they can't do much about it. The president needs to help those people, Dario. The country needs to help take care of them. Do you have any idea how the president can do that?" Raul asked.

Dario thought for a moment, then replied, "Can't he give them things they need, like a place to live and food and things?"

Raul smiled.

"Yes, but where will he get all the money that these things will cost? Who has it?" Raul asked him.

"People can share, couldn't they?" Dario replied. "They teach us here that we should share."

"Exactamente, Dario," Raul said. "But, everyone who wants to be president doesn't think that the richer people should have to share very much. There is one person who is in the election, though, who thinks they should, and that's who I would like to win."

"What if the rich people don't want to share, though? We have some kids here who don't like to share," Dario asked.

"Well, when you're the president, sometimes you can make people do the right thing when they don't really want to," Raul answered. "That's called being a leader."

A curious expression crossed Dario's face, and Raul could see a question forming in the 11 year old's mind.

"Tío, you said you were poor like me, but you aren't. You live in a big house now and you have a nice car. Aren't you one of the people who should share a lot?"

Raul was both startled and pleased by the boy's question. An 11 year old had challenged him with his own simplistic parable, albeit unwittingly. Coming up with a good response proved difficult, and Raul quickly settled on a less than honest answer.

"I have more than most people, yes, Dario," he said, downplaying his wealth. "But if the president decided that I had to share, that would be fine with me."

"But you could just do it, anyhow. Why does he have to tell you to do it?" Dario asked, taking the conversation farther than Raul wanted it to go.

"Yes I could, and I do share already in a lot of ways. But everyone who's rich isn't as kind as I am."

***

Pleased with himself, Raul turned toward Cuernavaca on ruta 183 after dropping Dario off at the orphanage. He'd intended nothing more than to give the boy a simple look at politics. Dario had handled that, and then some. The boy was quick, and developing nicely.

Although headed toward home, Raul's visit wasn't quite over.

A few miles outside of Cuautla, he pulled off of the highway and waited for the traffic behind him to pass. When he could see no other vehicles in either direction, he turned onto a narrow dirt road that turned off into the countryside just ahead of where he'd pulled over. He slowed to a crawl, not wanting to generate a trail of dust. The road ascended a gentle slope, through a hardscrabble area of sandy soil, scrub trees and shrubs. After a half mile, the vegetation grew larger and denser, and soon the leaves at the tips of tree branches were brushing against the car, making a soft, swishing sound. A quarter mile farther on, he came to a small shack, stopped the BMW, and turned off the ignition. He sat in the car for perhaps a minute, listening. He got out, stood motionless for a moment, and then looked around. There was no movement or sound, nothing at all, except for a light breeze and the sound of a few birds. Lit by dappled sunlight filtering through the trees that crowded it on all sides, the shack rested in front of him where the road had abruptly ended.

This wouldn't be a bad place to spend a few days if you just wanted to relax.

A simple structure of one room, with rough plywood walls and a corrugated metal roof, the shack had a small uncovered porch and a few cloudy windows that barely let in enough light for someone inside to see. As far as the government's real estate records showed, the land it occupied was owned by a land development company with an address in Monterrey which, if anyone bothered to check, didn't exist.

On the porch, Raul inserted a key into a padlock that hung on a crude wooden door, and pushed. It opened with a creak.

Why do I bother to lock the door?

Inside, he looked for signs that anyone uninvited had been there since his last visit a month earlier. The single room held only a table and three chairs, and a small cupboard in one corner. Everything seemed just as he'd left it. The legs of the chairs and table still rested within the faint pencil marks on the floor that he'd placed there to tell if they'd been moved, which he assumed anyone exploring the cabin might do. His men, of course, had been here, but he'd instructed them not to go inside unless they were meeting with him.

Satisfied, Raul locked the door and returned to the car. He removed a small pry bar from the trunk and walked to the rear of the shack. Shielded by some bushes and crouched on one knee, he pried a small piece of corrugated metal from near the base of the shack's rear wall. Reaching his arm inside up to his shoulder and pressing hard against the wall, his hand searched the space under the cabin floor until it found the handle of a large suitcase. He dragged it toward him. After the suitcase was clear of the cabin, he replaced the metal siding, stepped away from the building, and spread the soil with his foot to cover any sign that he'd been there. Well away from the cabin, he laid the case on the ground, opened it, and checked its contents. Inside were bundles of fresh, 1000 peso notes, 10 bundles in all. There were also four plastic covered one kilo bricks of pure cocaine, intended for delivery as gifts to a few well-placed government officials. The street value of the cocaine, if it had made it to the United States, was in excess of $45,000.

On the way home to Cuernavaca, Raul minded his speed.

Chapter Twenty-Two

For several days after his encounter with Ana at the zócalo, Scott avoided her. Spending most of his time in the artifact processing trailer, it wasn't difficult. Her work took her down into the excavation, working the soil and the stones with Arturo's archaeologists. The thought of being close to Ana made Scott uncomfortable, yet he didn't understand why.

"Buen día, Jorge," Jerry said to the expressionless Jorge as he pushed past him into the trailer.

Jorge said nothing, only watching Jerry as he passed. "Does this guy speak any English at all, Scotty?" Jerry said, smiling at Scott's dour looking assistant as he asked.

"Not that I can tell."

"Good. Then I don't mind telling you that I think he has the demeanor of an undertaker. How the hell can you stand being trapped in here all day with Mr. Excitement?"

Scott laughed.

"Jorge grows on you. He actually does a decent job with the work I've asked him to do. And we have these great conversations. I talk, and he listens. It's refreshing. Nothing like our conversations."

"Well, keep his ass in here with you, then. I prefer working with people who have a detectable personality," Jerry said as he continued to smile at Jorge and searched for any sign that the insult was understood.

Jerry's work took him all over the site, and Arturo had an endless list of things for Jerry to do. Whether because he'd come so far to help, or because he seemed so confident about everything he did, the locals respected Jerry, exactly as Arturo had hoped. Jerry's steady hand had begun to impose order and the frenetic pace had settled. His early morning job conferences planned the day's work, and at the end of each afternoon he made them share all they'd done and the problems they'd encountered. During the day he was everywhere, asking questions and making suggestions. Increasingly, the local professionals looked to him for guidance.

"Break time, junior," Jerry said. "Coffee and fresh air."

After covering the short distance from the trailer, they had the tent to themselves.

"Where does Mr. Personality go when you leave the trailer, Scotty?" Jerry asked between gulps of black coffee.

"Good question. Most of the time I think he just stays there until I get back. He's usually waiting for me," Scott said.

"That strike you as odd, even for him?" Jerry asked. "I mean, it's pretty obvious that he's supposed to watch over you and the stuff in the trailer, but when you're gone wouldn't you think he'd like to get out for at least a little while? Stretch his legs, get some air? So, what's he doing in there by himself when he's not watching you?"

"No idea, Jerry," Scott replied.

Scott shifted a little on the bench and looked down into his coffee mug.

"You run into Anarosa much when you're out and about?" he asked.

"Some," Jerry replied. "Tell you what's funny, though. I see Jorge's boss around her all the time. I can't see that connection."

"Cathedra?" Scott asked, remembering Arturo's comment about Raul and Ana.

"Yeah. Just about every day," Jerry said. "The guy ought to behave better. He has to have most of 20 years on Ana and he looks like a dirty old man when he's standing next to her."

The thought of Cathedra hovering around Ana unsettled Scott.

Arturo's voice growled through Jerry's portable radio.

"Gotta go. See you at lunch?"

"Sure."

Jerry walked away, leaving Scott alone under the canopy. Resting his head on the table and closing his eyes, a warm breeze filled the space around him. Suddenly, he felt weary. It often came over him this way, unexpected.

**

Scott had gone to the hospital without telling her. He'd made these lunchtime visits often during the three months they'd been seeing each other. He called them their "dates" since Lisa's shift schedule meant that for weeks at a time coming to the hospital was the only way he could spend time with her. He usually called, but today he planned to surprise her. Stopping at a floral shop near the hospital, he'd picked up a single rose. Wrapped in white tissue, Scott carried it through the hospital's main entrance and down the hallway toward the cafeteria.

He always got nervous just before he saw her, and he always forgot that he'd felt that way the moment she appeared.

Massachusetts General had a massive cafeteria, large enough to hold a sizeable number of its employees at one sitting. At a regular meal time like this one, employees filled almost every table. From the main entrance Scott looked out over the crowd, the occasional white lab coats looking like whitecaps on a sea of hospital green scrubs. His eyes searched methodically from table to table, looking for the long blonde hair and the familiar face. He'd had no idea there were so many blondes at Mass General, and, somehow, the din of hundreds of simultaneous conversations made it harder to find her.

Giving up on the surprise, he reached for his cell phone just as he spotted her at the far end of the room. He started toward her, stopping when he noticed the young man dressed in a white lab coat sit down next to her. At a table in the farthest corner of the dining hall, the pair had as much privacy as could be had in the place. The stranger didn't sit across from Lisa, but, instead, sat close, alongside of her.

Scott studied them after retreating back toward the doorway. His heart began beating noticeably faster when he saw the man reach his arm around Lisa's shoulder, lean toward her, and say something in her ear. They were smiling, laughing. The man had something around his neck. Was it a stethoscope? A doctor? Hard to tell from this distance.

Locked in place, Scott couldn't move toward her, but couldn't leave.

After a few minutes, the man rose, and Lisa stood and turned toward him. They each said something, embraced, and then the man walked quickly across the room toward the doorway where Scott had concealed himself. As he passed, Scott saw that his guess about the stethoscope had been correct, and he caught just enough of a glimpse of the embroidered name on the front of the crisp white coat to see that it ended with "M.D." Scott also noticed that he wore no wedding ring.

Looking across the room at Lisa, alone now as she finished her lunch, Scott couldn't bring himself to go to her. He felt wounded, but knew he had no right to question her. Perhaps he had assumed too much about where they seemed to be headed. Maybe what he had just seen was not what it appeared to be. Or maybe she just wasn't who he thought she was. In the short time he'd had with her, he'd grown so secure, so comfortable, that the notion that this woman he'd only met a few months ago had the freedom to do exactly as she pleased simply hadn't occurred to him. No, he decided, he wouldn't ask about it.

When he saw Lisa leave the table and head toward the entrance, Scott quickly turned and left ahead of her, tossing the rose into the first trash bin he passed.

***

Scott didn't really have a work schedule, and he often took time to walk through the project site, stopping to talk to the Mexicans. He'd developed a cordial relationship with many, and enjoyed asking their opinions about the election, the project, and, lately, about Raul Cathedra and his cadre of funcionarios who seemed to be everywhere. At first he found the workers reluctant to talk about Raul, but, as Scott became a familiar face, they opened up.

Raul had arrived after it became obvious the site was rich with artifacts, they told him. His staff followed soon afterward, and since then most of the project's workers felt as if they were being watched. The government had placed Raul in total control of the processing of all the recovered antiquities, responsible for identification, cataloging, and their eventual safe shipment to the National Institute of Anthropology and History in Mexico City.

There were as many rumors about Raul as there were people to repeat them. Some thought Raul was involved in the drug trade. Others thought him an agent for the Policía Federal, sent to make sure they didn't steal anything. Someone even said that he was going to be put in charge of all of the archaeological projects in the country when the Xochicalco project ended. What was clear to Scott was that no one liked or trusted him.

As he walked along the rim of the excavation, Scott searched for Ana down below. How strange, he thought. He didn't want her near, yet he looked for her.

In a few minutes his eyes found her, bent over a wooden box screen, sifting soil, looking for something of importance in a small piece of sandy earth. He was about to turn away when he saw Raul appear out of nowhere and approach Ana from behind, standing over her as she worked.

He reminds me of a vulture.

Tall and dark, to Scott he looked sinister, as though he could spread his arms out, grab her, and fly off. Scott wondered if Ana even knew he was standing there.

Ana stopped her work and stood, facing Raul. Scott watched them talking, then, without thinking, took a few steps down the path into the excavation. He caught himself, stopped, and watched for a few moments more as Ana and Raul continued their conversation. When he thought he saw Ana smiling, he started down the path again. He'd had no intention of reaching out to Ana when he left the tent. Raul's presence had changed that, although Scott had no idea why he was heading toward her or what he'd say when he got there.

"Scott," she said with a broad smile as she saw him approach. "I was wondering when I'd see you again." She embraced him. It was a polite embrace, but the contact pleased Scott just the same.

"Have you met Raul?" she asked.

"I've had the pleasure," Scott said as he forced a smile and looked directly at Raul.

Raul returned the eye contact with an emotionless look, nodded toward Scott, then turned to Ana and said, "Dr. Flores and I have spoken several times, Anarosa. I have a lot of respect for his knowledge, and we're very happy to have him here for the summer."

I'll bet he is.

"We're truly grateful for your help, doctor. It has to be difficult to work in a foreign place, with all the handicaps you'll face," Raul said.

"Handicaps?" Scott asked.

What the hell does that mean? He's starting this again?

"Well, apart from the cultural and language differences, I only mean that you may find it somewhat difficult to place all of our discoveries in the proper context," Raul replied.

"Context?" Scott asked, annoyed but not yet sure whether he should take offense. "I'm sorry, but I don't get your point."

"By that, I mean you can't be expected to understand fully the significance of our patrimonio in the larger, cultural sense. It's difficult for anyone but a Mexican to truly appreciate this," Raul said.

"What makes you say that?" Scott asked.

"I'm sure your training was the very best, but native anthropologists have a special perspective. There's a connection to the land and its history. I know this doesn't sound scientific, but I believe it's real enough."

What nonsense. He has no credentials and knows nothing.

Scott's blood was instantly up. He realized he ought to back away, but couldn't. Raul had insulted him for the second time. That he'd done it in front of Ana made it worse. Energized by his anger, he hadn't felt so alive in a long time.

"Con respeto," Scott shot back. "I disagree. I've spent my whole life appreciating Pre-Columbian civilization. I spent every day of eight years studying your patrimonio, and I teach it every day to my students. What more do I need to do in order to understand context?"

Raul glared at Scott, his face starting to flush as his hands closed into fists, signaling to Scott that Raul either had thin skin or wasn't used to being challenged. Scott stared back, daring Raul to continue the exchange. He decided to press further.

"I hear that we norteamericanos are arrogant and chauvinistic. And now I hear that if I wasn't born in Mexico I can't possibly understand the meaning of an artifact that I spent eight years preparing to understand?"

Shaken by the sharp and unexpected exchange, Ana rushed to change the conversation before things got worse. Raul leaned forward, about to answer, when she interrupted.

"Raul, Scott, please. There isn't any need for this," she pleaded, stepping into the space between them.

"I apologize for my tone, Ana," Raul said. "Perhaps it's the difference between the languages that caused Dr. Flores to take offense. I'm sorry if I sounded patronizing, doctor. That wasn't my intention. It was just a harmless point of view, nothing more."

Ana looked at Scott. It was clear to Scott that she expected him to say something equally gracious.

"Apology accepted. And I should have thought better before showing my temper like that," Scott said. Still angry, it was as far as he would go with Cathedra.

Raul excused himself, and, as soon as he'd gone, Scott tried to explain.

"I'm sorry about being so aggressive with him, but this isn't the first time he's insulted me. Maybe it's my culture that *he* doesn't understand, but where I'm from you don't insult your guests, particularly if they've dropped by to help you with something," he said. "It's almost as if he wants me to feel uncomfortable about being here."

"No," Ana said. "In the states you don't attack your hosts, either. You could have disagreed with him in an entirely different tone and still made your point. I'm surprised at you."

"I know what you're thinking Ana. You're thinking I'm a typical gringo who's too quick to fight and argue. Some kind of cowboy. But..."

Ana cut him off.

"Please don't presume to know what I'm thinking," she said. "And no, I don't think that at all. I think he insulted your work and you defended yourself. I also think that maybe your emotions are a little raw."

"I suppose I did over react some," he said.

"I'd say more than some," she continued. "Raul is a strong personality but he has an important position and responsibility. He isn't used to being talked to like that, but at least he had the sense not to continue it. You wanted to take it farther. You also might remember that the Mexican government, which he represents here, is your host. You could show at least a little respect for his position."

Scott assessed the morning as a disaster as he trudged up the ramp to the top of the excavation. Quite certain now that Cathedra would look for a way to get even, he'd managed in a few moments to create an enemy and to convince Ana that he was some kind of testosterone-laden cowboy. An uneventful afternoon in the trailer alone with Jorge, would be a relief.

Chapter Twenty-Three

Raul seethed as he walked toward the old house trailer in a remote corner of the excavation that served as his office.

He tossed his cigarette onto the ground and yanked open the trailer door. Slamming it shut behind him, he picked up a stack of files and shuffled through them for a few seconds, then threw them down on a table and pounded it with his fist. He fumbled in his pocket for another cigarette and coaxed the last one from a gold cigarette case.

Get control. You need to be... in control.

He lit the smoke with a trembling hand.

I wonder how the gringo would have made out if he'd been born in my place. Hell, he never would have survived. He's probably had everything handed to him. And if he did survive, it would be because he made the same choices I made.

The small size of the trailer didn't stop Raul from pacing the short distance between its walls, back and forth as the space filled with smoke.

He has no idea what it's like to have nothing. Money makes everything possible. You need money to have food in your stomach and a decent place to live. You need money to do things for people so they respect you. You need money to get a woman.

143

Raul sank into a recliner and took a long drag. He remembered the time before he was rescued from the street. He remembered being hungry and alone.

No, you don't forget that. Never. And if I have to move the drugs, so what? If I don't do it, someone else will, and nothing will be any different, except that Raul Cathedra will have to live in some crummy apartment with a toilet that doesn't work and no way to be sure the rent will be paid. So why should I let someone else make the money? Besides, it's the norteamericanos' money that I get. I'm not taking anything from a Mexican.

His thought about his Zeta cartel business partners. As a part of the transportation network the Zetas maintained to run drugs from the coast near Acapulco, or the Guatemalan border to drop off points near the border with the United States, Raul's men made pick-ups and deliveries, over and over again.

Would the gringo doctor ever deal with those people? Damn right he would if it would give him what he wanted.

He snuffed out the cigarette, stood up, and opened the door to clear the smoke laden air. Raul stood in the doorway and looked across an open field toward the excavation's working face.

And those precious little statues and pieces of clay that we fuss over all day. The museum in Mexico City is loaded with them. And there are thousands more buried all over Mexico. A few less won't make any difference at all. So let the rich collectors have their fun. They'll end up in a museum someday, anyway. I'll take their money, too.

Raul thought of the confrontation with Scott in front of Ana.

That was so stupid. Now I'm screwed. I'm going to have to apologize and it will have to be a good one. That's what happens when you lose control.

CHAPTER TWENTY-FOUR

Jerry couldn't understand much of what the scratchy voice coming from the portable radio was saying.

"Say that again?"

"Jerry. I'm down in the southwest corner. You'll want to see this." It was Max, one of Arturo's men, and this time Jerry heard him clearly enough to sense excitement in his voice.

"What do you have, Max?" Jerry asked.

"Just come, Jerito. You'll see."

Max and a few others worked in one corner of the excavation where a jumbled pile of large stones, once a part of the structure, protruded from undisturbed soil. The excavation teams had faced the situation before at Xochicalco, and the team assigned to it had little choice but to use heavy equipment to dislodge the stones.

As he approached, Jerry saw six men crowded closely together. One gestured wildly, waving his arms, while several bent over one of the large stones and seemed to be looking down at something on the ground in front of the group. Jerry found Max in the middle of the group, on his knees, peering at a small hole in the ground.

Max stood and tried to brush off the dark soil caked on the front of his sweat soaked shirt, but accomplished little more than making himself look like he'd been rolling in mud. He pulled a bright red bandanna from a rear pocket of his jeans, wiped the sweat from his face, then motioned toward a spot between two large stones.

"There, Jerry. See?"

Arturo had selected one of the large stones for removal by a small backhoe, and after Max's crew pulled it away from the others, an opening into the earth the size of a basketball appeared. Inside was darkness.

"I've sent one of my men for a flashlight, but we reached inside with a cigarette lighter and it looks like a sizable cavity. It should be easy enough to enlarge this so someone can get in there and look around."

"See anything inside with the lighter?" Jerry asked.

"Not much, it's not enough light. But I can see enough to tell the cavity extends some distance in and turns downward," Max answered. "And from what I could see, inside it looks man-made."

"You're thinking we're going to find something in there?" Jerry asked.

"I'll bet you lunch we do, Jerito," Max said, smiling.

A look inside with the flashlight revealed a large space, at least 40 meters deep, but narrow. The sides were regular, clearly hewn from stone. It was a man-made passageway, a small part of the interior of a structure, with a floor covered with jagged rocks. At the farthest end of what he could see, Jerry thought he saw something lighter in color and regular in shape that seemed out of place amid the rocks and bits of the collapsed structure lining the floor.

146

"There. Toward the back, Max. You see that?" Jerry asked, as the beam of the flashlight played on a small area of lighter colored debris.

"Yes. Something's back there beside rock," Max replied.

The opening proved more difficult to enlarge than Max had thought. An adjacent area of soft soil could be scooped out, but solid rock ringed most of the perimeter of the opening. No one questioned Jerry when he volunteered to try to squeeze through.

Getting his shoulders and upper body inside didn't take long, although squirming through the abrasive stone had cost Jerry one of the sleeves of his shirt and some skin on each arm and shoulder. His lower body proved much more challenging.

With the entire top of his torso through the hole, Jerry pushed down as hard as he could on the stone that lay to either side of the opening, trying to force his hips through. Laboring in darkness, he regretted not placing a flashlight in ahead of him. His arms aching as he strained, he stopped to rest a moment, then pushed again. The jagged edges of the stone that formed the sides of the opening now tore at the skin on his hips, and ripped small holes in the side of his pants.

"Jerry, you've eaten too many quesadillas for this type of work."

Arturo's familiar voice sounded far away and barely audible, muffled by Jerry's body plugging the opening that separated them. Jerry smiled at the comment, but said nothing, doubtful anyone outside could hear.

He considered giving up and sending someone smaller in his place, but the situation had become personal. Impatient, he wanted to be the one to find whatever was here.

Because the cavity fell away several feet below the opening, when he finally managed to pull his hips through, because his hands were braced against the rock, pushing as hard as he could to force the final few inches, he had nothing to use to break the fall as his body shot forward like a cork popping out of a bottle. Unable to get his hands down fast enough, he fell to the rocky floor face first with a crash, striking his head and opening a gash above his right eye. He held his hand against the cut, felt the dampness on his hand, then pulled it back, startled at the amount of blood covering his fingers. He thought for a moment about going back out.

Why the hell didn't I go in feet first? Did I cut the class where they taught that?

Arturo poked his head inside the opening after Jerry's legs disappeared.

"Jerry. You alright?" he yelled into the darkness. "Max, hand me that flashlight," Arturo ordered. "Jerry?" Arturo shouted again. "Jerito?"

Arturo tried to get his shoulders past the opening but couldn't. As he surveyed the crew, looking for the smallest man to send in, Jerry shouted from inside, his voice echoing off of the walls of the cavity.

"I'm fine. I couldn't push down to force my way in and break my fall at the same time," Jerry finally said. "So I made a dramatic entrance. I got a few cuts and scrapes is all. Toss me the flashlight and the tool bag."

Jerry had more than a few scrapes and cuts. The slice on his forehead bled heavily and his khaki pants were torn in a half dozen places. Scrapes and bruises covered his hips and arms. He looked like he'd been in hand-to-hand combat.

Arturo passed a tool bag and a flashlight through the

shoulder width opening. Jerry scanned the inside of the cavity with the light and saw that it ran more than 40 meters deep. Perhaps five meters at its widest, it had a floor consisting of small, broken stones, and a ceiling not high enough for a man to stand. It would be hands and knees all the way to the back. His body sore, scraped and bleeding, he winced at the prospect of crawling so far in the dark on jagged rocks, hunched over and beat up.

I'm too old for this.

Jerry ran his hand over a seam between two large rectangular stones that formed part of the sidewall of the passage. They were, without question, man-made. He ran the flashlight's beam farther along the passage and saw seams at regular intervals, every five or six feet.

As Jerry realized that the stale air filling his lungs had been trapped in this space for at least 800 years, the thought gave him a rush. The place smelled ancient. Forgetting how much he hurt, he felt victory and validation.

He crawled 30 meters forward and stopped abruptly when his head slammed into a piece of the jagged ceiling he hadn't seen.

"God damnit!" he cried, holding the top of his head.

His hair felt wet. Another cut had opened, this one on his scalp. Laying prone on the floor, rolling onto his back, he wiped his face in the sleeve of his wet shirt. A combination of sweat and blood had soaked it through.

I must look like I just went ten rounds with the champ.

He rolled back onto his stomach and panned around the small space with the light. He saw nothing except natural looking stones, mixed with chunks of broken structural stones whose squared corners belied that they'd been shaped by human hands. The light beam found the end of the cavity and Jerry searched for the lighter colored object he thought he'd seen from the outside. His eyes focused on something small, something that didn't seem to belong. He could see now that the out of place object had a dirty yellow color. When he realized what it was, he cried out.

Jesus!

Jerry scampered forward as fast as he could on his hands and knees to the end of the passage, ignoring the sharp shots of pain running through his palms and knees as he hurried over the rocky floor, tearing the knees out of his pants. Reaching the end of the cavern, he knelt, hunched over the object. Partially buried in loose stones, it had a rounded, oblong shape. Jerry caught himself just as he was about to tear away the rocks to expose the object fully.

No. Now discipline, Dwyer. You know what you should do. Don't screw this up.

Jerry took a deep breath and reached for the digital camera in the tool bag. He began photographing the object from every angle the small space allowed. Up close, he now realized it was part of a larger series of objects that extended perhaps five feet, with some protruding from a shallow blanket of small stones along its full length. Jerry quickly took measurements from the visible portions of the object to various parts of the small cavern and recorded them in a notebook. Only after all of this did he carefully remove a few small stones to confirm what by now was obvious to him. As Jerry's flashlight pierced the darkness under the soil of Xochicalco his face was not more than two feet from the skull of an Aztec who had died almost a millennium ago.

The aging anthropologist knelt over the remains, in no mood for wisecracking now, not even with himself, moved by the realization that he was the first person in at least eight centuries to share this space with a man who had probably died here. As Jerry sat in the quiet darkness, paying his respects, he considered the magnitude of the moment, and the privilege of entering the last place of an indígena, lost to history, who had walked with the Aztecs so many centuries before.

"Jerry! What can you see?" Arturo's voice boomed through the small cavern, shattering the moment.

Jerry had forgotten about the others standing above ground, waiting to hear something, and he shouted as loud as he could, his voice pounding off of the rocky walls.

"¡Momentito Arturo!"

He carefully replaced the few small stones he'd displaced and started crawling back toward the opening. It was a long way back on bruised and cut knees.

Breathless from the effort it took to reach the opening, from just inside it Jerry looked up and saw Arturo, Max and the others crowded around, pressing against one another as they tried to get a glimpse of him in the darkness below.

"You look like you've been in a fist fight, Jerry," Arturo said, peering down through the opening.

The blood caked on Jerry's face looked strangely out of place on top of his broad smile as he reached through the opening and handed the camera to Arturo. Jerry looked almost giddy, despite his battle scars.

"Take a look for yourself," Jerry said.

"¡Dios mío!" Arturo cried, scrolling through the photos on the camera's LED screen as the others crowded around for a look.

"I'm pretty sure the entire skeleton is here, just under the surface," Jerry said through the opening. "It looks to be twisted some, so it's hard to say whether he was buried here or whether he was killed right there when the structure came down in the quake, if that's what happened. I'm betting he died here. Either way, I'll be surprised if we don't find personal items all around him."

"You want me to send someone else in to help?" Arturo asked.

Jerry held his wrist up so that the light streaming through the opening landed on his watch. It was already late afternoon and he was exhausted.

"No, I don't think so," Jerry replied, looking up into the fading light. "It can wait till tomorrow morning. Then we can take some time to widen the access so we can get in with a full crew and some gear and start working. Just help me get out of here. And make sure you send someone to find Cathedra or one of his men before they leave to let them know what we have. I'm not sure how the institute wants human remains handled, but before we start disturbing things tomorrow, we'd better be sure we don't do something they won't like."

CHAPTER TWENTY-FIVE

Sitting on a large rock, Jerry sipped from his second cup of black coffee and watched the sun throw streaks of pastel across the brightening Mexican sky.

A crowd had already gathered in front of the shoulder-width entrance to the cavity. Jerry yawned as he watched Max's men chisel and dig to enlarge the entrance, their shirts already soaked through with sweat. A warm morning promised a torrid afternoon. Both of Jerry's bandaged arms ached, and a large piece of antiseptic gauze covered his forehead above his right eye. His knees and hips were sore to the touch and almost all of his body hurt from yesterday's ordeal. Draining his cup, now impatient and fully awake, he stood, anxious to get on with it.

The discovery of human remains had energized the project's entire crew of archaeologists, and more than a dozen had gathered before sunrise, waiting for details of the cave's contents and an opportunity to take a look inside. Arturo had decided that he and Jerry, Max, and Scott would be the first to enter.

Although enlarged enough to allow an average sized man to slip through, the fit at the opening was still tight, and pain shot through Jerry's bruised hips as they rubbed against the side of the entrance. One by one, the other three dropped down after him into the darkness, and, despite Jerry's warning, each of the others managed to bash his head against the low, jagged roof, producing a variety of expletives.

"Told you," Jerry said, no sympathy in his voice. "Watch the profanity, please. This is some poor fellow's final resting place," he added, not intending the comment as a joke.

With an electric lantern raised in his right hand, Jerry crawled downward toward the end of the passage, this time his knees covered by knee pads. The others followed close behind as Jerry's light bathed the narrow space in a soft, eerie glow that cast larger than life shadows of the crouched men against the walls on either side of them. It was a scene fit for cinema, the archaeologist, dressed in dirty khaki pants and wearing an old beat up hat, lantern in hand, crawling through a cave.

No one spoke as the four inched along the passage. The only sound was the soft, crunching of their knees on the small stones of the rough, broken floor as they followed Jerry the length of the cavern. At the end of the tunnel they bent over the exposed top of the skull, three lanterns now illuminating the cave, casting overlapping shadows that danced on the walls as the men shifted positions. Jerry examined the surface along what he estimated to be the length of the remains, leaning within a few inches of the ground and examining the loose stones that covered the bulk of the form. The other men stayed back, watching as Jerry finished his inspection.

Jerry sat up and announced, "Something's wrong."

"Wrong? What's wrong?" Scott asked.

Jerry pointed to several stones near the base of the skull.

"See these? They've been disturbed since I left yesterday. I was very careful about what I touched. When I left the skull was not as exposed as it is now. And the orientation is slightly different. It's been moved. Someone's been in here since yesterday."

Jerry dug the digital camera out of his tool bag and scrolled through the photographs he'd taken the day before.

"Here. Look at this," he said, showing Scott and the others a close up of the skull on the camera's viewing screen. "See there, the way that rock appears at the base, and look at how much of the skull is clearly visible above ground? It's changed now. So has its orientation."

Scott looked at the photo, down at the skull, then back at the photo. "Damn, you're right," he said.

"I think the entire body's been disturbed," Jerry said, scrolling through more photos. "Look. All along the length of it the stones look like they've been moved. Like someone picked them up and then tried to put them back into place. They're definitely not the way they look in the photos."

"But who would have done this?" Arturo asked. "And why?"

"I have a thought about why," Jerry said.

"I recorded all the provenience data and took the measurements yesterday," he continued, "so let's do as we planned and expose the entire thing, but if my guess is right, we won't find anything but bones. There'll be nothing else. No personal artifacts, no weapons, no jewelry, no nothing."

"The site has been looted?" Arturo said. "Dios."

"That's my guess," Jerry said. "Or at least someone wanting to loot it came to see what might be here. I can't be positive, because I don't know for sure what was here under those stones yesterday, or for the last thousand years for that matter, but it's unlikely this guy ended up here bare ass naked. And I'm positive that someone's been poking around here since yesterday afternoon."

Jerry's prediction proved correct. Carefully setting aside all of the stones and debris covering the entire five foot length of the remains, they found no object of human manufacture — no remnants of clothing, metal, or ornament, no weapon or implement of any type, only bones and fragments of bones.

No one spoke as they photographed the full length of the exposed remains from various angles. They were all thinking the same thing, that someone on the project staff had corrupted the site.

Leaving Max behind to guide the others who wanted to come inside for a look, Jerry, Scott and Arturo left the cavern. They huddled out of hearing range of the project staff gathered around the mouth of the cavity.

"Any suspects in mind?" Jerry asked.

"It's difficult to imagine any of my people doing something like this," Arturo answered, shaking his head. "I have my problems with some of them, and I won't say no one has ever slipped anything into his pocket. But something this brazen?"

"You must have an idea," Jerry asked. "You've told us you thought things were disappearing."

"Cathedra," Arturo said, under his breath. "Or one of his men."

"Wouldn't surprise me," Scott said. "We've all been thinking it. Why not?"

156

CUERNAVACA

"Well, Cathedra heard early last night about the discovery here, so there was plenty of time for a private expedition to be arranged before this morning," Jerry said.

"So, Cathedra is involved in this," Scott said, looking at Jerry.

"I'd bet on it," Jerry said.

Chapter Twenty-Six

The confrontation with Scott worried Raul for days afterward, his anger now directed at himself for foolishly insulting the gringo in front of Ana. Why hadn't he realized it would make him look arrogant? Clearly, he'd both underestimated the man and been taken off-guard. He vowed not to make either mistake again. He sensed the gringo as a threat, and he'd have to find a way to deal with it.

Raul needed an opportunity to talk to Ana alone. She sat in a corner under the project canopy, taking refuge from the hot sun and working on her notes, when his opportunity came.

"Ana, can we talk?" he asked.

"Of course, Raul."

"I want to apologize again for my behavior the other day," he said. "I'm sorry you had to get into the middle of that. It was unfortunate, but Flores has a hot temper and has trouble controlling himself. I had no idea he'd react as he did, or I wouldn't have spoken so."

"There's no need for another apology. It just went a little too far. I wouldn't necessarily say that about Scott, though. You spoke to him rather sharply and he has personal reasons to be upset easily. But I understand that you wouldn't have any way of knowing about those."

Raul recoiled at the thought that she knew details of Flores' personal life. It meant she must have spent time alone with him. He also noted her reference to Scott having "personal reasons" for being edgy.

Would they make a man drink heavily?

"Perhaps I did get aggressive, but Flores is still a typical arrogant yanquí, Ana. He comes from a place where people always have the best of everything. He's not had to struggle. That was my point, although I didn't make it very well. I just think it will be hard for someone like him to appreciate what pride in our patrimonio means to us."

"You're quick to judge him," she said. "He's a norteamericano, surely, but I've seen another side of him that isn't at all like that. And Raul, he's taken the trouble to learn our language, and well enough to turn your words back on you. So he's hardly typical. "Besides," she added, "I was born into a family of wealth, too. You don't believe that I'm not capable of appreciating el patrimonio, do you? I just don't see the point, Raul."

"But you're Mexican, Ana. That matters."

It was the best he could do.

"I'm sure he can be charming if he wants to be," Raul continued, "but it's their nature to order us around like we all work for them. The other one, Dwyer, he's only been here a few weeks and already he acts like he runs the project, telling everyone what their job is, and giving orders."

"Does he challenge your authority, Raul?" Ana replied. "I've not seen that. Everyone knows the government is in charge and that you've been given responsibility. Jerry is only trying to help. Besides, he's an expert and knows more about this work than anyone here. Have you checked into his background? Jerry's a legend."

She even calls the older one by his first name.

Attacking the gringos wasn't going to get him anywhere, he realized.

"I'm not sure we're going to agree on the Americans, Ana, but I don't want you to think poorly of me because of that one conversation. You know I think the world of you." Hopeful, he added, "I would go out of my way to be generous toward them, if only to please you."

"Just be yourself, Raul, and treat them as you'd want to be treated if you were in their country. Pleasing me shouldn't be a concern."

"It seems like nothing I say is coming out right. I don't care about the Americans. What they think of me isn't important. But what you think of me is."

It was the most aggressive thing he'd ever said to her. He thought he read surprise in her face, but, whatever she thought quickly disappeared behind a polite smile.

"Raul, I'm flattered that my feelings matter so much. Truly."

His heart sank when she said nothing more, and, carried further, he knew the conversation would go badly.

Anger roiled inside of Raul as he left the tent and retreated toward his office.

That was horrible.

Ana obviously liked the two Americans, and the conversation hadn't gotten him any closer to her. He'd been close to offering Ana a dinner invitation, waiting until he sensed the time was right. That seemed out of the question now. Flores had complicated things.

CUERNAVACA

Raul closed the door of the trailer harder than he needed to, and threw his hat against the wall.

Fucking gringo.

He lit a cigarette and inhaled deeply, then reached for a bottle of Petrón and a small glass that rested on top of a file cabinet. He filled the glass, sat back in a soft recliner and took in a second deep lungful of hot smoke. After taking a long drink, he considered what to do about this Dr. Flores.

Raul stood, walked to the window, and looked out across the project grounds. He turned and twisted the end of the cigarette, snuffing it out in the ashtray on the desk before a self-assured smile crossed his face.

Yes. It would be a little risky. But so satisfying. Perhaps this could fix everything.

Raul opened one of the desk drawers and reached toward the back, retrieving an envelope. With the ring of keys he took from inside, he unlocked a cabinet in a corner of the trailer. The cabinet held four small relics, each neatly packaged in a thick plastic bag. He picked up each item, feeling its weight and heft, holding it up to the light and examining it. They were all quite beautiful, he thought, and would fit neatly into an oversized briefcase.

Raul lit another cigarette, pulled his cell phone out of his trouser pocket, and dialed a number in Mexico City.

CHAPTER TWENTY-SEVEN

Raul walked up the steep grade of Avenida Miguel Hidalgo and, where it ended, paid the small admission to enter the 300 year old home of a nineteenth century Hapsburg emperor. Once inside Jardín Borda, he started down the long stone walkway toward the fountain and, past it, to an artificial lake. When he wasn't at the Xochicalco excavation he sometimes came here during his afternoon meal, bringing lunch from a street vendor. Eating wasn't on the agenda today.

The Borda garden was a Cuernavaca landmark, but as Raul worked his way through the intricate series of narrow walkways that intersected the complex garden, he had little appreciation of the fact that he was in the middle of one of the western hemisphere's greatest botanical collections. He only knew that it was large, quiet, and, for Raul's purposes, perfectly private. Lush vegetation of all descriptions lined each of the narrow crisscrossing walks, shielding visitors from each other. Going deeply into the garden, he could easily get lost in the maze of this organized jungle, and staying unnoticed was the point of his visit.

CUERNAVACA

Raul glanced at his watch and saw that he was ten minutes early. After assuring himself that no one was close by, he sat on the bench nearest to his appointed rendezvous place, pulled the day's edition of the Diario de Morelos out of his large brief case, and pretended to read it.

In a few minutes he saw a familiar face approach down the narrow pathway. He rose to offer the man his hand. "Buenas tardes," Raul said.

The man ignored his gesture and said nothing.

Raul had always thought that it would look more natural if the two of them appeared to be friends who were meeting for lunch in the Jardín, as many others did. Ernesto didn't agree. He wanted to get the transactions over with as quickly as possible and had no interest in stage acting.

After sitting, Ernesto looked around, confirmed that no one was able to see them, and handed Raul a thick envelope. Raul opened it, and counted the bundles of large denomination bills inside.

"It seems in order, then," Raul said, as he tucked the envelope into the pocket of his suit coat.

The courier looked around again, reassuring himself that no one had seen the exchange, stood, and walked away, taking Raul's case with him. He disappeared as quickly as he had appeared and had never said a word. Raul thought the whole thing too dramatic.

After Ernesto left, Raul sat back down on the bench, picked up the newspaper, and, this time, actually began to read it. The front page article about Rodrigo Oro trailing badly in the national polls was of particular interest to him.

Chapter Twenty-Eight

She was late, but Scott didn't mind.

He waited, leaning back against the gate of his housing compound, marveling at the unbelievably pleasant evening surrounding him. It was perfect, warm and clear. Cuernavaca was called the City of the Eternal Spring, and, judging by this evening, Scott thought it deserved the description.

Determined to show Ana that he wasn't the overwrought gringo he appeared to be during his confrontation with Raul, Scott had suggested dinner and, to his surprise, she'd accepted. A lot of thought had gone into what to say about the argument with Raul. He'd decided to let her draw her own conclusions. A brief apology would be his only mention of the conversation with Raul. He'd just be Scott, show himself to her, and, if that didn't work out, well....

When the VW beetle pulled up to the curb, Scott saw her smiling at him through the window as he reached to open the door.

"Don't you look nice, all cleaned up and out of those dirty khaki pants and that sweaty shirt?" she joked.

"Nothing less for the señorita," he said, settling into the passenger seat.

He noticed the soft aroma of the scent Ana wore. It was subtle and sweet, not intended to make a big impression, but impossible to miss. Scott found himself relaxed, and expecting nothing more from the evening than to convince Ana he wasn't an arrogant yanquí.

"Where are we going, anyway?" he asked, as Ana pulled the VW away from the curb and out into traffic with an aggressiveness he hadn't expected. She drove fast, and appeared to be comfortable doing it.

"The ex-hacienda. You've been there?" she replied.

"No. What's the ex-hacienda?"

"That's what it is. An ex-hacienda. Of Cortés, no less. The original home of Hernán Cortés, el conquistador. He turned it into a sugar mill when he finished living there and now it's a hotel and a restaurant. Pricey, but I'm not going to let you pay for me. You told me to pick."

"You might be a modern Mexican woman, but I'm an old fashioned American male. I invited you, so I pay," he said.

"Norteamericanos."

Their table was outdoors under a large umbrella, on a patio surrounded by the tropical plants that bloomed during much of the year in Cuernavaca. From his seat, Scott could reach out and pick a pastel colored blossom for her if he'd wanted. Late in the day for dinner by North American standards, the sun was just setting, coloring the sky. The evening had just gotten more and more beautiful.

Anxious to get the apology behind him, Scott said, "I don't want to dwell on this, but I'm sorry for my behavior in front of you and Raul. I'm a guest here and I should be more careful about reacting to things that perhaps I don't understand properly."

Scott looked at her, hoping he'd said enough about the incident and could leave the subject quickly. He feared that he'd sounded too formal and polished, revealing that he'd rehearsed his comment.

"There's no need to talk about it. It wasn't important anyway. But you might find it interesting that Raul told me much the same thing the other day," she said. "Everyone seems to be so concerned with offending me. You men and your conflicts."

Scott found it disconcerting that she referred to him and Raul as though they were equally to blame for the encounter.

After a moment, she asked, "Do you mind if we talk about something personal? You asked me that question once."

"That's fair. Go ahead."

"How long were you married when your wife passed?" she asked, her gentle tone suggesting worry that she might do harm by asking.

"Almost four years," he said. He paused, looking down at the table, then at Ana. "You'd like to know about her, about how it was?"

"If you don't mind, yes. I was hoping you'd be willing to talk. But if it's difficult, I understand."

"It's alright," he said. He smiled, looking down at the table again. "It's always difficult. But I've told enough bartenders. I don't mind talking to you about it."

Scott brought his hand out from underneath the table, opened his palm, and laid in front of Ana the tiny figure of the Aztec child he'd been holding.

"It's beautiful, Scott. It looks authentic," Ana said, picking up the figure and holding it near the candle that now provided light for the table.

"You wanted to know how it was," Scott said. "This is part of it. And that's the same thing I said the first time I saw it. It *is* authentic. Lisa gave it to me the night she told me she was pregnant. It was two weeks before the accident."

"It's legal, don't worry," he continued. "The government approved the exportation."

"This is preciosa then," Ana said. She cradled the figure in her hand for a moment, running her fingertip over it in the soft light, then carefully returned it to the table in front of Scott. They sat in silence, each realizing that Scott had opened a door that led into a private place.

"You know, this tiny artifact is a link to a past of almost a thousand years, but that seems unimportant, doesn't it?" she said. "After only a few months, it must mean so much more to you. You shared this with me?"

"Well, it helps with understanding how things ended for me back there," he said. "Better than I could explain with words. You wanted to know. We tried to have a child for two years and it was very difficult for her. Lis was an amazing woman, Ana. Devoted. Loving. And she wanted it so badly for us. Then, just when things were right, we lost it all. To be honest, I thought my life ended. I wanted to die, too."

"You no longer feel that way? Like your life is over?" she asked.

"I'd be lying if I just said 'no.' There are times I feel exactly that way. Too many of them." He looked at Ana and forced a smile, then said, "That's not how I feel tonight."

"You're a sweet man, Scottsito," she said.

Ana's comment lifted his spirit.

"I see you still wear your wedding ring," Ana said. "I can't begin to imagine how much it must have hurt."

Scott's eyes turned away from her as his mind started to drift backward to a place he didn't want to go.

"Yeah," he said. "It hurt more than I thought anything could."

Their conversation for the rest of the evening engaged them so much that it kept them from noticing the tall man who had been watching them intently through the doorway that led to the bar. Raul emptied the last two inches of top shelf tequila from his glass in one swallow, looked at the couple for a final time, then turned and walked toward the door.

The ride home was strangely quiet after an evening that had been full of conversation, so much of it personal. How odd, Scott thought, that at his age he found himself nervous like a pimple faced teenager on a date, trying to decide exactly how he should say goodnight when they reached the gate of his home.

Maybe she's wondering the same thing.

When the time came, he leaned toward her and placed his arm around her shoulder, but could only manage to pull her toward him, resting his forehead against her for a moment as he said goodnight.

Scott watched the tail lights of the VW disappear down the dark street and wondered whether she'd expected him to kiss her, and what she'd thought when he didn't. Perhaps he'd made a mistake. After the sound of Ana's car faded, he turned to key the lock in the gate, then hesitated. He looked about and saw no one. The street belonged to him, and the night was wonderfully warm and clear. He wasn't the least tired, and, lit by only a few street lights, the quiet, empty street invited him to stay. Accepting, he walked toward the end of the block. He saw no one, and no car passed.

As he turned the corner and walked deeper into the deserted barrio, Scott turned over his reaction to Ana. She was lovely, charming, intelligent. He could make a very long list of things about her worth noticing. He couldn't deny being attracted, yet he wanted her at arms' length, where he'd be safe.

This all feels so strange. Like I'm paralyzed. Moving makes sense, and I want to, but I can't.

As Scott walked on, giving no thought to his location, or the hour, his mind wandered. He thought of Lisa, as he often did at night, random images crossing by with no sense to them, just glances of her, and pieces of memories.

After walking for a long time, he tired, and turned toward home.

Chapter Twenty-Nine

Inspector Federico Salinas of the Policía Federal took a swig of cold coffee before turning back to the computer screen that had occupied his attention for the past hour. Paperwork always made him wish he'd stayed a sub-inspector. June had already been an unusually difficult month for the local Policía Federal, and it wouldn't be over for ten more days. His sector had lost two good men to the narcos, one in a gun battle with drug traffickers and the other only a few days before during an arrest gone bad. The reports occupying his afternoon seemed unimportant.

"Boss wants to see you," the sector commander's clerk said as he brushed by Federico's desk without bothering to stop.

Grateful for the reprieve from his computer, Federico rapped once on the inspector jefe's door and stepped inside without waiting for an invitation. "Sit, Rico," the jefe said through a mouthful of sandwich, without looking up.

The jefe's job involved endless forms, reports and paperwork. Neat stacks of files and folders covered his desk and both large work tables that lined one wall. It all reinforced Federico's long ago resolve that he would never apply for promotion to the jefe's rank.

As Federico waited, patient, Pedro Jimenez, Inspector Jefe of the Policía Federal, Morelos Sector, finished his mid-day meal and wiped the corners of his mouth with a paper napkin. He set aside the paper plate that occupied the center of his desk and, with a neat, deliberate manner, placed it, and his empty soda can, in the trash. His desk finally cleared and orderly, he reached for the top file on a stack that sat in its far corner. He placed the folder directly in front of him, opened it, and studied its contents for a moment. The jefe never did anything casually.

"This is a bit out of the ordinary, Rico," Jimenez said, his tone serious. "In fact, I don't think we've had anything quite like it. And it came in to us in an unusual way."

He pulled a single sheet of paper out of the file and slid it across the desk toward Federico. Jimenez folded his hands and waited for Federico to finish with it.

"A norteamericano?" Federico asked, surprised. "Trafficking in artifacts? Are they serious?" With two dead officers he had no time for trafficking in artifacts.

"Now, Inspector Salinas," Jimenez said with a smile, "you know trafficking in antiquities is a serious crime against the republic that has to be punished. Where's your devotion to la patria? We've had cases like this before."

"As I recall, Pedro, but now? And a gringo?" Federico pleaded. "You know the embassy will get involved. This guy is a professor on some kind of an exchange from an American university and it will be nothing but a big pain in the ass. So, I'm going to have to waste an afternoon chasing him down just to find out he has some convincing explanation for whatever it is that caused this file to be generated. It will all be some big misunderstanding, we'll let him go, and I'll just have to write another damned report."

All humor disappeared from the jefe's face as he said, "No, Rico that definitely is *not* what will happen here."

Puzzled, Federico looked at Jimenez in disbelief.

"You're going to take this man into custody and we'll keep him, at least until he gets a lawyer and manages to get a judge to issue an amparo for his release."

"Custody? You're not serious?" Federico asked.

"Custody. Exactamente," Jimenez replied.

"Why, Pedro?" Federico asked, thinking of the time this would cost him.

"As I said, we got this case in an unusual way. It came directly from Mexico City and we have to do this just so. That's why I'm giving it to you, Rico. Because I want it handled just so."

Federico now studied the sheet of paper more carefully. It told him the suspect was Scott Flores, a college professor working the summer at the Xochicalco excavation site, and that a "reliable informant" had reported that Flores had in his possession an authentic relic, which had been diverted from the excavation. The report claimed he intended to remove it, and others, from the country without government permission in violation of federal law. The artifact was described as small enough to be concealed on his person and it was thought possible he would have it with him when questioned. The authorities at the site had prohibited anyone from removing recovered antiquities from the project's processing facilities. The report also suggested that Flores be confronted at the excavation site, although there was no indication of the reason for that advice. Nothing on the summary sheet mentioned an arrest being required.

How could anyone be sure that he'd have evidence on him days after the report was filed? This doesn't make sense. People who steal things don't walk around with them.

When he'd finished reading, Federico asked, "You're telling me to bring this man in and keep him no matter what I find and no matter what he says? The report doesn't address taking him into custody."

"Yes. You are to do it, no matter what. This isn't on paper, Rico, but along with this file came a call from Mexico City with very specific instructions for what we're to do. We're supposed to detain this Flores until his release is ordered. It's clear we have no flexibility on that. None at all. The only other thing I was told was that we were to follow without question whatever instructions are given by the procurador who's assigned to prosecute the case."

He handed the file to Federico.

"Just bring him in, Rico, then let the procurador handle it. Don't get any more involved than that. It's simple enough."

Back at his desk, Federico examined the full contents of the thin file, but learned little more. He found a physical description of Dr. Scott Flores, a brief biographical summary that looked as though it had been pulled from the Internet, and the usual forms that were part of every investigation. Nothing seemed out of the ordinary, until he came to the information the procurador would have to use to justify the arrest and detention when Flores' lawyer sought an amparo to secure his release. Federico thought it odd that the file contained such a detailed description of the single artifact that formed the basis of the charge. He was particularly struck by the fact that the informant, who was not identified, seemed very sure, positive even, that when the suspect was arrested he'd have the evidence literally in his pocket.

If this Flores was smuggling artifacts out of the country, what would he be doing carrying one around in his pocket? Wouldn't the things be hidden somewhere?

It seemed likely that the charge was a pretense and that someone familiar with Flores, someone with considerable influence in Mexico City, was setting him up.

But who? And why?

CHAPTER THIRTY

Six-year-old Roncito wrapped his arms around his father's leg as Federico came through the door.

"Papá," he cried, over and over, sending a smile across Federico's face.

"Roncito," Federico replied, reaching down to hug the boy. "I missed you, little one." As his embrace around the boy tightened, the day's stress disappeared.

Federico and Felicia had only one child, but had plans for another. Together since school, neither had ever paid much attention to anyone else. And that was fine with them. They had all they wanted.

When Federico finally let Roncito free, Felicia quickly replaced him in Federico's arms.

"Tough day?" she asked, pulling back. She asked the same question every day, and always wanted a real answer.

"Not really," he replied. "Paperwork mostly. But toward the end it got interesting. Instead of the narcos, they have me chasing after some norteamericano college professor who's supposed to have stolen an Aztec relic."

"A relic? Really?" she asked.

175

"But I think there's more to it than that."

"Oh, he's really a big time crook? A smuggler or something?"

"I doubt it. It's some type of political case. That's what makes it interesting. Jimenez got a phone call from Mexico City ordering him to give it some special treatment. So there's something going on here. I just don't know exactly what, yet."

Felicia moved in close again, and kissed him.

"It's not important, then, Rico," she said. "Put it away, querido mío"

I need this. I need her.

After the late evening meal, Roncito was tucked into bed, and Federico returned to the table for his usual evening drink of tequila. It helped him sleep. The television intruded into Federico's privacy, the coverage on the Milenio cable news channel dominated by the presidential election, and Oro's claims that the upcoming election would be rigged against him. Federico had tuned it all out well before he reached for the remote and switched off the television. He sat back and reflected on the day's events. For Federico, work couldn't be turned on and off as easily as his television. He was devoted to it. A serious man, Federico loved Mexico with all his heart, in a way that most in the force didn't. It wasn't just a job to him. He was Policía Federal, a guardian of the Republic, he felt, and he actually believed in it.

He emptied the glass and poured another, his limit of two.

What to make of this gringo professor I'm ordered to arrest and send to jail? Odd.

Felicia's soft hands on his neck interrupted his thoughts. He sat back and let her fingers press into him, banishing all of the tension that remained. After a while he reached back with his hands and placed them on top of hers, caressing them.

"You feel good, bebe. You always do."

She leaned down and kissed his temple.

"Rico, I want to talk again. Please," she asked, as she leaned over him, her hands massaging his neck.

"We've been through this a dozen times now. Nothing's going to change," he replied, his voice calm and patient. He couldn't be angry at her, no matter how many times she brought it up.

"But there are so many reasons that make sense, Rico. Postings for inspector jefe don't come up very often and, God knows, you deserve it. We can use the salary, especially if you want another little one here when you come home."

"Not fair," he said, still no anger in his voice. "It's not about the money, or whether I deserve the promotion, and you know it."

Federico turned toward her and realized his attempt to sound matter-of-fact had failed.

"I'm sorry, bebe, I didn't mean it to come out that way," he said. "I know you want me off the street. If I were you I'd want the same thing. But you married a cop, not a paper pusher who spends all day writing reports and going to meetings. I couldn't be happy that way."

"And what about me, and Roncito, when Jimenez knocks on the door someday and tells me you're not coming home? What then? You only owe them so much Rico. You've given them enough already."

"Amor, I hate that you worry. But it's what I am. Nothing's changed, nothing at all. I'm the same man you married."

"No," she answered, bludgeoning him with truth, her voice firm. "You're not the same. The man I married wasn't a father."

She's right. She's always been right about this.

"Felicia," he said. "What about all of the others? What about them?"

"Others? What others?"

"The people who depend on people like me? Some are fathers too."

"Please don't give me that 'it's for Mexico' speech, Rico. I don't care about Mexico. The country will survive without Federico Salinas risking his life every day. You can be replaced. Let someone else do it now. You took your chances. You've done enough."

He saw her eyes glisten with tears as he stood to hold her. She wrapped her arms around him, burying her face in his shoulder.

"Sometimes, I just get so worried."

"Tranquilo, amor mía," Federico whispered in her ear as he stroked her long dark hair. "Forgive me for this."

She pulled back, just far enough to look into his eyes. "If I can't forgive you this, amor," she said through her tears, "I don't deserve you."

CHAPTER THIRTY-ONE

Donors filed through the suite at the Fiesta Americana Hacienda Hotel, each trying to convince the candidate that Rodrigo's success was the most important thing in his life. As the ninth, and final, person in line, Raul extended his hand to Rodrigo.

"Raul, so good to see you again," Rodrigo said, forcing a smile. It had been a long day. "Sit, please."

Rodrigo was tired of it all, the begging and manipulating. It never ended.

"An honor again, Rodrigo," Raul replied, the excitement in his voice betraying that he was ever so impressed with his ability to meet privately with a national political figure. "I'm surprised you remember me. We've only met once."

"Yes, several months ago, here in Cuernavaca, at that hush, hush meeting." Weary of the afternoon's task, Rodrigo faked a laugh. "I hope being involved with me hasn't caused any problems."

"Not at all. In Morelos you're going to win easily, so no one cares."

Rodrigo knew that, in spite of his local support, many prominent citizens of Morelos, including Raul, had supported him only quietly.

"My advisors say I'm wasting my time coming to Morelos. We're polling strong here, so they think I should be campaigning elsewhere. But I'm not so sure. What do you think?"

"You've excited the city," Raul replied.

"Yes, but politics is a practical business, I'm afraid. Excitement doesn't necessarily win elections. You work for the Gobierno Federal, don't you — the National Institute of Anthropology and History, isn't it?" Rodrigo asked.

"Yes. But Mexico City might as well be a thousand miles away for all they care about local politics. I'm too unimportant for anyone there to notice what I do or say," Raul said.

Rodrigo sensed the opening he needed.

"You'd like to change that, wouldn't you?"

"Of course. That's only natural, isn't it?" Raul replied.

"Mexico's full of talented people like you, Raul, who fought their way up as we did and who can handle positions of authority but will never get the chance. It's never going to open up to us unless we force it open. That's the reality. But I need your help."

"May I speak candidly?" Raul asked.

"Of course."

What's this now? Candid talk?

"I'm sure you have more accurate information, but the newspapers say that you're going to get barely 30 percent of the vote and the PRI candidate Ruiz is approaching 45 percent. There are only a few weeks left.

Realistically, do you still think you can win? I hate to sound this way, but you're looking like a questionable investment."

Surprised by Raul's question, Rodrigo wondered if Raul was really the star-struck sycophant he'd assumed him to be. Then he remembered their first conversation, when Raul had told him that he would sign on to Rodrigo's campaign as long as there was something in it for him.

The man's simply evaluating an investment. Perhaps I should let him understand a bit more about my intentions. If he's worried about this election, he doesn't even have a faint idea of the real plan.

"You're quite right," Rodrigo replied. "I don't expect to win. Not this time, or this way. But time is on my side, and on the side of those who come with me. Make no mistake. We'll win eventually. I'm going to get between 30 and 35 percent of the vote nationwide, as you said. Perhaps a bit better than you think. But Ruiz is going to fall well short of a majority, and that's the key. The PAN candidate will come third, but his party will raise hell along with us because the PRIs can't resist stealing votes. The election will be a fraud and we'll be able to prove it and flood the streets with demonstrations to undermine its legitimacy. You see where this is heading?"

"No, not exactly," Raul replied.

"Six years pass quickly," Rodrigo explained, "and after the sexenio there will be another election. In the worst case, we win the next time. But perhaps the entire system collapses well before that if people are convinced it needs to be replaced with something else," Rodrigo said. "Either way, we need your help and won't forget you. And we will win, Raul." Rodrigo waited a moment, then added, "Surely, you've made more speculative investments that this."

An uncomfortable silence separated the two men for a moment as Rodrigo watched Raul process the conversation before continuing.

"Raul, if you want to be a part of what I'm doing, we have to be able to speak plainly to one another. Let's have no secrets between us. I know you're a wealthy man," Rodrigo continued. "Very wealthy. I also know how you've made your money."

The muscles in Raul's neck and face tightened as his face began to flush.

"All of your money. And I don't care," Rodrigo said, his voice reassuring. "What I care about is Mexico, and nothing more. It takes money to run a campaign and it will take more money to do what will come after the campaign. A lot more."

"You know then..." Raul stammered.

"I know all about you," Rodrigo said calmly, cutting him off. "Relax. You're with a friend here. But a friend who needs you. What I'm doing is more important than the war against the narcos. Let the gringos buy all the drugs they want. They can poison their country and ship their money here. Who cares? Instead of fighting the narcos, the government should be figuring out how to benefit Mexico from the gringos' addictions. Now, you tell me, Raul, how much of an investment can you afford to make in your country?"

Raul hesitated, then said, "I can handle 500,000 pesos now, Rodrigo, and perhaps more depending on how events unfold. Does that convince you that I'm serious?"

"Indeed it does, Raul."

As his business with Raul concluded, Felipe opened the door without waiting for an invitation and announced, "Time to go. The zócalo's already filled and we'll be late as it is."

Rodrigo turned to Raul. "Would you like to ride with me to el centro? I'm sure we can find a spot for you on the stage as well."

That should shake even more money loose.

As their car approached the center of the city, Rodrigo felt the energy build. He lived for these moments, when thousands shouted his name. He watched as Raul marveled at the frenzied crowds outside the car's window. The crowds shouted "¡Oro, Oro, Oro!" Overwhelmed, Raul pressed his face to the window, childlike.

"You feel this?" Rodrigo said, leaning toward Raul, rubbing his shoulder into him. "I see it every day. This is how I know we'll win in the end. It can't be stopped. It's just a question of how and when."

"¡Oro, Oro, Oro!" the crowd screamed louder as they approached the square, the police clearing a path through the center of the street. As the police line pushed the crowd back, Rodrigo's heart beat faster. In a few moments he would be on the temporary stage that had been set up in front of the statue of Zapata at the far end of the zócalo, facing thousands of people who would believe every word he spoke.

"¡Oro, Oro, Oro!" The crowd rolled on, louder still when they saw Rodrigo leave the car and climb the few stairs to the platform. Trailing behind, a member of Oro's staff diverted Raul to discuss his donation to the campaign in more detail, then directed him to a chair near the rear of the stage. The crowd extended the full length of the square, to the state office building at the opposite end, perhaps ten thousand in all. Rodrigo looked over the sea of faces, to its farthest end, and saw dozens of national flags, green, white and red with the national emblem emblazoned in the center, waving in the sunny afternoon. His heart raced. He loved it so.

He leaned over toward Felipe, sitting next to him, and said, "I know what you're thinking. That these people are all going to vote for me no matter what, so why the hell are we wasting our time here. You're such a practical person, Felipe, but we need to see this. Crowds that believe in us and shout it." Rodrigo paused. "It keeps us moving. You know what, Felipe?" he said, smiling. "This makes me hard."

Felipe couldn't help but laugh.

"Please don't use that line in your speech, Rodi."

Rodrigo endured the turns of several local party officials and candidates, each of whom was supposed to be limited to five minutes. The shortest droned on for twice that, the sight of the packed square irresistible. The governor, from Rodrigo's party, was allotted 15 minutes, and he kept to the schedule.

When Rodrigo's turn came, a deafening roar rose as he stepped to the podium, the statue of the revolutionary Emiliano Zapata, rifle held high, silhouetted behind him. When Rodrigo raised his arms to the crowd, it roared louder still. The rhythmic chant rose again, "¡Oro, Oro, Oro!"

When the crowd began to quiet, Rodrigo grasped both sides of the podium and held his head as high as he could, chin thrust forward, as though he wanted the person at the farthest end of the square to have a clear look. Then he held his hands up, and shook his head from side to side, asking for silence. The square grew silent, and the moment belonged to him.

"Mexicanos."

The public address system sent his first word cascading off of the buildings bordering the square.

"Mexicanos," he repeated, his words echoing again. "Are you ready to reclaim your country?" he shouted, piercing the quiet.

The crowd erupted.

"¡Sí, Sí, Sí! ¡Oro, Oro, Oro!"

Rodrigo let it go on for a moment, then raised his hands again, shaking his head from side to side, again calling for silence. He could control the crowd, he saw, and when the crowd settled, the Oro music really started.

"I hear you, Mexicanos! And soon all of Mexico will hear you!"

This time, he let the crowd have its way, thundering on until the energy was spent of its own accord, and the square had grown quiet and anxious, waiting for more. He let them wait, allowing the anticipation to build before continuing.

"For 100 years we've lived in the shadow of the United States, exploited and walked over, our people cheap labor for the foreigners as the riches of our country are sent around the world, all to profit a few corrupt politicians in Mexico City and their friends. It is time that Mexico was restored to the Mexicanos, to whom it rightfully belongs!"

With each provocative phrase he turned, the audience grew more excited, punctuating Rodrigo's speech with more chants of "¡Oro, Oro, Oro!" The national flags waved back and forth, urging him on. The mass of bodies pressed against the front of the stage as if drawn to it magnetically by his words, the crowd a giant organism, reacting to each provocation. Over and over

Rodrigo let the crowd's emotion rise, then recede, waiting for him to lift it again

After 30 more minutes, a spent Rodrigo let the crowd settle for a final time.

"Mis amigos, I love you for your devotion to your country. It's the love of Mexico that each of you feels in your heart that keeps our hope alive. Together, we will win this fight. God bless each of you and God bless our country! ¡Viva Mexico! ¡Viva la patria!" Rodrigo raised his arms triumphantly, fists clenched, as the thundering approval of the crowd echoed off of the buildings and washed over him.

As they settled into the back seat of the car taking them to the airport, Rodrigo turned to Felipe with an exhausted, but contented, look and quietly asked whether his confidante still felt coming to Cuernavaca was a waste of valuable time.

Felipe grinned. "No Rodi, it wasn't. It surely wasn't. This was so damned much fun."

CHAPTER THIRTY-TWO

"We should have left home sooner," Jerry grumbled, as he and Scott trudged up the steep incline of Calle Salazar. Still two blocks from the top of the hill and the edge of the zócalo, they fought their way through close-packed groups of walkers, all competing for space on the edges of the street and the narrow sidewalks lining either side of it. Ahead, in the direction of the square, Jerry and Scott could hear the loud but indistinct hum of a large crowd, hundreds of conversations blended together as one sound. With the walks barely wide enough for two people to pass, it had become a task just to make it to the square.

At the top of Calle Salazar stood the Palacio de Cortés, the building from which the conquistador had ruled Mexico almost 600 years earlier and now a museum. The Palacio faced a large courtyard which lay just below and in front of the end of the zocalo where Scott had mused over the statue of Emiliano Zapata.

"Good God, look at that," Scott said as they turned toward the courtyard. Packed with hundreds of people, the courtyard held the overflow from the completely full zócalo. From the statue, all the way to the state office building at the far end, a sea of humanity waited for Oro.

"I doubt we'll even get to see the great man," Scott said when they crested the top of the street.

"We sure as hell will," Jerry replied. "I didn't walk all the way up that damned hill to turn around and go home. I came to see the show. Follow me."

Jerry plunged into the crowd, pushing and shoving across the courtyard and up the steps leading to the square, drawing angry looks and a few retaliatory elbows. Scott's "perdón" and "con permiso" didn't help much as he followed in Jerry's wake, trying his best to smile and apologizing as Jerry bulled his way through.

"We lucked out," Jerry announced when they reached the edge of the main square. "The stage is on this end. All we have to do is get just a little farther in and it'll be perfect."

The speeches by local politicians had already begun. Near the end of the second speaker's turn the crowd reacted as Rodrigo Oro climbed the stairs to the makeshift stage and took a seat in the front row. At the sight of him, the crowd began to chant "¡Oro, Oro, Oro!" drowning out the final words of a federal diputado's speech. Jerry and Scott watched as the seated Oro raised a hand to acknowledge the crowd, which only caused the chant to grow louder. After a few moments, beaming, Oro raised both hands as if to tell the crowd to settle and let the program continue.

"Look at him," Jerry said. "Just look at him. He's a beauty. That's no fake smile pasted on his face. He gets off on this. You can tell. I'll bet he gives a hell of a speech." Jerry turned and surveyed the crowd. "This is great theater. Told you elections down here were fun to watch."

When Oro finally took the podium Jerry could feel the roar of the crowd ripple through his body. It reminded him of his youth when he'd crank up the bass on his sound system and let the music hit him in the face.

They watched Oro work the frenzied crowd with words that echoed off of the buildings surrounding the square. The echoes made it seem as though everything he said ran through the crowd not once, but two or three times, amplifying his message, and the crowd's reaction.

"He's a damn good speaker. He doesn't talk to a crowd. He seduces it," Jerry said. He leaned over and joked, "If he wanted to pass out the guns right now and ask them to take over that government building at the other end of the zócalo, I'll bet they'd do it."

"Probably," Scott agreed. "To be honest, this whole thing is a little scary. These people aren't thinking at all. This is just raw emotion and demagoguery."

"That it is. Tell me, though, is it really any different back home?"

"Maybe not," Scott said. "But this is an octave higher, I'd say."

After the rally, as they walked down Calle Salazar and turned onto Avenida Atlacomulco, heading for home, Scott hadn't said a word and Jerry could sense something troubling him. "You're thinking that looked a little like 1930's Germany, or some such imperfect analogy, aren't you?" he asked.

"It's just that there's an intensity here I don't see at home when we do our politics. I can see this getting out of control."

"It won't happen. Not here. Since elections here became real contests the people have taken them to heart, and they won't give it back. Besides, Oro's going to lose, probably by a lot. Morelos just happens to be a place where he has a lot of friends. But he does tap into something very basic. Mexico's coming out of a long, dark time when it seemed to be going nowhere, but the country's waking up and aspirational candidates like Oro can sense that. You have to look past all the Chavista bullshit and look at what he's playing into."

"Which is?"

"People here aren't so fatalistic anymore. They're beginning to realize that no matter how dark things have been, it doesn't have to be that way. They expect more. Actually, they're starting to demand it. I think that's Oro's real message. It seems to work for him, and I'm not surprised."

"You make him sound positive."

"Oh hell, I have no use for all the manipulation," Jerry said. "But he's a politician, after all, just like the rest. And he'd be a lousy president. But you have to look a little deeper to see what's really going on. And you have to admire the man's technique. It's masterful."

The street vendor who sold roasted ears of corn on a stick in front of the ecological park each night had started to close up shop as they crested the hill at the top of Avenida Atlacomulco. They made the old woman's last sale of the evening.

"You're thinking. I can tell," Scott said as he chewed. "You know," he added, "I'll bet we could franchise this back home. It's so simple."

"I was just thinking about you," Jerry said, growing serious. "About how you're doing. I worry, you know."

"I know, Jer," Scott answered. "I know."

"Is it any better being down here? Honest now. Tell me."

190

"Some days yes, some no," Scott lied, and as Jerry watched his friend, Scott's eyes betrayed him.

"I know you thought bringing me here would help, and it probably has, but..." Scott looked down at the pavement for a moment as his voice drifted off. "It's still just so damned hard, Jer."

Jerry could see that the mention of it had pushed Scott close to breaking.

He's still so fragile.

"Tranquilo. This will end. It damn well has to."

Chapter Thirty-Three

He smiled as he remembered his father calling such things "eating a toad." Papá had told him that when you had to eat a toad, sitting and looking at it didn't make it taste any better. It was still going to be a toad. The thought lingered as the marked Policía Federal patrol car pulled into the project's parking area at the end of the long access road. He'd put off meeting the norteamericano for as long as he could.

When Federico and the uniformed officer accompanying him walked under the canopy of the project tent, they found it empty except for a lone workman bent over a cooler full of ice, looking for a bottle of cold water. Federico took out a white handkerchief and wiped his brow. It was a hot, cloudless day at Xochicalco, and unusually humid.

"Señor," he said, interrupting the workman. He opened his credential. "Inspector Federico Salinas, Policía Federal. Can you direct me to the person in charge here?"

The workman looked up, startled. He glanced at the pistol resting on Federico's hip and the muscular young uniformed officer standing behind him. Neither visitor wore a friendly expression.

"Sí, inspector. That would be either Arturo Lopez or Raul Cathedra. Arturo is in charge of the work but Senor Cathedra oversees the project for the INAH. They're both here but I don't know where either is right now."

"Just find one of them, please, and bring him here."

Federico's tone left no room for discussion and the workman took off on his assignment without saying another word, choosing to head straight for the place he thought it most likely he'd find Arturo.

***

Arturo introduced himself and extended his hand to Federico.

"How can I be of service to the Policía Federal?" he asked.

"I'd like to know a bit about your activity here, if you can help me, Señor Lopez," Federico said. "I confess I'm not familiar with this project at all. From what I can see, though, it looks like you have quite an operation."

"Certainly. This is an archaeological site under the supervision of the National Institute of Anthropology and History. Most of the people working here are academics — anthropologists and archaeologists. Some are contracted workmen helping with the excavation work. There are almost 50 people engaged in all. We're exposing a structure that we believe may have been destroyed nearly a thousand years ago in some type of cataclysmic event. Perhaps a quake, or a military event. At least that's what we suspect happened here. One of our principal activities, and what the government is most interested in currently, is the recovery of artifacts. The site has been very rich."

"Artifacts? What type of artifacts?" Federico asked.

"Many different types. We've recovered weapons, jewelry, pottery, statuary, even items with gemstones and a few made of precious metals. We also just located the first human remains found at the site."

"What kind of statuary have you found?"

"Statuary, Señor? You want to know about types of statuary?" Arturo asked, unable to conceal his puzzlement.

"Yes, I do. Please," Federico replied, offering no further explanation.

"We've recovered all types. Some very large, several feet in length, and some quite small," Arturo said.

"How small? Small enough to be easily concealed, say, in clothing?" Federico asked.

"Yes, I would say we've had a few. Most are larger, but, yes, we've had a few like that," Arturo replied.

"Have there been any issues with the security of any of the artifacts?"

Arturo's ability to hide his anxiety had reached its limit with Federico's question. Federico noticed a slight trembling in Arturo's hands, which suddenly appeared to be searching for something to do.

"Inspector Salinas, may I know why you're asking these questions?" Federico could see the stress on Arturo's face. "Please understand, it's not every day we get a visit from the Policía Federal."

"I'll explain all of this after I get a little more information, Señor Lopez. Can I see some of these artifacts?"

Quietly relieved that Federico hadn't pursued the question about security, Arturo replied, "Of course,

Inspector. They're collected in a trailer dedicated to that purpose. We do the cataloging and recording there, and quite a bit of preliminary study and analysis before they're shipped to the institute in Mexico City. I'll show you."

As Arturo and Federico entered the artifact trailer a few minutes later, Jorge stepped aside and stood silently, eyeing Federico and his uniformed escort.

"This is Jorge," Arturo said. "He's with the government Institute — the INAH — and helps us look after the artifacts. Not quite 'security,' but the government likes to have more than one set of eyes on these objects. Some have very significant value."

Jorge nodded toward Federico, who nodded back. Scott looked up at the sound of the voices interrupting his work.

"And this is Dr. Scott Flores, a professor at a university in New York who's spending the summer with us helping to process what we've found. He's been most helpful."

Federico drew back slightly, reacting to the mention of Scott's name. He hadn't expected to be introduced to Scott without asking for him to be summoned.

"Scott, this is Inspector Salinas of the Policía Federal. He's interested in seeing what you have at the moment in the way of artifacts, and learning about what we do here," Arturo said.

"Surely," Scott said, smiling after shaking Federico's hand. Scott turned toward the storage racks that lined the walls of the trailer.

"Well, Inspector," he said, "all the recovered items are brought here from the excavation. We clean them up first. That's more complicated than you might think. Then we log them in, take a lot of different measurements and record a highly detailed description, including a complete photographic record. Then I do an assessment of the potential cultural significance of each one. That involves a lot of computer work — quick research, actually — and the preparation of a report. What you see here represents almost a month of effort by the people who do all the physical work. When we're finished with them they're sent to Mexico City for processing and then either storage or eventual placement in the national collection."

Federico studied Scott. Something troubled him about all of this. Good at sizing people up, and not easily fooled, he could sense already that this Professor Flores probably wasn't guilty of anything. Either that, or his nerve was exceptional. He saw no fear in the man's manner, as there should have been if Flores had something to hide and suddenly the Policía Federal appeared unannounced.

This gringo acts like he's speaking to a tour of school children. He has no idea what's coming.

Federico decided to talk to him a little longer to take his measure.

"May I handle some of them?" Federico asked.

"Certainly," Scott replied, pulling back the plastic sheeting that covered the racks, exposing the artifacts that had been fully processed and were waiting for shipment.

Federico picked up the smallest item he could find, a small piece of statuary perhaps six inches long.

"What can you tell me about this one, doctor?" he asked.

He listened patiently to Scott's explanation, then returned the artifact to the storage rack and turned to face Scott.

"Doctor, have there been any issues here about items going missing?"

"Missing?" Scott asked.

"Yes. Items that were recovered but have become unaccounted for at some point, before they made it to the institute in Mexico City?"

Scott hesitated and looked at Arturo.

"There is something you two would like to tell me?" Federico asked, noticing Scott's sidelong glance.

"Only rumors, inspector," Arturo answered. "I have no information for you, but perhaps you should talk to Señor Cathedra about that question. He represents the institute here and has total control over everything we recover. If anything is missing, he would know."

"I'll be sure to do that," Federico said as he turned and looked squarely at Scott. "Dr. Flores, now I must ask you to empty the contents of all of the pockets in your clothing, please, and place everything on the table over there." He gestured toward the small wooden table where Scott had been working.

Stunned, Scott stammered, "But why...I don't..."

Federico cut him off. "Please, just do as I say, doctor." The uniformed officer standing in the background took a step toward them and watched as Scott emptied his pockets.

Federico picked up the small figure of the Aztec child that Scott retrieved from his trouser pocket and examined it, finding its appearance to be exactly as had been described in the file the jefe had given him. The informant had, indeed, been reliable.

"I can explain that, inspector. It's not what you think. That was a gift from my wife. I brought it here from the states when I came to Cuernavaca in May. It was legally exported and purchased. I can prove that."

Perspiration that hadn't existed a few moments ago ran down Scott's brow.

"You'll have an opportunity to explain all of that later, doctor, but for now, I'm afraid you'll have to come with us. You are under arrest for violating Artículos 49 and 53 of the Federal Law of Archeological and Historical Sites, and corresponding provisions of the Federal Criminal Code."

Federico picked up the figure and placed it in his pocket.

"But this is all a mistake. I haven't done anything! I can prove it! You can't just take me away like this!" Scott's words tumbled out, his voice filled with panic.

"With due respect, Dr. Flores, I can, and I'm going to. You aren't in the United States now. You're in the Republic of Mexico, and a guest here. You'll be afforded the rights provided by our laws for someone accused of a crime but you may find our system somewhat different than what you're accustomed to," Federico said without emotion. "Normally we would place handcuffs on you, but as long as you behave properly I'll dispense with that. Will I have your cooperation?"

Scott struggled to understand what was happening. When he didn't respond, Federico repeated his question, more insistently. "Doctor. Will I have your cooperation?"

"Yes. Yes, of course," Scott said as he turned to Arturo, who looked as upset as if it were he who had been arrested. "Arturo, find Jerry and tell him what's happened. Tell him he has to find someone who can help."

"Sí, Scottsito. I'll find him," Arturo said. "Just stay calm and do what they tell you."

CHAPTER THIRTY-FOUR

The ten foot square holding cell at police headquarters contained a rusty metal cot with an inch thick mattress covered with a sweat stained sheet that hadn't been washed in months. The smells of the last several residents mingled on the pillow. A simple wooden stool with peeling black paint and a tiny opaque window braced by rusty steel bars finished the room. A small metal light fixture just outside of the cell held a bare bulb that filled the space with a harsh, unfriendly light. Scott had been the cell's only occupant since arriving hours earlier.

Sitting on the edge of the cot, he relaxed just enough to try to sort out what had happened. The exercise only produced questions.

How did the inspector know to ask him to empty his pockets? If he was really trying to smuggle artifacts, he wouldn't be carrying them around in his pocket. Anything worth stealing is much too large for that to be practical. And the way the inspector looked when he saw the figure? Like he knew exactly what he'd find. Why?

Scott leaned back against the gray concrete wall and closed his eyes. He'd heard stories about Americans getting into legal trouble in Mexico, usually with drugs, and these things never ended well. His stomach felt sick as he tried to reassure himself that this was all a big misunderstanding.

For Christ's sake, it's a tiny statue and I can prove it's legal. How much trouble can this be?

Scott's eyes snapped open at the metallic sound of the cell door opening. Inspector Federico Salinas stood in the doorway for a moment, looked at Scott, then pushed the door shut, the bang echoing down the hallway.

The wooden legs of the stool scraped along the rough concrete as Federico pulled it alongside the cot. Still silent, he sat facing Scott, studying him. The inspector leaned forward, elbows on his thighs, and rested his chin on his folded hands. Each man waited for the other to speak. When Federico finally spoke, his tone was direct, and his voice a bit louder than it needed to be in the cell's quiet.

"Dr. Flores. You've been charged with very serious offenses under Mexican law. Do you understand the possible consequences?"

"No one's explained any of that to me," Scott replied.

"Artículo 49 carries a penalty of up to 10 years and Artículo 53 up to 12 years. Those are years in a place like this," he said, glancing around the cell. "You're charged with both sections. You see, it would be best for you to be straightforward with me, doctor."

"In the United States my lawyer would tell me I'd be crazy to talk to you without him here," Scott replied.

"Likely so," Federico said. "I see that sort of thing on the television shows we get from the U.S. I suspect you'll have a lawyer here soon enough, who will probably tell you the same thing."

As Federico sat back in the chair and looked at Scott, Scott sensed some of the tension leave the room.

"I can't make you talk to me, professor, but no matter what you expect, we're not going to beat you with a rubber hose to get a confession. See?" He held out his empty hands. "Mexico is a civilized country, despite what your press reports. You can wait for your lawyer to appear, or you can talk to me. It's your choice. But if you have an explanation for this, the sooner I have it, the better for you."

Odd, but he doesn't frighten me.

"So, can we talk, doctor?"

"Inspector, I'd like to ask you some questions, too."

A smile crossed Federico's face.

"Good. Then we'll have a deal," Federico replied. "We'll ask each other questions. Actually, I don't want to question you about the relic I found hidden in your clothing. Not yet. What I'm most interested in is why you and Lopez lied when I asked if there had been issues at the excavation with items disappearing. I've been at this job a long time, doctor, and I'm no fool. I know when someone's keeping something from me. The two of you were obvious."

"Inspector, the relic wasn't hidden, and I didn't lie to you about anything. I just didn't tell you everything."

"A matter of semantics, doctor. This would be a good time to be candid."

"There's no proof, but I can tell you something's wrong at the project. Since the beginning the man in the trailer with me — Jorge — has been assigned to watch me every minute I'm working. I don't think he's there to keep me from stealing things. I think he's there to keep me from finding out what someone else is stealing. I'm getting in someone's way by doing my job."

"Who assigned this watchdog to you?" Federico asked.

"Señor Cathedra."

"As I understand, your job is to catalog and keep track of everything of value that's recovered?" Federico continued.

"That's right. But I only keep track of them for a while, until they're turned over to Cathedra. I give him everything — all of the analysis and reports, photos, everything. And before I arrived, the work that was done after the artifacts were recovered was very sloppy, very disorganized. I couldn't believe how casually they were being treated before they were supposed to be sent to Mexico City."

"Supposed? You don't think they're all being sent along?"

"As I said, I have no proof."

"But you suspect?"

"Yes."

"The items that are recovered aren't being treated 'casually' anymore?" Federico asked.

"No. Dr. Dwyer and I have changed a lot of the procedures at the project."

"And how valuable are these artifacts that you're handling?"

"Some are quite valuable...thousands of dollars. Some have jewels embedded in them, some are gold. Even the smaller clay artifacts have great value to collectors," Scott replied. "It's all black market value, of course."

Federico stroked his chin, then pointed at Scott. "You believe there's organized activity involving trafficking?"

"Many there believe it, but it's all rumors and innuendo," Scott replied. "Before I straightened things out it certainly would have been much easier to divert items without being noticed. I'm creating a detailed record of everything that goes through my work station, so at least there's a paper trail now."

"I asked what *you* thought, doctor. Please don't answer me like a politician. This will go better for you if you just tell me what you think. Who would be responsible? You have suspicions?"

Scott hesitated before saying, "I'd start by talking to Señor Cathedra, just as Arturo said," his suggestion clear enough. "He controls everything there."

"I see," Federico said. "And your questions, doctor? You said you had questions. I told you we have a deal."

"Inspector...I'm sorry, I forgot your name."

"Federico Salinas."

"When you came to the excavation you already knew that I'd have that little figure in my pocket and I think you even had a very good idea what it looked like, didn't you?"

"Yes," Federico replied. "That's so."

"And you came there with the specific intention of finding it and making an arrest. That says someone who's very familiar with me wanted to make trouble and told the police that I carried it with me."

"A logical conclusion, doctor, and essentially correct, at least the part about our suspecting that you had the artifact on you," Federico said. "I have no idea who provided that information. Not that I would be allowed to tell you if I did know, but, in this case, I don't. Perhaps you can give me some idea about who knew you were in the habit of foolishly carrying the little statue around in your pocket."

"Other than my colleague Professor Dwyer, and Ana Mendes, as far as I know, there isn't anyone who even knows about it."

"Ana Mendes? The daughter of Gabriel Mendes?" the Inspector asked, surprised. "She works at the project?"

"Yes, it's her. But neither of them would have had anything to do with me being here."

"I'm sure they didn't. Now tell me, if you're not a thief, what's the story behind the relic?"

"It was a gift from my wife," Scott explained. "She gave it to me the night she told me we were going to have our first child. That's the significance of the child figure. It was purchased back in the United States by Professor Dwyer. He can confirm that. I know it was legally exported with the approval of your government. All the papers are back in New York. I'm an anthropologist, inspector. I'm devoted to your patrimony. The last thing I'd do is steal part of it."

"You've the proper documentation, then, to prove this?" Federico asked.

"Back in the states, yes. I just don't have it here."

"That will complicate things for you, I'm afraid. You'll have to get the papers here as soon as you can. Perhaps your lawyer can sort it out. You don't have one yet?" Federico asked.

"No, but I sure as hell hope Professor Dwyer is getting one for me."

Federico smiled.

"I'm sure you'll have one soon enough."

As Federico rose to leave, Scott said, "Inspector, before you go, there's something else I need to ask."

"What's that, doctor?"

204

"The figure you took from me. The Aztec child. It's important when this is all over that I get it back."

"Perhaps. If things turn out to be as you say, I'll see what I can do."

CHAPTER THIRTY-FIVE

Luz commanded attention from the moment she strode into the procurador's office and announced her appointment. Tall, with finely chiseled features, she wore her hair tightly pulled back, signaling that she should be taken seriously. Her tailored suit, with a tight skirt that ended well above the knee, flattered a figure that men always noticed. Luz used her appearance as a tool, and she took great care with it.

Licenciada Luz Beltran had puzzled over the odd way the case had arrived on her desk — a personal telephone call from Gabriel Mendes, wealthy businessman, well known patron of the Catholic church, and close confidante of the President of the Republic. And a man she'd never spoken to. Why would Gabriel Mendes care about an American college professor who'd gotten himself in trouble in Morelos over a tiny piece of Aztec statuary? And care enough to guarantee the large fee she quoted, a fee more appropriate to her usual well-heeled clients — drug dealers, corrupt businessmen, and the ill-behaved children of wealthy families? The professor must be connected.

CUERNAVACA

A combination of the image of a terrified American college professor in jail, and the over-sized fee that Mendes guaranteed led her to the office of the procurador assigned to prosecute Scott Flores. Expecting to learn more about the case from him than from her client, she'd decided the professor could wait a few hours.

Inside the office of Procurador Ricardo Carroza, Luz settled into a soft leather chair and waited for Carroza to finish a telephone call. As he talked, he nodded to Luz and smiled. They weren't exactly close friends, but Luz had handled so many cases with Carroza they'd developed a comfortable relationship. They respected each other, and that he'd let her hear one side of his conversation with an unknown caller told her he trusted her. Although he'd never done or said anything forward, she'd wondered for some time if there might be more to Carroza's courtesies than professional respect. She liked Ricardo, and didn't think he'd ever lied to her — at least she'd never caught him — and, in her business, that counted.

As Carroza continued his call, Luz occupied herself with the photographs covering the walls and filling the end tables of Carroza's office, two of him with former presidents, several with governors of the State of Morelos, and a half dozen with lesser officials. Carroza had even managed to get into a large group photo taken with President George Bush when he visited Mexico City. Carroza was the last person on the left in the third row in that one, and it took Luz a while to spot him. With a long way to go, Carroza had well known political ambitions.

"Ricardo," Luz said after Carroza finished his call, but before he could start a conversation. "Why are you holding this American, Scott Flores? He shouldn't even be in custody and the man's been your guest for 48 hours now."

"I love how you get right to the point, Luzita. You could at least ask me how the hell I'm doing before you start in. I'd like to know what you're doing with a case like this," Carroza said. "A four inch long Aztec artifact? Really? The famous Luz Beltran?"

"Fair," Luz answered. "I have his case because someone agreed to pay me a ridiculously large fee to handle it."

"An answer that tells me nothing. Who's the 'someone'? It's not the professor?" Carroza asked.

"I shouldn't tell you, but I expect you to come clean as well, Ricardo. You know Gabriel Mendes?"

"Of course. What's he got to do with it?"

"He's covering it. And before you ask, I've no idea why."

Carroza made no attempt to hide his surprise.

"Gabriel Mendes? So we're both pieces in some game?" Carroza said, reaching for his coffee cup. "As for why he's still here, the Policía Federal had instructions from Mexico City to take this professor of yours into custody and hold him as long as possible. But, for some reason, I've already been told by the Procurador General's office to offer him a complete amnesty if he just leaves the country. Of course, he won't be allowed to ever re-enter. This should be the easiest case you've ever had. Make sure you charge for the result, and not the time."

"Why do you suppose they wanted the man held in custody so long?" she asked, ignoring his offer.

"Who knows?" Carroza replied. "They didn't tell me. And who cares? Perhaps to scare him, soften him up for the offer to let him run back to the states, which seems to be the purpose of all this. But I've no idea, really."

The case now made even less sense to Luz. Someone with enough influence in Mexico City to get the Procurador General to order Flores arrested and held as long as possible on a petty charge wants him out of the country? Why? All she knew about him was that he was a college professor doing some kind of field project over the summer, and he'd been in Mexico for less than two months. It was time to meet her client.

"Maybe so, Ricardo, but why does someone want so badly for him to leave?"

Remembering why she'd asked for the appointment, she leaned forward slightly, locking her eyes on him and continuing before he could answer.

"As you said, there's more to this than the charge against my client. It's rather interesting, don't you think? I'm going to want to figure this all out before I let him do anything, so we'll sit on that offer a while. Tell me, are you going to release him or do I have to go to the trouble to apply for the amparo? You can't hold him. You know that."

"I'm afraid I can't agree to it. My hands are tied on this one." Carroza smiled. "But I don't think you'll find my office investing a lot of effort in resisting your petition."

They looked across Carozza's desk, understanding without speaking exactly how the release of Scott Flores would be handled.

As Luz got up to leave, she said, "You'd best be careful how you handle this, Ricardito. I'd hate to see your career affected by such a small matter."

"Careful?" Carroza said. "Always, Luzita."

***

Luz hated visiting clients in jail. The Atlacholoaya prison where Scott had been moved was dark, full of people she didn't like, and smelled bad. The odor was the worst of it, like no other she'd experienced. Once you breathed the air of a prison you didn't soon forget it. You couldn't get the smell out of your lungs until you were in your car and heading home, and sometimes it lingered even then.

"I'm here to see a prisoner named Scott Flores," she announced, showing her court credential to the jailer at the entrance to her client's block. She looked out of place in the fetid jail with her tailored clothes and clean, crisp professional appearance. The jailer eyed her chest a little too closely, then nodded, wordlessly passing her through the security station.

Her high-heeled footsteps echoed off the hard floor as a second guard walked her down a dimly lit hallway to her client's cell. She glanced at the grubby, hopeless-looking prisoners in the cells she passed. They leered at her, some muttering lewd remarks she couldn't make out, stirring at her passage, the highlight of their day. As the jailer turned the key, the door to Scott's cell opened with a squeal.

"Señora," the jailer said as he held the door. "Speak loudly when you're ready to leave. I'll hear you."

Luz nodded.

After the door locked behind her, Luz found Scott sprawled on a cot, asleep. She surveyed the gray concrete block enclosure. No matter how many times she'd been here, she couldn't imagine her world consisting of a 12 by 12 foot space with a single cold light, a toilet, and a cot covered with a filthy blanket. Not even for a day.

Pobrecito. Well, he doesn't look like he's had too bad a time so far.

She'd expected him to be pacing the cell, filled with anxiety. Instead, Scott was asleep in the middle of the afternoon.

"Dr. Flores," she said, reaching for his shoulder. "Wake up. We need to talk."

Her client stirred and looked up at her, not quite awake. When his head cleared, he asked, "And who are you?"

"Luz Beltran. I'm your lawyer," she said, relieved when Scott replied in Spanish.

"My lawyer? I didn't know I had one. Jerry got you?" he asked, struggling to lean on an elbow and rubbing his eyes. "'Bout time."

"No, I'm afraid no one named Jerry had anything to do with it. I was asked — hired actually — to represent you, by Gabriel Mendes. Señor Mendes is a very important man in Mexico City. But then you must know him, since he guaranteed my fee. Apparently you're very well connected, doctor."

Scott wiped his face in his hands, still waking.

"No, I'm not. This might be a surprise to you, Señora...Beltran you said your name was? But I don't know anyone named Gabriel Mendes. And I don't know why he'd hire you."

"Really?" she said, surprised. "Well, I'll want to talk about that. Right now my job is to get you out of here, and that should happen soon. We likely can get an order for your release pending the processing of the charge, and, with luck, you'll be leaving in a few hours. Did the policía advise you of your right to contact the United States consulate?"

"I wasn't advised of anything, Señora Beltran. Were they supposed to do that?"

"Yes, along with several other things they probably didn't do. Sometimes the policía just forget to do that, and sometimes it's intentional. But either way, that will help us get the order for your release." She paused. "I need to know what happened, doctor. Why you had the figure with you, and what the explanation is. We'll need to present that information to get you out of here. You do have an explanation?"

As Scott explained why he had the relic in his pocket, just as he had to Salinas, it all made sense to Luz. He also told her that Salinas had confirmed that the Policía Federal knew all about the small figure he always carried before they had arrived to arrest him, and that Salinas seemed much more interested in what was going on at the project than what was in Scott's pocket when he was arrested.

"Perhaps this Inspector Salinas intentionally didn't tell you about the consulate because he wanted us to be able to use it. There's a treaty with the United States that requires it, and it tends to complicate things when it's not honored. Something like that isn't supposed to influence whether you get released, but the reality is that it can be a good excuse for the judge to use."

Luz patiently explained the procedure for securing the order which would release Scott from custody, which she called an amparo, the conditions that would be attached to it, and how she thought the rest of the procedure would play out.

"Doctor, I know this is all very confusing, but let me give you something else to consider. Someone wants you to leave the country. That's what's behind your arrest."

"What?" Scott asked. "How do you know that?"

"Because I just came from the procurador's office and he offered to make this all disappear if you simply return to the states. Your visa will be permanently revoked, but it all goes away without a trace."

"I don't understand. Why would anyone want me to leave? I'll be gone in a few months, anyhow."

"I've no idea yet, doctor, but you should think about the implications for your career. It's your life, not mine, but I don't suppose it will look good on the record of an anthropologist to have been formally accused of stealing artifacts from a host country, no matter how your case turns out. Wouldn't your university's administration have concerns? And keep in mind there's always the possibility that you might be found guilty, as crazy as that sounds. We have no jury trials here, and this isn't television. You should consider that someone with influence in Mexico City is behind this, someone who may be able to get the system to do what he wants. As you can see, this part of Mexican hospitality is rather unpleasant."

"Señora, my situation at home is complicated. I need the summer to collect the data to publish a research paper that's going to be critical to my career. If I leave now, without it, I'm going to have a serious problem."

Scott needed the data from the summer at Xochicalco to produce a credible research publication. That publication, which he planned to prepare in the fall, would explain his absence from active teaching for a semester, and help him as he searched for a new position.

"I'm going to have to deal with this here somehow. And there's something else, Señora."

"Something else?"

"Yes. This is personal now. It's not a transaction for me."

This is going to be more complicated that I thought. Personal, he says.

"No decisions have to be made just yet," Luz replied. "We'll be in front of a judge later today, and we'll have a chance to talk more before that. Try to relax."

"I'll try, Señora Beltran. No promise on that, though."

Far too occupied with wondering what her American professor had done to deserve such attention, Luz hardly noticed the gauntlet of catcalls as she left the cell block.

CHAPTER THIRTY-SIX

Scott examined what little remained of the jail cell — just a rusty metal door with thick steel bars and peeling paint, framed by two small sections of what had been the walls of the cell. Nothing else gave a hint that the Cuernavaca jail ever stood there before it was totally demolished.

Ordinarily, he wouldn't have paid any attention to a historical monument to the city's original lockup, but his recent two day stay in the jail's replacement had provided a sense of kinship with the old jail's residents. He imagined the gloom they must have felt, and how the place had looked and smelled. If the new jail was an improvement, he couldn't imagine how wretched the old one must have been.

Sitting on the bench with Ana and Jerry in the Acapantzingo ecological park, the irony of what the government chose to build on the site of the old prison surrounded him. A short walk from his home, every night the park's 100 foot long fountain put on a computerized display of music and colored lights. Now people came to relax and enjoy themselves, not to be punished.

"Ana, I can't let your father pay for Beltran," Scott said. "I can afford to pay her myself. And she's wonderful. She sure as hell got me out of that place fast."

Ana nodded.

"She's the best in the city. According to papá, that is."

"When Beltran told me that someone named Mendes had arranged the fee I had no idea it was your family. The name just didn't register. I expected my amigo Jerry to find some cut rate shyster."

"I was shopping for the best price when you managed to get out all by yourself," Jerry said. "I didn't see the point in wasting any of your money."

"Ana, I'm so grateful for what your father did," Scott said.

"There's not much he won't do for his daughter," she replied.

"How are the people at the excavation taking all this?" Scott asked.

"Mixed reaction," Jerry answered. "Arturo, Max and the people you've spent the most time with think it's all bullshit. Some of the others, who don't know you, wonder what it's all about. Not surprisingly, Cathedra is trying his best to make a big deal out of it, saying that you were stealing the country's patrimonio and all. The son of a bitch. I'm afraid he's going to ban you from the site based just on the accusation. He can pull that off, considering what you're accused of."

Scott hadn't considered the possibility, but a way to deal with it quickly formed in his mind.

"I may be able to do something about that," Scott said.

"Oh?" Jerry asked. "I figure he's going to kick you out straight away."

216

"When I was in jail the man who arrested me, an Inspector Salinas, came to visit and we had an interesting talk. He doesn't seem like a bad guy. And I think I convinced him that the relic is legit. If not, we'll be able to prove it soon enough. But he was real interested in whether there's been a pattern of things going missing at the excavation. I think I know why."

"Tell," Jerry said.

"Well, Salinas told me that the policía already knew before they came to arrest me that I would have the relic in my pocket. Someone must have told them that, but even he didn't know who. Apparently this case is being given some type of special handling with orders that came from Mexico City. Beltran, and maybe Salinas, too, thinks this has all been trumped up by someone with clout who just wants me to go away."

"Raul?" Ana asked.

"Who else would it be? Beltran told me that the procurador already offered to wipe the whole thing off the books if I just leave."

"Leave the country?" Ana asked.

"Yeah. Apparently the procurador will just erase everything if I agree to have my visa revoked and never come back."

"Interesting, but I still don't see how any of that can stop Raul from banning you from the excavation with the charge hanging over your head," Jerry said.

"I think Salinas is a conscientious cop," Scott explained. "He just wants to find out what's going on and catch the bad guys. And he's curious about who wants me gone and why. He's already figured out I'm not a smuggler and he's sharp enough to know that stuff has been going on at the site that no one's anxious to talk about. I'm guessing he wants to get behind it all now that he has the case. I might be able to convince him that I can feed him some information from the inside, and if I can't do anything else, just by being there I can make Cathedra nervous as hell. Maybe I can get Salinas to tell Cathedra that keeping me there will help his investigation of me. Cathedra won't like it, but he won't want to get on the bad side of the policía."

"Even if it's Raul who's behind that phony charge, how did he know that you carried the relic around with you?" Ana asked.

"No idea. I never told him about it, but he must have found out about it somehow. Speaking of that, to make sure I'm good with Salinas I'm going to need the documentation sent down here as soon as possible," Scott said.

"I'm working on that," Jerry reassured him. "I called back to Albany and your housekeeper is looking for it in your apartment. It would help if you'd call her directly and tell her what empty pizza box to look under."

Without warning, the fountain's light show erupted in front of them, to the delighted squeals of a group of children. A sudden breeze blew the fountain's cooling mist over the three as music blared from the park's sound system, making it impossible to talk without shouting. They retreated from the bench to walk on one of the park's pathways, away from the confusion and the shower.

As they walked on and the sound faded, Ana asked, "If Raul's responsible, why does he want you to leave so badly that he goes to all of this trouble? To ask people with influence in Mexico City to have you arrested? It would cost Raul a lot of what you norteamericanos call 'points', and probably a lot of money, too. You're leaving in a few months anyway, so why go to this trouble?"

"I've puzzled over that," Scott said. "At first I thought it might have something to do with you."

"Me?" she asked.

"I'm sorry if this comes out wrong, Ana, but he's interested in you and he feels I'm a threat. You had to notice him."

"Of course I know he's interested. He's so obvious, but that can't possibly explain something like this. Having you arrested? Really?"

"Perhaps," Scott said. "Like I said, I've turned this over. Then I figured maybe I shouldn't flatter myself with that theory."

He watched Ana for a reaction. Their eyes connected for a moment and he thought he saw the corners of her mouth turn up slightly before he continued.

"More likely, he's hiding something and he's afraid of it coming out. I'm some type of threat for that as well. Since I catalog all of the recovered items, and I keep a record of what we've found for my research, it must have something to do with them."

Jerry had been quiet.

"I'll give you my simple ass theory. I just think the guy's a crook. I can smell it," Jerry announced. "This goes way back to the emails Arturo sent to me in Albany, Scott. Remember those? And the way Arturo explained things the first day we got here? There was no damned way to check what's been recovered against what was properly cataloged and sent on to Mexico City until we got here. And you're the guy in the trailer making sure all the t's are crossed and the i's are dotted. You're getting in the way, plus, if our friend Raul is running artifacts on the black market, he can't be sure that you won't figure out exactly what he's doing."

Jerry's point hung in the air.

"Is he sharp enough to realize that you're keeping notes on all of this for publication?" Jerry asked.

"Not sure. He might be. It's common knowledge at the site."

"Then he knows, and he can't be happy with the idea that there's going to be a paper published, complete with pictures and descriptions of things that maybe never made it to the national collection. He's in a position to divert tens of thousands of dollars' worth of relics into the black market," Jerry continued, "and no one would ever know except for the paper trail you've created."

Chapter Thirty-Seven

"Señor Cathedra. I'm afraid you're going to have to make the time to show me this."

It had taken Federico a full half hour just to find Raul, and another 20 minutes to pull him away from what seemed to Federico the unimportant task of giving instructions to some of the site's workmen. Federico didn't have the time to waste. He considered the delay Raul's way of demonstrating his importance, and that didn't help Raul at all with Federico, who had only grown more irritated as he waited.

"I need to see the entire process that you go through with these artifacts, from the time they're recovered out in the excavation until they're gone from here and on their way to the institute. Including how the items are documented and accounted for. It's essential to our investigation of Dr. Flores. I prefer that you show me personally, so there's no possibility of any misunderstanding on my part."

"I just don't see the need for any of this, inspector," Raul protested. "Flores was caught with a relic in his possession. Isn't that enough? What difference does it make how we catalog these things and prepare them for shipment?"

"There isn't a choice. We actually have very little on Flores. He can have any number of good explanations for why he was walking around with a tiny piece of statuary in his pocket. And it isn't exactly the crime of the century, now, is it? To have any real chance of making something serious stick on the norteamericano we're going to have to try to tie him into something more organized, more...what's the word I'm looking for?...extensive. If he's really a thief, there should be more to uncover."

Federico watched Raul for some reaction to the prospect of an expanded investigation.

"In some ways this is an odd case," Federico continued.

"Odd? In what way?" Raul asked.

Federico thought he noticed a change in Raul's self-assured demeanor, and the slightest look of concern.

"I don't get orders from Mexico City very often about how to handle an investigation," Federico said, still searching Raul's face. "In this particular case, I've been instructed to do whatever it takes to see that the gringo is convicted of something. Someone high up wants this little case handled like the future of the republic depends on the outcome, and that's exactly what I intend to do with it. So I want to know everything that's happened here."

Choosing his words carefully, Federico added, "Including things that perhaps aren't so obvious. And if more than the theft of one little statue is involved, I'm going to find out what, exactly, that might be."

"I still don't see why all of this is necessary," Raul protested, clearing his throat. "Surely you can explain to your superiors how simple this really is."

222

Raul's hands fumbled with a pack of cigarettes he took from his shirt pocket. He finally pulled one clear and lit it. Federico thought he noticed the flame of the lighter trembling slightly in Raul's hand.

"You don't really think there's more to this than Flores' petty thievery, do you?" Raul asked.

"I've no idea," Federico replied. "But if there is, I'm going to find out. There seem to be a lot of nervous people around here."

Federico pulled a small notebook out of his hip pocket and, for Raul's benefit, jotted down a note as Raul watched. When he finished, Federico looked up at Raul and said, "Your career and position may be secure, Señor, but mine is not."

His eyes never left Raul's, who looked away.

"I don't know if I'll find out anything more about this Dr. Flores, but I can assure you I'm going to send in one hell of an extensive report on my attempt. And you're going to help me with it, aren't you?"

Raul fidgeted, but said nothing.

"Let me tell you something else," Federico continued, his voice suddenly taking on an intensity not part of the plan he'd had for talking to Raul. "This month I've lost two good men to the narcos. They both had families. I had to see them there, lying in the street. Both of them. I should be hunting those fucking animals, but instead, I have to spend my time trying to catch people who maybe, just maybe, are stealing little statues. And I'm under orders to do a goddamned proper job of it."

He paused as he moved to within a few feet of Raul's face.

"I need to know what the hell is going on here, so I can be done with this."

Frozen by Federico's words, Raul's hand shook visibly as he took the cigarette out of his mouth and let it drop to the ground. He stared at Federico, waiting for something to happen.

"Now," Federico said, lowering his voice and taking a step back. "We're going to start at the beginning, out in the excavation, and I want you to show me everything that's done, all the way back to the trailer where Flores has been working. And I want to know how it was done before Flores got here, and then exactly how things have changed since he arrived."

"Nothing has changed since he started," Raul said. Federico noticed Raul rubbing his pant leg.

"You mean the procedure for all of the documentation was fully in place before he got here, and he made no changes?" Federico asked.

"Yes, exactly," Raul replied. "I'll help in any way I can, of course. I'm sorry about your officers. The drug traffic is such a tragedy in so many ways."

"Flores changed nothing at all?" Federico asked, ignoring the comment.

"No, nothing," Raul answered.

"There's one other thing," Federico added. "Flores is out of jail and may want to return to the excavation project. I don't want you to interfere with his coming back."

"I don't understand," Raul objected. "How can I let him work here when he's under suspicion for stealing our artifacts?"

"Say whatever you want. Tell everyone the gringo is entitled to be treated as innocent until the court says otherwise. Tell them you've put security measures in place. I don't care what you tell them. I just want him

224

here working for a little while longer. It will help with the investigation in ways you may not understand."

No, I'm sure you won't.

CHAPTER THIRTY-EIGHT

It was past midnight when two men dressed in dark business suits entered the lobby of the Presidente Inter-Continental Santa Fe Hotel in Mexico City. They walked directly to the lobby elevator and through its conveniently open door. The taller of the two selected the top floor on the keypad as his companion shifted an attache case from his left hand to his right, belying its weight. They said nothing to each other, even after the door closed. In a few seconds, it opened onto a brightly lit, but deserted, hallway covered in plush carpet and bordered with expensive looking sofas and chairs. There were only a few doors on this floor, each one the entrance to a penthouse suite. After locating the number they were looking for, the tall man rapped lightly on the door.

When it opened, Felipe Bencivenga stood aside and motioned them in. "You're the representatives of Señor Guzman?" he asked.

The taller man nodded, his face cold, expressionless. "Yes. I'm Ramón Portillo," he said. "And this is Julio Zepeda. Señor Oro's here?"

"Yes, of course," Felipe replied, closing the door behind them. "He's expecting you. In the other room. Come."

Rodrigo stood on the balcony admiring the lights of the city. At the sound of Felipe's voice he walked back into the suite, and, smiling broadly, extended his hand. After the introductions, Rodrigo offered the two guests a drink, which they accepted with the same polite, but stoic demeanor that had greeted Felipe at the door.

Portillo took a long drink from his glass of Patrón, then set it down with a slow, precise motion on the coffee table in front of him.

"If you don't mind," he said, "I appreciate the hospitality, but can we conclude our business directly?"

"Of course. I assume you have the money?" Rodrigo asked.

"It's all in that attaché," Portillo said, gesturing toward the case that sat on the floor within reach of the silent Zepeda. "Go ahead and count it."

"Oh, that won't be necessary," Rodrigo said. "I'm sure he's good to his word."

"As you wish," Portillo replied, taking another swallow of the Patrón. "But most of the people with whom I make transactions take a more careful approach to such things."

Portillo crossed his leg and focused on Rodrigo.

"Before I release this contribution there is the matter of your understanding that we have to discuss. You were told that we'd talk about this?"

"Yes, and I had a preliminary discussion about the consideration you need from me," Rodrigo said. "I think I understand it very well."

"Things like this are never written down, of course," Portillo said matter-of-factly. "But the understanding must be as clear as if there were a written contract. If you achieve a position of influence we expect only that the government will not interfere with our business. We can tolerate purely cosmetic actions, but nothing must happen that has a serious impact on us. And anything that interferes, even for appearances, has to be disclosed in advance. And approved. That's clear?"

"Perfectly," Rodrigo replied. "You needn't worry, Ramón. Our understanding only asks me to do what I will do in any event. The government's suppression of the narcotics trade is nothing but a tragic waste of money and time. It serves the interests of the United States government, not Mexico."

"Your philosophy is really not any concern of ours," Portillo replied coldly. He stood, signaling that the meeting was over. "You can tell the people anything you want. Just be sure to honor your commitment to us."

After Portillo and Zepeda left, Felipe and Rodrigo walked out onto the balcony, surrounded by the warm Mexico City evening. Reading the discomfort on Felipe's face, Rodrigo asked, "You're really troubled by this, aren't you?"

"Hell yes, I'm troubled. These people you're accepting money from are cold blooded killers. And they kill Mexicans, not foreigners. Do you realize how many policemen they've murdered?"

"Those killings could have been avoided. They were all the result of the government's policy toward their business, and that policy was only adopted to please the gringo government. It will be different when we're running things," Rodrigo assured his aide. "No more Mexicans will die."

"All of this talk about their 'business,' as if they run restaurants or factories. These people sell death, and it doesn't seem to bother them much," Felipe replied before downing the drink he'd nursed while sitting in the corner of the room, watching the money pass. "And forget all of that. What happens if we get caught taking this money? Remember, we expect someone else to be running the government after the election and they'll control everything, for at least a while, including the procuradores. If any of this gets exposed..."

"You worry too much, my friend," Rodrigo reassured him. "I understand there's risk, and the whole business is unsavory, but remember what we're trying to accomplish. The good outweighs the bad, don't you think?"

Rodrigo's confidence never wavered. It didn't move Felipe.

"Don't you really mean the ends justify the means?" he asked.

"Felipe, Felipe. Things will work out. You'll see."

"I hope you're right, Rodi. I sure as hell hope you're right."

Chapter Thirty-Nine

The business card read "Luz Beltran, Abogado, Licenciada en Derecho, 235 Calle Rayon," the address matching the number on the wall of a well-maintained three story building facing a small plaza in downtown Cuernavaca. An unpretentious set of concrete stairs with a freshly painted iron hand railing led to a single wooden door flanked by a small, polished brass sign displaying the names of the several attorneys maintaining offices there. Despite their common quarters, the sign gave Scott the impression that each practice was separate from the others.

Scott had little experience with lawyers. He remembered his father talking about them at the dinner table in unflattering terms, and he recalled a time when his father had taken him along when he had business with one. He remembered a very large, fancy office, and that it seemed as though many lawyers worked there. The building that faced him looked nothing like the one his father had taken him to.

The directory in a glass case to one side of the vestibule told him that the office of Luz Beltran was on the very top of the building, third floor. He looked for an elevator, and, seeing none, he glanced up through the center well of a tall metal staircase.

She must not represent many feeble old ladies who want estate planning.

After the long climb, Scott paused to catch his breath before opening the only door he found on the third floor. Inside, a young woman greeted him, and as she took in Scott's appearance, a smile crossed her face that he thought a bit too animated.

"Buenas tardes," she said. "You must be Dr. Flores."

"Yes, I am. I'm a few minutes early."

"I'll let Señora Beltran know you're here," she replied. She smiled at him again before disappearing toward what Scott assumed was Beltran's private office.

In a few minutes Luz appeared from around the corner of the waiting room and extended her hand. Convinced of her formidable talent by the speed with which she'd managed to get him released, the sight of her reassured Scott.

Luz' immaculately organized personal office matched her appearance. Her desk was clear of papers, save for Scott's personal file, the matter at hand. It rested in the center of a perfectly restored antique wooden desk. The seating was comfortable, but arranged in the traditional way, with the client's chair squarely facing the lawyer's desk, signaling who was in charge of the conversation. There was an air of control about Luz that Scott appreciated, given his present circumstances. He supposed that she didn't like surprises, deception, or losing.

"I received the wire transfer from your bank in New York, Scott," she began. "Thank you for that. I've told

Señor Mendes' representative that his financial support won't be necessary."

"I've solved that mystery, Señora Beltran."

"It's Luz, please," she replied.

"Thanks. Señor Mendes is the father of a friend, a woman who works at the excavation with me. When she heard I'd been arrested she asked him to help. From what I can tell, Mendes is a very high powered person, which speaks well of his choice of you."

"I've gotten some results, yes," Luz said, smiling at the complement. "And Señor Mendes is more than high powered. He's one of the wealthiest people in Mexico and a very influential man in Mexico City. He's a close personal friend of the president as well. You know his daughter?"

"Yes. Anarosa. She's on the staff at the Xochicalco project."

"I was most curious about the connection to Mendes."

"Well, getting the amparo was the easy part, I'm afraid," she continued. "The government's case is weak, I know, but they have time on their side."

"I don't understand," he said. "Time's on their side?"

"It's June," she explained, "and you're supposed to return to New York by the end of August, correct?"

Scott considered whether to share with Beltran the fact that he had no job to return to, and no real plan. It seemed best to be honest, given his circumstances.

"Actually Luz, I don't have a position to return to. I resigned my appointment at the university before I left to come here."

"You have no position when the summer is over?" she asked.

"No, I was planning to search for something when I returned."

"That may make things easier for you, but you have to understand the case will sit on the court docket for a lot longer than the next few months. Things move slowly here as it is, and if someone with influence *wants* them to move slowly, it only gets worse. It can take months to get to the point where we can clear everything out. Meanwhile, I'm afraid you won't be able to leave the country with this charge hanging over you. I suspect that whoever wants you out of the country — if that's what he wants — will be able to force you to look at staying here indefinitely as the only alternative to what you're being offered. You either take the deal and leave, find a position and get on with your life, or stay and fight it out until God knows when. And with a record of all of this following you when you return."

"But in a few days I should have the documentation showing the relic is legitimate. Surely you can get this all taken care of as soon as the paperwork gets here," Scott protested.

"Ordinarily, yes. But we're dealing with politics and this is not an ordinary case," Luz said, assuming the patient, but direct, manner of a teacher imparting a lesson. "Whoever is behind this has enough influence to tie the procurador's hands up very tightly. He has orders to handle this in a certain way and my guess is that those instructions involve delaying the disposition of your case as long as possible. He's probably going to be able to manage at least several months, which is all they need to put you up against a difficult choice. Your documentation may eventually win for you, but eventually may be too long to wait."

She waited for a response before adding, "Remember what I told you at the prison. We have no jury trials here. The system doesn't always work as it should, especially when politics is involved. I'm sorry. Scott. This is going to be difficult."

Scott sat for a moment, silent.

"I can't make this decision," he said.

"If there's a bright side, it's only the end of June and I think the amnesty offer will be on the table all summer," she said. "Whoever wants you gone will likely be just as happy to have you gone a month from now, as tomorrow."

Luz sat back in her chair and rested her elbows on the arm pieces.

"Scott, I have one question which may, in the end, matter a great deal." Luz hesitated before continuing. "Or perhaps not at all. Who has a reason to want you to leave? You must have some idea."

Scott thought for a moment.

"I can only think of one person. Raul Cathedra."

"Who, exactly, is Raul Cathedra?"

"Raul's an official with the INAH who's in charge of the archaeological site at Xochicalco."

"Why would he want you to leave Mexico?" she asked.

"I'm not sure why he'd go to these lengths to do it. Maybe he's afraid I'll expose him."

"Expose him? For what?" Luz leaned forward, her curiosity piqued.

"My job at the project is to catalog all of the recovered antiquities. They have a considerable value on the black market, but they're all supposed to go into the Mexican government's national collection in Mexico City.

There are a lot of rumors about items going missing at the site and Raul would be in the best position to divert them, or look the other way, if others do. This is all rumor, now. But if Raul's involved, and that's just an 'if,' then I could see where he might think my job put me in a position to make things more complicated."

"There's something else," Scott added. "Gabriel Mendes' daughter Anarosa. Raul's been pursuing her, I think without much luck. But Ana and I have spent time together and he may have noticed. No, I'm sure he has. There could be jealousy behind it as well."

"Well, if this Raul is the cause of your legal troubles, you've managed to make an enemy of someone who apparently has influence. And right now, he's in control."

TERCERA PARTE

CHAPTER FORTY

Scott held up the thick gold bracelet and let the bright sunlight streaming through the open window reflect off of its polished surface. As he turned it over in his hand, the sun played with the precious metal, throwing sharp beams of reflected sunlight at his face.

Beautiful. And, at the present price of gold, worth thousands of dollars.

"You like this one?" he asked Jorge without looking up, not expecting an answer.

During the first few days after he returned to the Xochicalco project, Scott actually welcomed Jorge's cold, emotionless demeanor. Arturo had been right about the staff's reaction to Scott's arrest. The few people who knew him well — Max, Ana and a handful of others — acted as though nothing had happened. The rest were cordial enough, but kept their distance, not sure what to make of the arrest and accusation. Clearly, things had changed. Jorge, however, acted no differently. With Jorge just as stoic as he'd been all along, Scott found it oddly comforting that nothing had changed with him.

As Scott worked into the early afternoon, he kept glancing at his watch, impatient for meal time. With the break would come time away from Jorge's constant surveillance. If Jorge stayed predictable, he'd either disappear sometime after Scott headed for lunch, or remain in the trailer as he did most days. Scott had no idea where he went when he left the trailer, and didn't care, as long as today it wasn't to Raul's office. It was Friday, and, like most Friday afternoons, Raul's car had disappeared from the lot.

At 2:00 Scott finished up the work immediately before him and announced to Jorge that he was going to eat. He invited Jorge to come along, just as he did every day, and, just as predictably, Jorge declined.

"Suit yourself," Scott said, as he tossed his smock onto a chair and brushed past Jorge and out the door.

Jorge had yet to take a meal with Scott and the rest of the professionals and field workers, but, to be safe, Scott hurried to the headquarters tent and quickly gathered up lunch, making sure to be seen there. Fifteen minutes later he quietly excused himself from a table full of colleagues and slipped away from the tent. Satisfying himself that Raul had gone and Jorge wasn't coming to lunch, he walked directly toward Raul's private trailer, located in a far corner of the site, well away from any routine foot traffic. Raul had made sure that anyone approaching his private work space would have no reason to be in the area except to visit him.

The old trailer that served as Raul's office bore the national seal and the freshly painted words "Instituto Nacionál de Antropologia e Historia." As Scott approached he glanced back toward the tent and the working face of the site in the distance. Seeing no one, he quickly removed the key that Federico had given him and tried it in the lock on the trailer's door. He tried it several more times. Federico had called it a 'master key' which he thought might work on the door of an old house trailer. It didn't.

Damn. So much for skeleton keys.

Scott took a deep breath and remembered what he'd been told to do. He quickly circled to the rear of the trailer to check for an unsecured window. Finding none, he returned to the door and tried the key again.

He pulled hard on the aluminum door. When nothing happened, he pulled again. After the third try, he slid a thin, oddly shaped metal blade that Federico had given him into the space between the door and the jamb and manipulated it. He pulled as hard as he could on the door. Surprised when it popped open, he stepped inside. He turned and looked back toward the excavation again. Satisfied he'd made it into the trailer without being seen, he closed the door, relieved that once inside he hadn't run straight into Jorge.

This should probably be good for about 10 more years in jail all by itself.

Scott's ticket back into the project had been Federico's belief that having someone on the inside would be a better way to gather information than another visit from the policía, which Raul's men couldn't miss. If Raul was really into something meaningful, Federico wanted to make sure Raul didn't know that anyone was aware of it until Raul had been watched to see where he went and who he spent his time with. That, Federico had explained, would take a while because there were limited resources available for surveillance.

Stillness saturated Raul's trailer. Scott could hear only the soft ticking of a clock on a small desk that sat in one corner, and the rapid beating of his heart. The trailer had several windows, all darkened with blinds that admitted only enough light to provide Scott the dimmest view of the interior.

He'd never been in Raul's private workspace, and, as far as Scott could determine by discreetly asking, neither had anyone else at the project. Surprisingly comfortable, it had a pair of recliners that would look at home in a living room, two four foot square tables, each with a chair tucked neatly underneath, a desk, several large metal cabinets, and a set of file drawers. On top of the file cabinet were two bottles of Patrón tequila, one with only an inch of the top shelf liquor remaining. Stale cigarette smoke lingered in the air, and Scott saw that butts littered the linoleum floor.

The guy's a slob.

Scott opened the blinds on one of the trailer's windows, allowing enough light to work.

He started with the papers strewn over the desk, inspecting each. All of the paperwork related to the artifact shipments to Mexico City. Given enough time, Scott could have put together from them a fairly complete list of everything sent off to the institute during the past several months, but, with the short time he had to examine them, it was impossible to tell if anything he could remember having been recovered was missing from the manifests.

He remembered the gold bracelet he'd worked on less than an hour earlier.

No, there are some things that have to be in here somewhere. Things you just don't forget.

He went back through the papers a second time, looking for references to two gold bracelets and an emerald encrusted necklace that he was positive had been cleared through his work station within the past month. Unforgettable relics with intrinsic value that had made a lasting impression, he found no references to them.

Nothing, but it proves nothing. The paperwork could be unfinished, or it could be somewhere else.

A search of the desk's drawers revealed little of interest except a ring full of keys tucked inside of an envelope. It looked as though the envelope had been stuffed intentionally at the rear of the drawer full of files and writing tablets, perhaps as a crude attempt to hide it.

Scott pressed the "enter" key on a laptop that rested, open, in the center of the desk. He heard the hard drive click and whir. When he saw that the spaces between the computer's keys were filled with cigarette ashes, he wondered how it managed to work at all. He was even more surprised when a screen full of bright icons appeared in front of him without a prompt for a password.

He left the damned thing on.

Without anything like the time it would take to walk through all of the files he could access from the computer's desktop, Scott scanned the shortcuts for something promising in plain view. He paused when he found an excel spreadsheet labeled "deliveries." As his eyes ran down the first page, his heart raced.

Robert Levinson
220 Avenue of the Americas
New York, New York

Stone figure with cavities for inlays, 30 cm. Black-brown vessel with excised and incised decoration, 20 cm

Large jar with stamped decoration, 25 cm June 17 via our courier.

Peter Bergeron
2315 Aragon Place
Toronto, Ontario, Canada

Thin orange effigy vessel, 30 cm
Incensario with hourglass-shaped base and ornate lid, 45 cm.
Jewel inlays

June 20 via customer courier in Mexico City

Scott scrolled through the rest of the spreadsheet, counting 57 entries with dates as long ago as the past winter.

His hands fumbled with the top drawer of the desk where he'd remembered seeing a small cardboard box of thumb drives. He found one that looked unused and plugged it into one of the computer's USB ports. Finding no data on it, he copied the spreadsheet onto the drive.

His eyes returned to the computer's desktop, searching for more. Another shortcut caught his attention, this one labeled "pickups and handoffs, quantities."

Odd terminology for a guy selling relics on the black market.

Clicking on the icon, Scott watched as the screen filled with a two part document in Microsoft Word. The first part, labeled "pickups," consisted of a long list of entries, each containing a date and a location, many of which Scott recognized as near the Guatemalan border. Others, he knew, were places along the Pacific coast, near Acapulco. Next to each entry was a number, often "100," or "200," sometimes larger. Each entry also included a first name. Some said "Juan," others "Mario." The second part of the document, headed "handoffs," followed the same format, except that the locations were quite different. Most of them were towns well north of Cuernavaca, some close to the U.S. border. From the dates, it appeared the activity happened with regularity, at least once a week in both categories. Scott added the data to the thumb drive.

When he finished with the laptop, Scott considered whether he should leave it alive or shut it down. He'd found it on and unprotected. Perhaps that's the way Cathedra always left it.

Best to leave it just as you found it.

As he sat at the desk he noticed his hands trembling.

Thank God I don't do this for a living.

He walked over to one of the metal cabinets and tried the door handle. Locked. He remembered the envelope full of keys in the desk and retrieved it. He worked through the ring, one by one, until the door yielded.

Inside the cabinet Scott found a dozen clear, thick plastic bags containing artifacts that he remembered processing and which he'd last seen when Jorge had removed them from his trailer to deliver them to Cathedra. Each of the bags wore a detailed label and an envelope inside each contained all of the recorded data and analysis Scott had done on them. On the bottom shelf was a large cardboard box. Finding it surprisingly heavy, Scott slid it out of the cabinet and dragged it onto the floor, where it landed with a loud thud. Inside, Scott found children's books.

Now that's strange.

He picked up one of the books and had started flipping through the pages when he noticed a small piece of clear plastic protruding from a space between two of the books still in the box. Scott removed several more volumes, and, when he saw the contents underneath them, he pulled a chair away from one of the tables and sat, his shaking, sweaty hands wiping his face. He wanted to run from the trailer and forget all of this. In particular, he wanted to forget he'd ever seen the kilo-sized packages of cocaine wrapped in plastic resting in the box in front of him.

CHAPTER FORTY-ONE

Raul preferred working Saturday mornings when he needed to catch up on things. The deserted project guaranteed privacy, and, with it, came a measure of safety. He also enjoyed having the time to himself. It gave him time to think, and, this Saturday, he had a lot to think about.

He tossed his cigarette aside as he neared his office. The scene was quiet, peaceful, with no voices, no sounds of equipment working in the background. As he turned the key in the trailer's door, he noticed a slight indentation in its metal skin. Perhaps it had always been there and he just hadn't noticed.

After the door closed behind him, Raul looked around the room, taking it all in. He immediately sensed something wasn't right.

Someone's been here.

There were no obvious signs, but he could feel it, that the space had been violated. His eyes scanned the desktop clutter. Even in this lack of order, a person gets used to his personal space and can sense when things aren't where they should be.

Wasn't the laptop in the center of the desk? Now it's off to one side.

He tried to remember.

Yes, I'm sure it was.

He tapped the computer's power button expecting to wait while it booted and then prompted for the password. Startled when the screen lit up, fully engaged and ready for whatever he wanted it to do, Raul took a step backward.

I left the damn thing unprotected! Someone could have seen everything on it!

The thought of someone examining the contents of the laptop left him cold.

He retrieved a set of keys from the back of a desk drawer and hastily opened the doors to one of the metal cabinets. Everything inside seemed to be as he'd left it, the bagged artifacts, clip boards stuffed with documentation, and a large box on the bottom shelf, which Raul's nervous hands slid out of the cabinet and onto the floor. As he leaned over the box, the perspiration flowing freely down his face fell in large drops onto the children's books that covered the contents of the lower portion of the box. He pushed the books aside, and, as he'd hoped, found eight kilos of cocaine sealed in plastic cling wrap. Relieved that they appeared undisturbed, he dropped into one of the recliners. He could feel his heart pounding as he glanced around the room, his eyes coming to rest on one of the tables.

That chair by the table. Yes. It was under the table when I left, like it usually is, but now it's pulled away, facing away from the table, as though someone's been using it.

Looking past the table, he noticed that the blinds on one window were raised.

Did I leave them that way?

He lit a cigarette, and, after a few minutes, settled and began to think.

Who would be in here, and why?

He ran through the possibilities.

An unannounced visit by the policía? Perhaps. But someone would have seen them and told me. Someone from the project looking to steal something? They're all too afraid of me. Yes, of course. There's one person here who definitely isn't afraid of me.

The game had changed. With the possibility that his private affairs were no longer completely private, he considered something that he had only mused about. It involved a business he'd thought many times of getting into, always backing away because of the risk.

He considered the danger posed by the policía's expanded interest in investigating the project and what he knew to be Scott Flores' non-existent black market activities. It had been on his mind for days since Salinas forced him to let the gringo Flores back onto the project grounds. His life would be ruined if Salinas stumbled onto any of the details of either of his businesses. There was only one way to put a stop to it, and that meant eliminating the reason for Salinas' attention to Xochicalco.

Why didn't the gringo just go back home? Well, he made his own trouble. The risk is worth taking now.

He keyed a number into his cell phone and waited.

"Juan, I need to talk to you and the others. I have a special project. Something different. How soon can you have everyone together?" After listening for a few moments, he continued. "No, I don't want to wait that long. Tomorrow. It has to be tomorrow. Can you be there at two? Good. At two then. And yes, it will be worth it. Remember, we'll need everyone on this."

Chapter Forty-Two

The appearance of Raul's men didn't do justice to their efficiency or their ruthlessness. The four were a disheveled lot, all dressed in well-worn jeans and dirty tee shirts. One wore a weathered ball cap with a New York Yankees logo, another a shirt that bore the logo of Sol beer. None of them had shaved for several days. Three of them had killed a man, and one had killed a police officer.

Juan, the oldest and in charge, emptied a glass of beer and sat back in his chair.

"Something's up, I know," he said. "There's some special deal he wants."

"How do you know?" asked Mario, the youngest.

"Because he told me so, asshole," Juan replied. Juan was confident in his role as the leader of the group and the person in whom Raul confided. He enjoyed acting the part. "He told me there was a special project that he wanted done and that it had to be done perfectly."

"Special project? What the hell does that mean?" Mario asked.

"Who knows? And I don't give a shit, as long as it pays," Juan replied. "Neither should you," he added, remembering the extra bills that found their way into his pocket for keeping Raul's men in line.

Two beers later, Raul entered the small private room above a Cuernavaca bar named Los Tatuajes on Calle Abasolo. Raul commanded the room from the moment he entered. Here, he had undisputed authority. He reached into his jacket pocket and drew out the source of that authority.

"Here," he said, producing four envelopes stuffed with large denomination bills. "And I have something else for you to do, something a bit different, but important."

He tossed the envelopes onto the table in front of the four. Each envelope bore a name, Juan's a bit thicker than the others. Preoccupied with opening the envelopes and counting the bills, none of the four reacted to what he'd said.

"What would that be?" Juan finally asked.

"A kidnapping. Of a gringo."

Raul waited, unsure how the men would react. He'd never asked them to do much more than run narcotics from southern Mexico to the Zetas in the north. It was dangerous work at times, but not very complicated. To his surprise, they showed little reaction to his announcement.

Good. They aren't intimidated.

"A kidnapping? For a ransom then?" Mario asked.

"Sí," Raul said. "For a ransom. Why the hell else would we do it?" He paused, staring at Mario before continuing. "The gringo is a college professor working at the archaeological site I'm assigned to, and he has a lot of money. A lot. He'll get someone to pay to buy his freedom, and when he's frightened enough, money will be no object. We'll divide everything evenly on this one,

251

one fifths all around. I'll take the same cut you get, so it should pay very well for you."

"This will take some planning," Juan said.

Juan's matter-of-fact tone pleased Raul, who'd been worried that Juan might be reluctant to try something so bold.

"Kidnapping is complicated. We have to figure out where and when to take him in, then where to keep him. And how to pick up the payoff. That's the risky part. It's not so easy or fast," Juan added.

"I want it done as soon as possible. I want you to come up with the plan quickly, in the next few days," Raul said.

"A few days? You're asking a lot, Raul," Juan said. "And if the gringo can arrange payment we're going to let him go? That will be dangerous. Arranging a release will complicate things. And increase the risk."

Raul hesitated.

"We're not necessarily going to do that. It may be better if he just becomes a desaparecido."

Raul had considered that it might make sense for Scott to disappear permanently, and the prospect didn't alarm him. Even he was surprised at how casually he'd considered that possibility.

Juan smiled. Raul knew there was little Juan wouldn't do if the job paid enough, and that the thought of a premeditated killing likely didn't concern him.

"How much do you think this gringo's worth?" Juan asked, ready to divide by one fifth in his mind.

"It's difficult to tell just how much money he has, but I doubt if 250,000 US dollars would be out of the question on short notice. He's sure to be worth much more, but that should be an amount that can be raised quickly in cash, from what I've been told about him," Raul answered. "I'll have to give that some thought. Perhaps we can even push it to 300,000."

"We can do it, no doubt," Juan said. "But this is more complicated than our usual work. It all has to be carefully planned. We'll likely have to grab him when he's in a car going somewhere, and unless we know that he's going on a sight-seeing tour of the countryside, there's going to be the issue of other people being around when it happens. Then we need to set up a safe place to hold him while the ransom is arranged. I need at least a week minimum to handle all that. And right off, I'll need you to tell me what the man's habits are, where he lives, how and when he moves around. And I'll need to trail him a while to get his routine down."

"I'll have all of the details for getting him," Raul replied confidently.

With Juan showing such immediate command of the problems they'd face, Raul began to wonder if Juan had done this sort of thing before.

"Getting him is the easy part," Juan continued. "Once we have him, we need to know how to ask for the money, and then, how to pick it up. And we have to keep him somewhere, feed him, and guard him, in case we have to prove he's still alive. We have to figure out how to do all of that..."

"...and then dispose of him," Juan added without emotion.

"The Policía Federal will be all over this," Raul said, thinking out loud as the idea of the policía pursuing them aggressively entered his mind for the first time. In fact, he hadn't thought through many aspects of his plan, and, as they occurred to him, he found the risks didn't cause fear, as much as excitement.

Maybe I should have asked the Zetas to do this. No, those greedy bastards would have wanted to charge me for it and then keep the ransom. We can pull this off ourselves.

"Of course," Juan said, interrupting Raul's thoughts. "If this gringo is a rich big shot the federales will chase after him for a while. You've raised the stakes on us, jefe. Perhaps 10 per cent for you just for identifying him is enough? You're not going to be risking having your ass shot off like we are."

"Don't try to negotiate with me," Raul said dismissively. "Without me you don't even know what he looks like. Just figure out how to do it right, then pull it off, and you'll make plenty. If you do this well, it can open up a whole new business for us. We can work through this one and then look for other opportunities."

As Raul gave them details about what he knew of Scott's personal habits, a plan began to form. They'd take him as he moved to or from the excavation site. He'd be held in a small, lower class flat on an alleyway in Cuernavaca to avoid having to move him a long distance by car. They'd hide him right under the eyes of the policía. The ransom demand would be in the form of a letter delivered to his friend Dwyer, and the ransom would be left in a package at a hard to watch location in the town of Taxco, a village with crowded streets 40 minutes away by car. On Raul's orders, Scott would either be released, or, as seemed increasingly likely from the conversation, disposed of.

Chapter Forty-Three

By 9:00 a.m. the morning after the presidential election the crowd had already reached several thousand at the great traffic circle that surrounds the Plaza del Ángel de Independencia in the center of Mexico City. By noon the police had blocked off traffic from all of the streets that fed into the plaza as the angry crowds swelled to more than ten thousand and spilled out into the broad avenues that ran out of the plaza like the spokes of a wheel. By early afternoon the police had to deal with widespread reports of vandalism and violence against businesses, the crowd particularly hostile toward banks and financial institutions. At its outside rim, it had taken on the unsettled, edgy character of a mob, and military vehicles with armed soldiers had started to assemble there.

Rodrigo had come second in the voting, just as he'd predicted to those he confided in, but, with 38 percent of the vote, he finished far better than he'd expected, and, by his reckoning, good enough to cause a great deal of trouble. In the middle of the night, on national television, he'd delivered a passionate speech denouncing what he

255

claimed was massive voting fraud on behalf of the victorious Ricardo Ruiz, and urged his followers to show the next day that they refused to accept the result. Although many didn't need encouragement, Rodrigo's organization had provided plenty of it, as organized cadres of agitators turned out thousands of prearranged protesters in the central squares of virtually every Mexican city of any size. Strategic bribes had assured that police response in some places would be slow and restrained. The natural momentum of the moment had accomplished the rest.

"We almost made it to 40 percent," Rodrigo said, beaming at Felipe as he watched the crowd below from the penthouse window overlooking the Plaza. "And just look at it."

"I'm surprised, Rodi," Felipe replied. "I confess. I didn't think we could do it. Not the way it looked. That's four whole points higher than the best poll we had last week, and I wasn't really convinced about that one."

"With Ruiz at only 42 percent he has no mandate at all. He barely beat us. He's a minority president. A eunuch," Rodrigo said, beaming. "And if we can de-legitimize him with what's going on out there, we can destroy him. You'll see."

Felipe stood alongside Rodrigo at the floor length window, watching the scene unfold beneath them, no joy reflected in his face. Rodrigo expected to see his friend sharing the exhilaration of the moment as their plan unfolded below their window, and Felipe's pained look surprised him.

"You're still troubled by the money from the narcos, aren't you?" Rodrigo asked.

"I am," Felipe replied. "But perhaps it's more."

"What then? We've been through all of this, Felipe. What's done is done. We have the money and we've used it. You see the results."

"That's just it," Felipe answered. "Now that I see it, it's unsettling."

For the first time since Felipe had joined his cause, so many years ago, Rodrigo wondered whether he could count on him. The very idea of doubting Felipe hit him like a body blow. Felipe had been the one absolute constant in Rodrigo's years' long campaign. He'd shared his innermost fears and plans with Felipe. Felipe knew everything.

"Look down there," Rodrigo said, wrapping his arm around Felipe's shoulder. "All of those people are there because of us. They're doing what we've willed them to do. There's power down there, real power. If we can control it, the country can be ours. We can remake it into what it should be. If not for all of this, the bastards in the PRI will run the country for themselves and to hell with the barrios and the pobres and anyone who isn't one of them."

Rodrigo searched for affirmation.

"Felipe, the cause is as just as it's always been."

"Can we control it?" Felipe finally asked. "I think that's what bothers me now. I understand the game we're playing, but what if it all gets out of control? Look at them down there. It's a mob, Rodi. We'll need order and authority. Not this chaos. What makes us think we can simply tell them, 'enough' and they'll just snap to attention and do as we say?"

"It needs to be this way for a while," Rodrigo said, his voice calm. "Trust me. It's like a bull in the ring. It runs wild and makes a fuss for the benefit of the crowd, then in the end, the matador steps in and everything is as it should be. It will be the same thing here. Control won't be a problem. They'll listen to me."

Rodrigo sensed that Felipe hadn't been convinced.

"It's the same with all great movements. When the excitement dies down, everything is ordered and disciplined. People fall into line and do as they should. And when they do, we can get to work."

The two stood at the window, looking down on what they'd done together, one with supreme confidence, the other wondering what they'd set loose on their country.

CHAPTER FORTY-FOUR

There was little rest for him, even with the election over. Felipe walked through the lobby of his hotel and down a sidewalk toward no place in particular. He just needed to be away from it, and alone. Orchestrating the unrest continuing in a dozen different cities, this day Rodrigo had dispatched Felipe to Puebla to see what trouble he could encourage. Felipe finished his business by late afternoon and had a rare, precious evening with no place he had to be. He craved time to think, to clear everything from his head and reorder things. Responsibility fled for an evening.

An intellectual, Felipe usually saw things as he wished them to be. He thought way too much, but tonight he couldn't help himself. Rodrigo was right about everything, perfectly in sync with Felipe's vision for Mexico. How could Felipe doubt him?

The drug money is dirty. Filthy. I can't get it out of my head.

Felipe walked on, battling back and forth between what he knew, and what he felt, until something familiar stirred deep inside, pulling him away from the politics and the doubt. He knew what he had to do when he felt this

259

way. He searched for a cab, and, after a time long enough to annoy him, a radio taxi pulled up to the curb.

"¿A donde, Señor?" the driver asked as he got in.

"Not where, what," Felipe answered.

A puzzled look crossed the driver's face.

"Señor?"

Felipe had anticipated the reaction.

"I'm sorry. I wouldn't expect you to understand. I need a woman to be with tonight. You know where I can find one?" Felipe said as he felt his need growing.

Startled, the driver didn't respond. He glanced at the small statue of the Virgen de Guadalupe he kept on the dash of the cab, then looked down at the pouch where he kept the day's fares and tips, far less than normal. The pouch sat next to a picture of his children taped to a spot just above the radio.

"Sí Señor, I know a place I can take you. It's not far, and you might find what you want there. But I can't guarantee it."

"You've done this before?" Felipe asked.

"Sí," the driver replied.

"Then I trust you," Felipe said. "Take me."

Dropped off 20 minutes later at an intersection in a dark, nondescript neighborhood, he had no idea of the location. A single, dim street light illuminated the corner. Felipe had checked for a cell phone signal and taken down the phone numbers of both the driver and the cab company before the taxi drove off, careful to secure a connection with the world outside of the unknown barrio. The driver had advised him to stay on the corner and wait.

Only a few minutes passed before a woman turned the corner. Mid-thirties, he thought, as she approached.

She looked tired, her eyes taking him in through dark circles. She wore a skirt that only covered to the middle of her thighs, and a tee shirt that was mostly pulled out of the waistband of the mini skirt and stretched tight across her chest. Felipe noticed that she wasn't wearing a bra, the tips of her nipples visible against the tightly drawn fabric. With strands running down to the middle of her back and over her ears, her long hair looked as though it hadn't been combed since morning. Felipe found her acceptable, as he would have just about any woman who approached him this night.

"You looking for some company?" she asked.

"Maybe," he answered. "You have a place we can go?"

"Sure do."

She took his hand and led Felipe around the corner toward the entrance to a second floor flat.

***

Felipe let his head sink into a damp, sweat stained pillow as a long breath escaped. The tension that had built through the evening's exercise finally drained out of him as he savored the deep relaxation that follows robust sex.

There's nothing quite like it.

He looked at his partner, smiled, and wrapped his arm around her shoulders. She curled into him, still awake, taxed by her night's work and whatever had come before it.

"Can I stay the night?" he asked, realizing that what he'd asked was not a part of the usual transaction.

She turned toward him, surprised, and said "Of course." She kissed his cheek.

Felipe always treated his encounters with tenderness and respect, and he'd learned that the men who preceded him usually didn't. He didn't understand exactly why his manner seemed to touch something in them, but he sensed it did. As far as he'd thought on the matter, they were in their own way precious, and he saw nothing wrong with letting them know it. Rough as many were around their edges, they provided him with make believe warmth and affection, and physical pleasure, certainly. If he could make the affection real for a while by treating them well, so much the better. Everyone wins this way, he figured.

He didn't know her name, such had been his eagerness when they got to her flat.

"I'm sorry. I should have asked your name. It's just that I was..."

She cut him short with a laugh.

"It's Frida, and it's okay. Most of my clients never ask. You're different."

"Different? How?"

"Lots of things. The way you touched me, the words you used. The way you took the time to pleasure me. I don't see that much. And you didn't want to leave when you finished. Men never act like that. With you it wasn't like fucking. It was like making love, at least how I remember it."

"It's Felipe. I'll take that as a compliment, querida. How long have you been this way? Doing this, I mean?"

"Four years. I work a restaurant during the day and keep my eyes on the street corner from the window at night. It keeps our bellies full at least, but that's about all. It's a long day, usually."

"Bellies? You've got a family?" Felipe said, surprised. He'd seen no sign in the flat that she wasn't alone.

"A daughter. She's asleep in the next room."

Jesus. I can't stay.

"Then I can't be here in the morning. I have to go before she sees me."

Frida left his arms, rolled onto her side, and leaned on an elbow, watching him.

"You're sweet, but she's only four and she's used to men being here, even if she doesn't understand it. If it really bothers you, she isn't up till eight, usually, so you can just leave a little earlier."

"Where's her father? Won't he help you?" Felipe asked.

"He's dead. I was pregnant when he was killed. That's what landed me here."

"I'm so sorry, Frida."

Felipe often talked to the women he slept with about their personal stories, and frequently found in them reinforcement for his politics. Frida's tone had seemed matter of fact enough about the subject of her husband's death, so he saw no harm in asking her about it.

"You said he was killed. Some type of accident?"

"Hardly. He was a police officer. He was shot by a narco."

CHAPTER FORTY-FIVE

A long day had become more difficult after problems with the site's portable wireless Internet service interrupted Scott's research. With only sporadic access to his professional databases, he had to shift back and forth between the tedious work of recording physical characteristics of the relics, and the work he truly enjoyed, analyzing the recovered artifacts.

"That's about all of this I can take for one week, Jorge," Scott said as he cleared his work bench. Deciding to play with Jorge, he added, "Hey, it's Friday. You gonna hit the bars and try to get lucky, amigo?" Scott couldn't imagine what Jorge did on the weekends.

When Jorge didn't react, Scott said, "Didn't think so. Suit yourself. But you look like you could use some excitement. Know what I mean?"

Scott didn't expect an answer, and Jorge didn't offer one.

"Sorry if I got too personal. Just thought I'd ask. Thanks for another week of stimulating companionship."

Scott headed for the canopy and the usual Friday afternoon get together after the week's work ended. Since he'd returned from his arrest, things had been strained when Scott was among the workers. He'd said nothing to them directly, and made no attempt to explain himself or his situation. It was all best left unsaid, he'd decided. But the sidelong glances bothered him, and the very idea that the Mexicans thought he might be involved with looting their heritage upset him. Scott searched the gathering for Ana.

"Plans tonight?" he asked.

"No, Scottsito. You?" she answered.

Scott smiled. "I do now, if you'll let me."

"You gringos. So charming, and so direct. Of course. It's a beautiful night, there isn't any work to do for two days, and an evening with you sounds wonderful."

An evening with you sounds wonderful?

Ana was to drive Scott to his billet so that Arturo, his usual chauffeur, could go directly home to his family. She would return to Scott's home later, pick him up, and then Jerry, and the three were to find a place for dinner and then some live music.

As Scott and Ana made their way to her VW, Scott, without thinking, took her hand into his. He'd done it unconsciously, surprising himself. Her fingers tightened around his as their hands embraced. It felt good, her hand warm and soft. She offered no reaction, as though she expected it. It would prove to be all the invitation she would need.

The VW sped away from the excavation, through the crowded city streets with their frantic Friday afternoon traffic, toward Scott's billet on Calle 16 de Septiembre.

Scott watched Ana as she concentrated on driving. A wonderful combination of intelligence, style and beauty, Arturo was right about her.

So why do you keep your distance? You feel guilty because

you're attracted to someone? It's not as if you can control how you feel. It's been seven months. How long is enough?

"Scottsito, you've been looking at me like there's something on your mind," she said in a quiet, soft voice, her eyes still focused on the roadway.

"I'm sorry. I didn't mean to be rude."

"Don't apologize. I don't mind. Really. But there's something you want to say, isn't there? Please don't be afraid to talk to me. It's hard for me to explain this, but sometimes you seem so, how can I explain it, formal. Or polite. That can't be you. Just talk to me. Please," she continued, glancing over at him. "It bothers me that you can't open to me."

Scott took a deep breath.

Why is this hard?

"I'm sorry I sound that way. There I go again, apologizing. I can't seem to help myself."

He felt awkward, off balance.

Ana pulled the VW off of Avenida Atlacomulco into an OXXO convenience store parking lot and stopped the car in a space at the farthest edge of the lot. She turned off the ignition, and, without saying a word, turned toward Scott. Her expression was serious, but not stern, or threatening. She looked at him for a moment, and, still without speaking, leaned toward him, took his face in her hands and kissed him. The kiss turned deep and warm. She pulled away a few inches, her eyes never leaving his. He felt her warm breath against his face. She kissed him again, her lips lingering, inviting him in. Scott ran his open palms along her neck and then along the side of her head, running his fingers through her hair. It all felt wonderful.

She pulled away and looked at him, their eyes locked on each other. Her face intrigued him. She wasn't smiling, she wasn't upset or angry. There were no tears. Yet her face seemed full of intensity. He felt certain that what she had just done was not something she ever did casually.

I remember that look. Kiss me like you mean it. That's what she used to ask me to do.

He willed the intruder out of his head.

No. Not now. Please. Go.

Neither of them had spoken a word since the car pulled into the lot, until Ana said, "Maybe I shouldn't have done that. But I wanted to. Maybe it was selfish."

He'd never seen Ana less than totally confident and in command.

"It's just that I'm not sure what to make of you, Scottsito. I don't want to do the wrong thing. I don't want to go where I shouldn't. But I wanted to kiss you, and I didn't think you were ever going to do it. So I took what I wanted. Was it wrong? Tell me."

For the first time since he'd met her, she seemed to need reassurance.

"No Ana. It's alright," he said. "I've wondered how I'd feel if this happened, and I was afraid of it. I must look like a coward."

"You're not a coward. You're a man who has to deal with a past. Tell me, Scottsito. How did it feel?"

He leaned forward and kissed her, and then held her close. "Like I'm alive again," he whispered in her ear.

With his arms around Ana, Scott's sudden ability to think of Lisa without the thought of her pushing everything else aside surprised him. How different these two women were, he thought, Lisa the energetic, fun-loving caregiver, and Anarosa, the intelligent, stylish, elegant, and, until a few moments ago, reserved Latina.

"You've no idea how out of character that was for me, Scott," Ana said. "I'm not a typical modem Mexican woman. I was raised in a very traditional family and to be honest, I'm comfortable with myself that way. But if papá knew what I just did, he'd be furious."

"Then we won't tell him."

"So, my gringuito lives after all," Ana said, smiling as she cradled his face in her hands.

"Maybe I'm the old fashioned one," he said. "I think about the time I have here. It's so short."

"Sweet man," she said. "We have almost two months before you have to go. Let the time do what it will. It will tell us whatever we need to know."

He pulled her close again, kissing her forehead and holding her for a long time, content to feel her warmth and breathe her scent.

***

As they drove to Scott's billet, filled with thoughts of the evening's promise, neither of them noticed the well-travelled Honda Civic that followed them, turn for turn. When they turned onto Calle 16 de Septiembre in Acapantzingo, just past the ecological park, a car that had been parked on the side of the street abruptly pulled out in front, blocking them. Ana braked hard and the VW skidded to a sudden, awkward halt. The Civic pulled up close behind and stopped. Two men with ski masks covering their faces jumped out of the Honda, 9 mm Glock pistols in their hands. Each took a position at one of the VW's doors, pointing his weapon through a window.

"Get out. Onto the street! Now!" the masked man on the driver's side shouted into Ana's face through the open window.

Terrified, Ana opened the door and started out of the car. The masked man grabbed her by the collar and threw her to the pavement, tearing her blouse. When she struggled to her feet, he struck her on the side of her head with the pistol, knocking her to the pavement again. The masked man on the other side of the VW didn't wait for Scott to open the door. He yanked it open, grabbed Scott by the shoulder and dragged him out onto the street, pointing his pistol at Scott's head as he lay flat on his stomach on the roadway. He pulled on Scott's shirt, dragging him to his feet.

"Into the car. Now!" he shouted, pushing Scott toward the car that had blocked the street in front of them. "Now!"

Scott tumbled into the back seat, his mind racing through a jumble of confused thoughts.

What is this? What are they doing to Ana? Are they taking her too? Who the hell are these people?

The Honda backed up, made two swings across the road and sped away in the direction it had come. The car in front, with Scott in the back seat, tore down the street as soon as he was inside. Scott only had a quick glimpse of a man in the back seat before a black hood covered his head, cloaking him in darkness.

"Who are you?" Scott asked through the dark fabric. "What do you want with me?"

The silence upset him as much as the answer would have.

As the car bounced along Cuernavaca's uneven streets, Scott sank from the high of Ana's adventurous kiss, into oblivion.

Ana. My God, what's happened?

CHAPTER FORTY-SIX

The bright red trickle of blood ran out of the cut on his scalp and snaked down his forehead, along the bridge of his nose, and onto his cheeks. If he could have seen it, he would have noticed that it streaked all the way down his throat and onto his shirt, turning its wet collar a sickly salmon color.

Scott judged that a full day had passed since he'd been taken from Ana's VW in the middle of a residential Cuernavaca street. With the hood over his head he hadn't seen anything since being thrown into the kidnappers' car, but he'd had the presence to start counting after the initial shock passed. He estimated that it hadn't taken more than a half hour to drive to his present location, and, by that reckoning, he must still be somewhere in Cuernavaca. He also knew he was on the second floor of a building, because he'd been alternately dragged and pushed up a long flight of stairs before being thrown into a room and handcuffed to what he guessed was a bed.

His body ached. He'd been thrown to the pavement, pushed headfirst into the backseat of a car, cracked on the head with a pistol butt, dragged up a flight of stairs, shoved through a doorway and onto the floor, then handcuffed with his hands pulled so tightly behind his back that the slightest movement sent pain surging through his arms and shoulders. He'd had nothing to drink or eat since the day before.

Sitting on the floor in darkness, tethered to something so heavy he couldn't hope to budge it, Scott assessed his situation. He didn't have any options, but he knew that sooner or later his captors would have to interact with him. If nothing else, they'd either have to kill him or feed him. He began to think things through.

If they wanted me dead they'd have just killed me, so I'm going to live, at least for a while. Ransom. Yes. They're going to ask someone to pay to get me back. They have to keep me alive, at least until they have the money. They might need me to do something to prove I'm still alive. That makes sense. I have to get them to take this hood off and allow me to move around. I'm dead if I stay chained to whatever this thing is.

He laid his head back and let out a long sigh.

God, I hope she's alright. I hope to God they didn't hurt her.

His mind raced ahead, thinking of what would likely come.

Baño. Yes, the baño. They're going to have to let me go to the bathroom at some point. That might be a chance at least to learn something about where the hell I am. Maybe talk to them. I have to be ready for that. Focus, Flores. Focus. Focus.

Blind, hearing became his most useful sense. He remembered reading that blind peoples' other senses became more acute to compensate for the loss of sight, and so it seemed for him. A window in the room had been left open, and through it, he could hear what sounded like the voices of children playing some type of game. There seemed to be a group of them. Occasionally, he could hear loud truck engines revving, but they sounded far away, as though this building was a distance from the street. The sounds were frequent, though, so he must be near some type of major roadway, or at least one with a lot of truck traffic.

Second floor of a building somewhere near Cuernavaca, located fairly close to a road that a lot of trucks use, and with children living close by. Even if they let me phone that in, it wouldn't do any good. This is going to be hopeless.

He sank back against his anchor, exhausted, and closed his eyes. He hadn't slept since he'd been taken. He tried to concentrate on something positive. Instinctively, he knew he had to have a point of focus, something to hold on to, a reason to fight.

Ana.

He let out a deep breath and erected an image of her in the front of his consciousness. He saw her long black hair, her almond colored eyes.

His shoulders slumped and he slid as far toward the floor as the handcuffs would allow until the aching in his arms forced him to sit up. Quietly, he began to sob as tears mixed with the blood from the cut on his head washed down his face. He shook his head as fast as he could from side to side.

No. No. This is just starting. Come on, Scott.

His head cleared and he began to think again.

***

As near as Scott could tell, another night had passed before he heard the door open. He had urinated on himself during the night and needed the baño very badly.

After he heard the door open and then close, an unseen face announced, "Here's something to eat."

He felt the hood slowly lift off of his head. After two days in darkness, the piercing light tortured his eyes, forcing him to close them tight as he turned his head away, toward the floor. Unable to cover his eyes with his cuffed hands, he pressed his eyelids together and winced, his face contorted. The warm, foul smelling breath of his captor enveloped him as the man bent over and laid a plate on the floor next to him. Strangely, he welcomed the offensive odor. Squinting, Scott struggled to get a look at the man's face, and saw that he looked too young for his business.

"I need to use a baño," Scott said, "If I don't, things are going to get unpleasant in here for both of us."

The kidnapper looked puzzled, as though he hadn't thought about this. Without a word, he turned and left the room, reappearing a few minutes later to unlock the handcuffs.

"Come with me," he said, his voice stiff and formal.

Scott thought the boy tried too hard to sound confident and in control, and filed the information away.

Can he be manipulated? I'm betting I'm a whole lot smarter than he is.

Holding a pistol as he led Scott through an adjoining room that appeared to be a combination living room and kitchen, the kidnapper directed Scott into a small bath. He stayed while Scott relieved himself. Scott noticed that the baño had a small window, far too small for a person to fit through. Wide open, it served as the room's meager ventilation. When his captor led him back through the middle room Scott looked longingly at a crumpled bag from McDonalds and the remains of a hamburger lying on the table.

"Eat," the young man commanded when they reached the bedroom, motioning with the pistol toward the plate on the floor. "Do it now."

Scott ate slowly, assuming that the cuffs and hood would be replaced as soon as he finished, throwing him back into darkness and restraint. Milking this opportunity, he played with the cold beans and small pieces of fatty beef he found on the plate, fighting off the urge to consume them quickly, as the pain in his belly demanded. While he ate, Scott took the measure of his young captor. The man couldn't have been over twenty. Tall and skinny, he had a bad case of acne. With black hair cut short and trimmed, he didn't look as Scott had imagined Mexican kidnappers might. Scott studied his face.

What can I see here? Anything? Is there anything here I can use? What do I know? He's young, insecure, probably frightened, or at least overly excited about what he's doing.

"What's your name?" Scott asked, trying to sound matter-of-fact. "My name is Scott Flores. But then you probably know that already, right? You recognize that name? Flores? It's Hispanic. My grandfather was born in Cuba."

The young man stood silent.

"Oh, come on, you can at least tell me your first name. What the hell. It can be Emilio or Lorenzo or Miguel. Who the hell cares, anyway? Make one up. At least we can have a civilized conversation," Scott said, as he chewed on another forkful of beans and looked up at his captor, trying to manage a grin.

Stiff, with the pistol at his side, the man still said nothing.

"Does it surprise you that I speak Spanish so well?" Scott asked, his words distorted by a mouthful of chewy, fatty beef.

He finished with it and swallowed.

Trying to provoke a reaction with profanity, he asked, "What did they tell you about me, anyway? I'll bet they told you that I'm some rich gringo who doesn't give a fuck about Mexico. Is that what they told you? If that's what they said, it was all bullshit, Alfredo, or Roberto, or whatever the hell your name is."

Scott's empty stomach growled at him as he fought the urge to clean the plate.

"You know what I do for a living? I protect the heritage of your country. You know, el patrimonio? Ever heard that word? And I get kidnapped for doing it. You think that's fair? Do you?"

Scott surrendered to his hunger, finishing the last scraps of food before continuing.

"I spend all day studying little pieces of your history so that they aren't lost forever, and this is the thanks I get," he said as he studied his captor's face for some reaction. "You got Aztec blood in your veins, amigo, and I'll bet you don't even know what that means."

Back off. This is too strong and it's not working. He has no idea what you're talking about. Try something different.

Scott's voice softened. "You know anything about the Aztecs? I can tell you all about them if you want." Scott waited, looking at the young man intently. "Jesus, man, can't you at least say hello or anything? Come on. What will it hurt? Be a man."

"Mario," the young man said. "My name is Mario."

"Mario. Good. Now we can talk to each other like men," Scott replied. "I'd say I was happy to meet you,

275

Mario, but under the circumstances, that won't work for us, will it? Thanks for the meal and the use of the baño."

Scott looked around, thinking that Mario had brought something to drink with the food.

"Can I have some water or something to drink, Mario? I haven't had anything to drink since yesterday."

"Don't move," Mario ordered as he turned and left the room, returning a minute later with a bottle of water.

Surprised, Scott noted that Mario had left him completely unattended and free to use his arms and legs. He could have jumped Mario when he came back into the bedroom, and wondered if he should have tried. He'd learned that Mario wasn't thinking.

He might have shot me, too. This kid has to be new at this. He isn't old enough to have done much of it. That was really stupid to leave me here.

In one drink, Scott downed half of the bottle of water.

"Thank you," Scott said, trying to sound grateful.

He looked at Mario and wondered if he'd made any connection.

"Mario, can I ask you something?"

Mario looked down at him, the Glock still gripped menacingly in his right hand, and said, "Sí. So ask."

"Look, Mario. I'm not going anywhere, so why do you have to cover my head with the hood? You have to take it off to let me eat anyhow, and I have to use the baño every day a couple of times, and I can see you when you do that, so why don't you at least let me have my head free? And you can cuff me to a part of the bed up top with one hand so I don't have to sit on the floor, can't you? It's not like I'm gonna run away on you dragging a bed."

Mario looked at him, seeming to consider what Scott had said.

"Mario," Scott said, changing his tone again. He was pleading now. "I don't know what you're going to do with me, but for the love of God, if my life is going to end here, can't you at least let me see?"

***

As Scott laid his head back on the small pillow and closed his eyes, he began searching his surroundings for opportunity. He thought briefly of trying to rush Mario during a meal or a bathroom break, but dismissed it as too dangerous, particularly in his weakened condition. He'd now made a dozen trips to the baño and during half of them he'd heard children playing below the open window. Mario had tired of watching him sit on the toilet, and, during the last two visits, Mario left Scott alone in the room for several minutes. Scott did his best with his hygiene habits to make sure his visits to the toilet were an experience Mario wouldn't look forward to sharing. With Mario gone from the room for precious minutes, Scott would have access to a small portal to the outside world. He needed a way to use it.

***

It's strange. I haven't moved for days, but I'm exhausted.

Fighting off fatigue, he tried to think of something good, something to keep him alive. Wandering far, his mind led him away from the room, to somewhere in the past. He saw the faces of desaparecidos, the pictures he'd seen in the zócalo.

Jesus, I'm one of those.

He remembered what Ana had said about them, about the pain of losing loved ones.

What's she feeling? Jerry. What's Jerry thinking? Blaming himself for bringing me here?

His mind went blank, then snapped back into consciousness.

But it's so hard to think now.

His eyes filling with tears, he started to feel control slipping away. Scott shook his head, trying to ground himself.

Think this through. Grab onto something. A plan. Get a plan. You need a plan. A damn plan. Something to work on.

Scott looked at his raw left wrist, handcuffed to the bed frame. After what he guessed had been at least a week of captivity, it bled freely now from the cruel tightness of the cuff. He stared at his hand, and the cuff, unable to move his eyes off of them.

He pulled his wrist hard against the restraint, sending shards of pain into his forearm. He did it again, this time more violently, crying out as the metal chafed and burned his skin. Then he tugged a third time, then again and again, until he started to smile. Giddy now, he began to laugh, softly at first, then louder, as he yanked and jerked his hand as far as the short travel of the cuff's chain allowed.

Bleed, you son of a bitch. Bleed. Keep bleeding.

When he could stand no more, he collapsed into the pillow, rewarded with a deep, dreamless sleep.

CHAPTER FORTY-SEVEN

She looked fragile, sitting across her apartment's kitchen table from Jerry. He would need measured, patient words.

"Please tell me about it, everything that you remember. I know it's hard."

Jerry knew Ana would struggle to reconstruct the kidnapping, but, heartsick and worried beyond imagination, he needed to know everything. It was all his fault. He'd brought Scott here. He'd engineered it. Now this.

Before breaking down Ana managed to describe in detail the street maneuver the kidnappers had used. He let her calm, waiting for the rest of the story.

"Ana," he said finally. "You need to be strong."

She sobbed, resting her face in her hands. If she came apart, she would be of no help to him.

"Have you talked to your papá?" he asked, hoping that redirecting the conversation for a moment would help her deal with the highly personal question he'd come to ask. She lifted her face and looked at him, her expression a mixture of worry and grief.

"Sí, Jerito. He's talked to the Policía Federal in Mexico City, and to the embassy. He even called the president. He told me that the policía would do everything they can. They know my father is involved and he promised to keep calling them.

"The president? Lord, that should help. What are the policía doing with it?" Jerry asked.

"Inspector Salinas is wonderful. He remembers Scott from the detention and seems to care about finding him. But Jerry, they have no idea where he is or what to do! Salinas told me that. They can't do anything until we hear from the kidnappers."

She broke again.

"I'm so scared Jerry! I'm so scared! What are they doing to him?" she said, as she buried her face in her hands. "They're going to kill him."

Jerry let her cry for a while, not sure what to say. She might be right.

"Maybe this is the wrong time to ask about this," he said. "But we need to be honest with each other. Scott and I, we're a lot more than colleagues. You noticed that, didn't you?"

Ana's red eyes looked up at him.

"I knew that," she said, wiping the tears from her eyes. "Everyone can see it."

"I love Scott. He's like a son. And I'm as afraid as you are."

Jerry paused.

"It would be none of my business to ask this, except for what's happened. Forgive me. Scott is special to both of us."

Ana looked puzzled.

"Ana, I know Scott so well, better than anybody in this world does. But I need to know what he's thinking now, what he's feeling, and I need you to help me do that. I don't presume to know about the two of you, what was between you. But, if you can, tell me...please."

Embarrassed at how awkwardly he'd asked her about her relationship with Scott, Jerry waited for the information he desperately wanted.

"I'm not sure what to say," Ana replied, hesitating. "This is difficult to talk about...why do you need to know about this?"

Ana stood and walked to the kitchen's small window, settling herself.

"The night he was taken, it was the first time we kissed...but it wasn't like it sounds. It was more. Like it had been building inside for a long time and then just came out." She buried her face in her hands again, struggling to continue. "Scott was holding back, afraid of me. The night they took him it was finally different for us. This is so hard...to talk about this with someone...."

Jerry stood and moved toward her. He placed his hands on her shoulders and leaned close.

"I'm sorry to ask about this. I know how personal it is. But I had to know. We've been forced together now, you and I."

She turned and faced Jerry. "I don't know how to tell you," she said. "I just know my heart is broken and I'm so afraid Jerry. I'm so afraid."

She buried her face in his shoulder.

"Ana, he's strong and resourceful, but he's also vulnerable, and what he's dealing with now is overwhelming. I don't think he'll give up easily — no, I know he won't — but I needed to know what the two of you felt because if there was something there, something important to him, it will make him fight. And that's what he needs to do. The more reason he has not to give up, the better his chances are. I was hoping that he was more than just a friend, and that he felt that before he was taken. It may make all the difference."

"He knows that. I'm sure of it," she said.

"Good," Jerry replied, relieved. "Then you've helped him more than you know. That kiss just might have been enough."

CHAPTER FORTY-EIGHT

Dragged into the adjoining room, Scott saw another of his captors for the first time. Seated at a small table, Juan oozed machismo. Wearing a muscle shirt and a days' old beard, a cigarette dangling from a mouth that looked as though it bore a perpetual sneer, he could have been a character in a bad movie. The pistol resting in front of him on the table made him seem real enough.

Mario stood aside Juan and slightly behind him, their positioning leaving no doubt in Scott's mind that the man seated at the table was in charge and that this respite from his shackles would be different. Mario motioned for Scott to sit in a chair across from Juan.

"Who are you?" Scott asked as he sat, hoping to engage the ugly man across the table and doing his best to seem collected.

Juan ignored the question and slid a pen and two pieces of paper toward Scott, one blank, the other with a paragraph written out in long hand.

Scott took in the writing.

Addressed to Jerry, it said that Scott would be killed unless Jerry arranged to have $250,000 in US $100 bills

283

with non-consecutive serial numbers dropped off just inside the doorway of a building on a side street in the nearby town of Taxco. The delivery was to be in a backpack and made at exactly 10:00 a.m. on August 12, 10 days away. It also made clear that if any surveillance was detected, or if the package was interfered with in any way, Scott would die.

Lovely.

When he saw that Scott had finished reading, Juan gestured toward the blank paper and the pen lying beside it.

"Write what it says, in your hand," he ordered.

"It doesn't sound like me," Scott protested, trying to provoke a conversation.

"Just write it, gringo. Exactly as it says," Juan responded, his face expressionless.

"Don't you need it to sound like me, so they'll believe it?"

Juan picked up the pistol from the table and racked the slide, noisily chambering a round before resting his index finger inside the trigger guard as he pointed the gun at Scott's forehead, barely two feet away.

"Write the fucking note," Juan said, his voice cold, emotionless.

"All right. All right. But we ought to talk about this. I don't think Jerry's going to able to get $250,000 together in 10 days. That's a lot of money. And he can't get at my money. No one can do that back in the United States but me. It's all in a bank and a trust. There's no family at all. Jerry can't do it by himself."

"He'll find a way, or else you'll die," Juan said, his voice now elevated and sounding impatient. The pistol was still pointed at Scott's head.

"Have you thought about how hard it will be to get that much in US currency in Mexico, for God's sake?"

Juan angrily pounded the butt of the pistol onto the table, then stood and quickly reached forward and swiped it past Scott's face, cracking it hard against Scott's cheekbone. Scott cried out in pain, reeled back in his chair and fell to the floor, writhing, clutching the side of his bloodied face, cradling its shattered bone. Mario grabbed Scott by the shoulders and dragged him to his feet, then shoved him back into the chair. His hand trembling, Scott wrote the note exactly as Juan had wanted. A drop of blood dripped from his face onto the paper.

When Scott finished, Juan made him stand. Juan tucked the pistol into his belt and reached for Scott's left hand.

"Let me see your hand, gringo," he demanded.

When Scott held out his hand, Juan roughly pulled the simple gold band from Scott's left ring finger and pocketed it.

CHAPTER FORTY-NINE

Federico stared out of the inspector jefe's office window at the cars down on the autopista that ran next to the sector's headquarters. He and the jefe had spent the last 20 minutes on the phone with the President of the Republic, and, still stunned at having received the call, neither of them had spoken a word since it ended.

"Well," the jefe finally said, clearing his throat. "I guess that was direct enough. This is now the most important case in the sector. Maybe the whole country. The problem is, what the hell are we supposed to do, exactly, to find this Flores?"

Jimenez looked for the fourth time at the ransom note found a day earlier under the windshield wiper of Arturo Lopez' car. "Two hundred fifty thousand dollars is a lot of money to raise in so short a time. These people have no idea what they're asking. And you know what that probably means. I wonder if this Dwyer can even pull it off. Have you gotten in touch with him yet?"

"He should be here in a half hour," Federico answered. "Along with Señorita Mendes, too, I imagine. Someone from the American consulate is coming in this afternoon as well. To express their concern," he said in a sarcastic tone, "and to ask if there's anything they can do to help."

"Sure. They can tell us where the hell Flores is," Jimenez said as he tossed the ransom note onto the desk. "He could be anywhere in Mexico by now."

They'd gone over the details of Scott's abduction several times, and had officers grill everyone who lived on Calle 16 de Septiembre. No one had seen anything useful. Federico spent several hours with Anarosa Mendes, pulling out of her everything she could remember of the evening of Scott's kidnapping and the days leading up to it. He'd learned all about their personal relationship and all of the details of Scott's life in the states that Scott had shared with Ana.

There just wasn't much to work with. They knew the ransom demand would come, and now it mocked them from the jefe's desk.

"Have you sent someone to Taxco to check out the drop point yet?" Jimenez asked.

"He's on his way. He'll have the neighborhood scouted by the end of the day," Federico answered.

"Good. And Cathedra? We have someone watching him?"

"We have off and on since Flores gave us the information he took from Cathedra's office. We wanted to see where he went, and who he saw, before we brought him in. But I still think it's a long shot that he's involved in this. The computer records that Flores gave me, and the cocaine he found, make clear Cathedra's into some bad stuff, but a kidnapping in broad daylight, in downtown Cuernavaca, with Pedro Mendes' daughter roughed up? That all takes a lot of balls. To me, this guy just smells like a crooked functionario with an

287

overcooked ego and a small side deal to move drugs, not some macho narco with a personal army."

"I want him watched now twenty-four seven. Don't be so sure, Rico," Jimenez said. "If you're right and he's just a low level trafficker that would be consistent with the amateurish look of this whole thing. Maybe it's something new for him. But whoever took Flores knows he comes from money. That tells me someone who worked with him identified him as a mark. He's only been here for a couple of months, so the list of people who even know anything about him has to be pretty small, and probably limited to the project and the family that's housing him. Plus, they knew where he would be driving and when. Somebody at the excavation has to be in on this, and Cathedra's the only bad guy we have there."

"But there are over 50 people involved at the excavation in Xochicalco," Federico said. "Any of them could have set him up."

"I know," Jimenez replied. "But we have nothing else to go on at the moment, do we?"

If Raul was behind the phony criminal charges against Flores, as now seemed likely to Federico, Flores must have done something to offend or threaten him. And that made him a suspect in the kidnapping as well.

Cathedra. Maybe we can find Flores after all.

***

"Please, have a seat, Dr. Dwyer, Señorita Mendes," Federico said, motioning toward the chairs across the interview room table. "Thank you for coming so quickly."

He noticed that Ana Mendes' red, swollen eyes hadn't improved in the days that had passed since his interview with her. She still had a bandage on her forehead and another on her elbow, her face showing bruises from being thrown to the pavement.

Hell, she's had a damn tough time, hasn't she, dragged into the street by thugs and watching her boyfriend carried off?

"This morning the President of the Republic himself called our office to express his concern over Scott's abduction. You can probably imagine that this case is the most important thing we're working on now."

Federico took off his reading glasses, rubbed his face in his palms, and looked at them.

No, that's not how. It sounds phony. Tell them what you feel. He regretted mentioning the president's phone call. How do I say this? How?

"I'm so sorry about this," he said, holding up his hand as Jerry was about to speak. "Please. Let me explain before you say anything, doctor."

"I care a great deal about finding Dr. Flores," he began. "Believe me when I tell you that. It's not because we got a phone call from Mexico City. The men that took him are likely tied into the narco traffic in some way. They often run kidnappings as a side business because there's a lot of money to be made and because they're equipped to pull it off. I've lost two good men to the narcos in the last month, men with families. So this is personal for me as well. I hate these bastards."

"Inspector Salinas," Jerry said in a quiet voice. "Without you, we don't get him back."

Federico felt the responsibility press down onto him.

Without me they have nothing? Dios mío. I can't do anything.

He knew the chances of getting Scott back alive, of even finding his body, were almost non-existent. He searched for a way to tell them that they'd probably never see Scott alive again.

Not now. I can't do that to them yet.

"The ransom demand, Dr. Dwyer. It came addressed to you. Is there any way you can comply?"

"Scott's money is tied up in a trust and he has no family with any authority to get to it on short notice, but, if it's necessary, I can get the money myself from my personal funds. You'll have to arrange for me to transfer it to Mexico and then produce the currency here. You can do that?" Jerry asked.

"Of course," Federico replied. "Then we're going to want the payment to be made in Taxco exactly as they demanded. That is, if you're sure you want to do it."

"Hell yes, I'll do it," Jerry answered. "If I don't, they'll kill him."

Federico sensed the resentment in Jerry's voice.

"I'm sorry. I didn't mean to suggest you didn't care about your friend. It's just that it's a lot of money and you're not family. I don't know your exact relationship with Dr. Flores, or your personal financial circumstances. Please remember, we're all being thrown into this suddenly, even us."

Federico dreaded explaining the full details of what they faced now that the demand had come.

"We've dealt with a lot of these cases," he said "Unfortunately, the reality is that sometimes even after the ransom's paid the victim is never seen again."

Ana recoiled at Federico's words.

"I'm sorry, Señorita Mendes. But I'm trying to be honest. You see, the men who run kidnappings want to make sure that they can't be identified by the victims, so, after they get the money, sometimes they make sure that can't happen," he said, putting it as delicately as he knew how. "Of course, if they get into the habit of never releasing their victims, they run the risk of not being paid when they do this sort of thing again, because people get wise. It's a cruel business to analyze, but it would be better for Scott to have been taken by professionals who have done this many times, than to be taken by novices. The professionals know we can recognize them by their methods and at least they know how to play the game safely, from their point of view."

"Do you know whether the people who have Scott are 'professionals,' as you put it?" Jerry asked.

"No, we don't, but there are some troubling things about the ransom note." Federico replied.

Federico could see their alarm growing as he continued.

"For one thing, I don't like that the demand is only 250,000, and that you are to produce it in only 10 days," he continued. "And to insist on US currency is odd. Also, there was no method set up to communicate back and forth, to negotiate. With the sophisticated ones, the gangs that do this as a regular business, they only take wealthy people and usually ask for a lot more, so that it's worthwhile to run the risk. They might wait months before making an unrealistic demand, and then they set up some way to negotiate, often through coded messages in newspaper classified ads. There's none of that here. And picking up money is a risky business for them. Two hundred fifty thousand dollars may seem like a lot, but pros probably wouldn't take such a risk for that much. And this drop off in Taxco. That's not how the experienced gangs do it. Too easy to surveil. This has the signs of amateurs, I'm afraid."

"The ransom note says that if you interfere with the payment or they detect any surveillance Scott will be killed. What are you going to do in Taxco, exactly?" Jerry asked.

"I have a man on his way there now to check out the drop point and the neighborhood. He'll be careful, though, not to be obvious. He's very good. He'll look for a place to set up surveillance. Taxco is a very old pueblo with narrow streets and crowded buildings, so probably there'll be a place we can use safely, although it will be difficult to follow anyone there. We'll see what this spot is where they want the money dropped. Very likely, we'll be able to film the whole thing, but we might not learn much from it. We won't do anything to interfere with whoever picks the money up, but we'll try to follow him if we can."

"And if they see you doing that?" Ana asked, her face etched with worry.

"Señorita Mendes, I know how worried you are." Federico's eyes met Ana's. "I do. But we have very little to work with here. We have to take chances, or we'll have no chance at all. We'll be as careful as we can," Federico said, as he weighed the cruel calculus of risk and reward that he couldn't share with them. "But we have to get these people, if we can. It's the doctor's best chance."

"Do you have any suspects at all?" Jerry asked.

"I'm afraid there's nothing concrete yet. But I did want to ask you about someone."

"Us? Who would we know that could be involved?" Ana asked, surprised.

"As I said, we haven't anything specific. But I'm curious about whether there was ever any trouble of any sort between Scott and Raul Cathedra. Any tension, any disagreement, anything at all?"

292

"Raul resents us — both of us — for some reason," Jerry answered. "I think he might have a problem with North Americans in general. He seems to have an attitude about us. But I never saw anything happen between him and Scott."

"Señorita Mendes? Anything?"

"Yes. There was something. Several weeks ago Scott and Raul had an argument. It only lasted a moment, and I made them stop."

"An argument about what?"

"Raul insulted Scott. He said that because Scott wasn't Mexican he couldn't fully appreciate the work at the project, something crazy like that. Scott didn't handle it well and they traded words."

Ana hesitated.

"And there's something else. I'm embarrassed even to bring it up."

"Please, Señorita, I need to know anything that might help."

"Raul's been interested in me for a while now. I've never encouraged him, but he's been obvious. I told you that Scott and I have been together. It's possible Raul knows about it. It's probably nothing."

Federico began constructing the case for Raul as a suspect, starting with the inconvenient arrival of the two professors in the middle of his black market activities. That could explain his hostility. Add a touch of jealousy when Ana Mendes prefers a young, good looking foreigner to Raul, and finish it off with fear that on-going police attention at the project because of Flores' alleged, but fictitious, activity might expose evidence of both his smuggling and his drug connections. All of that could drive him do something desperate.

Federico still thought the more likely explanation lay elsewhere, but the jefe was right. At the moment, Cathedra was the only bad guy they had to work with.

CHAPTER FIFTY

Allowing him to use the baño twice each day turned out to be just enough freedom.

After using his teeth to rend a corner of the thin sheet that covered the bed, Scott tore off a piece. He'd considered using a piece of his clothing for the message, but tearing away part of his white shirt might be noticed, and his underwear had a print pattern that would obscure the writing. The scrap of sheet would do. Scott had his message board.

Fortunately, his captors had cuffed the right handed Scott Flores' left hand to the bed post. With a fingernail dipped into the blood that he urged from his raw, left wrist each time he pulled it hard against the bed frame, he managed to tap the barely legible words onto the scrap of bed sheet.

Lleve a policia Flores esta aqui secuestrado por favor.

Working over five days to produce the message, he wrote in tiny spots of blood, each of which had come slowly, in precious, single drops. The "por favor" had taken an entire pain filled afternoon. The words on the five inch square scrap of fabric looked pathetically faint and hopeless, but they were all he had.

Finding something with heft to wrap it around had proven more complicated than the unpleasant, tedious work of producing the message. The only place Scott was ever left alone with his hands free, he had surveyed the baño for the last thing he needed, and had come up with nothing usable. With the baño stripped of everything except toilet paper and a waste basket, Scott had been reduced to considering wrapping his precious piece of bed sheet around a piece of his own waste. Then Mario made a mistake, although it hardly seemed one at the time.

A small spoon usually came with Scott's lone daily meal. When Mario appeared distracted, Scott slid one under the bed after he'd finished eating, hoping that Mario wouldn't notice it missing from the plate when he retrieved it. Although under the bed, he'd placed it barely out of sight so that the attempt to conceal the spoon wouldn't appear deliberate if Mario went looking for it. Although Scott usually ate his meal seated on the bed, he'd started placing his cleaned plate and utensil on the floor, so it wouldn't seem odd if Mario discovered the spoon there. When Mario left the room without noticing the missing spoon, Scott waited three days before retrieving it, just to be sure Mario had forgotten about it.

Convinced that his captor had no idea what he'd done, Scott bent the spoon onto itself into as small a package as he could manage and wrapped the piece of bed sheet around it. He tied it off with a strip of elastic he'd torn from the waistband of his underwear, tying a secure double knot, and tucked the small package in his pants pocket.

Mario had stopped watching Scott sit on the toilet and had fallen into the habit of stepping outside for a few minutes while Scott used the baño. There was no way out, and, after all, Mario had the gun. When Scott undid his pants, Mario usually took it as his cue to leave.

Scott waited patiently through five trips before he had his chance. He often heard the sounds of the children playing between late morning and early afternoon, and he'd timed his requests to use the baño to coincide with this rough schedule. For several days after he prepared his message, he'd heard nothing through the window. He waited, impatient, realizing he'd only have one chance.

When it came, he fought to conceal his excitement, his heart racing at the sounds of the children somewhere down below the open window. As soon as Mario predictably stepped out of the baño, Scott stood and stepped toward the small, open window, his pants still around his knees. He'd have to manage an accurate throw of at least 10 feet, and hit an opening perhaps two feet square. If he missed, Mario would surely hear the result. After glancing toward the open door, he reached back and hurled the precious package as far through the window as he could. He thought he heard a dull thud, but couldn't be sure. The sound of the children became muted.

Below the second floor window of the tenement, a group of four boys, the oldest barely 12, formed a circle, kicking a soccer ball back and forth, joking and laughing. Dressed in shorts and tee shirts, they shouted at each other as they passed an old, scuffed ball. Scott's package landed among the four boys, nearest to a child named Marco, who pulled back, startled.

After the odd-looking bundle landed at his feet, Marco looked up at the second floor window and shouted, "Hey. Who's there? What are you doing?"

Hearing no answer, he picked up the strange little package that resembled one of the small bags of candy that fell out of the piñatas he'd seen at birthday parties. Marco turned it over in his hand, examining it. It felt heavy and had a tie at one end, but he couldn't tell what was inside. Something hard. His curious friends gathered around.

"Open it," one of them said. "There's something inside."

Holding off being rushed, Marco studied the package.

"Come on. Open it," his companion urged. "Maybe it's got money inside."

Marco scowled at his friend. "Right. Why would someone just throw money out the window? You're stupid."

Marco looked up at the building again. "Who lives up there, anyway? You guys know?"

"Who cares?" his friend said. "Just open it. Come on, Marco, open it up."

"Okay, okay," Marco said, as he undid the tie. A twisted, distorted spoon fell out.

"Shit, it's only a spoon. Damn," Marco's friend said, pleased that he'd managed to use two profane words in quick succession. "It's just some kind of joke," he said, looking up at the second floor window.

While his friends had lost interest and moved away, passing the soccer ball again, Marco wasn't so sure about the strange package. Even at 12, Marco realized that people don't just throw odd things like this out of windows for no reason. Wondering if there might be more to the cloth that had covered the strange, twisted utensil, he turned it over in his hand several times and bent down, moving his face to within inches.

He saw something.

"Come on, Marco," one of his friends said.

Marco ignored him, his focus on the tiny scrap of fabric. They were barely legible, nothing more than faint, pink lines really, but he thought he saw words. His eyes moved over them, once, twice, then a third time. When he realized what he was reading, his eyes opened wide with excitement, and he shouted to the others.

"¡Dios! ¡Miren! ¡Es de un desaparecido! ¡Dios! ¡Mirenlo! ¡Este es enorme! ¡Tenemos que tomarlo a la policía!"

He looked up at the window again, now terrified, then ran, far and fast, the cloth gripped in his hand.

CHAPTER FIFTY-ONE

Barely two days after Scott launched his precious message through the small bathroom window, impatience had already turned to despair.

He'd guessed it would take at least a day or two for whoever picked up the note to go to the police, and for the police to come for him. That is, if anyone found the note and took it seriously. So he waited, hoping. He hadn't heard the children playing since he'd sent the message, which he tried to convince himself was a good sign. But it was all such a very long shot, and a plan B didn't exist. Handcuffed to a bed, he could do nothing more. Writing the note had been monumentally difficult, draining what little energy remained, and he knew he couldn't do it twice. He couldn't concentrate enough, nor summon the will. When the package sailed through the window, Scott's hope rode with it.

Give it time. Maybe. Paciencia. Paciencia. Y ten esperanza.

But patience and hope competed on vastly unequal terms with despair in the small room that defined Scott's world.

The worst part was the emptiness of the days, all completely devoid of anything, with everything but breath and a little food, and precious little of that, sucked out of them. His days contained nothing — nothing to do, nothing to think about, no-one to be with. Chained, with only two, or at most, three, brief chances each day even to stand, Scott drifted in and out of mindless, un-thinking semi-consciousness as day and night ran together. At the beginning of it, when he could think clearly, he supposed the first sign he was losing control would be when he lost track of time. When he drifted into full awareness now, less and less frequently, his mind cleared just enough to appreciate, by that measure, that his cause had already been lost. He now had no idea how long he'd been here. He'd lost the detail of his very existence. It wouldn't be long before he no longer cared, and that, he knew, would be the end of him.

It's all so terribly sad. To end like this.

He fought the surrender hard, as hard as he could, for as long as he could, but he felt powerless. He tried to create images in his mind that would keep his spirit from falling. At the edge of despair, still he fought.

Ana. There wasn't time. It's so sad.

He had to find something to hold onto. Anything.

Lis. Yes, I remember now. Lis. Help me, baby. Please. Help me. I need you now.

Exhausted, he fell into sleep.

***

He saw her leaning over him, her face filled with love as she ran her soft hand over his battered cheek.

"You dear man," he heard, barely able to make out her words. Then, more clearly. "What have they done to you? My poor baby. You know I love you so much."

Scott tried to move his lips, to make some sound come out, but, like every other time she'd come to him, he had nothing. He wanted to talk to her so badly, the words screaming inside of his head. He wanted to say so many things. He wanted to tell her how his life had ended when she left him, how he wanted to be with her. He wanted to reach with his arms and hold her, but he couldn't move them. He could only listen.

She pressed her fingers against his lips and looked into his eyes.

"I know, love, I know how you feel," she said. "Can you see I'm here with you, baby? Do you believe I still care about you? You have to believe."

He felt her caressing his face and felt her warm lips on his forehead. He felt the ends of her long blonde hair brush against his face as she leaned over him. Her kiss felt as real to him as her touch the night she cleaned his wounds in the Cambridge hospital. His heart exploded. He had never wanted anything as much as he wanted to hold her, but his arms wouldn't move.

"Tranquilo," she said, placing her finger to his lips again. "Tranquilo? Remember that?"

He relaxed and looked up at her. She looked so real and so beautiful. He needed to touch her. He tried again to move his lips, but they were as useless as his arms. He could only watch, his heart aching.

"Live, Scotty," she said. "I want you to live. Live, baby."

***

"Lis..." he said in a whisper. "Lis..."

Scott didn't so much wake as drift back into consciousness. Even though the second floor room was stifling, his sweat soaked shirt, clinging to his chest, sent a chill through him as his eyes opened. Slowly, as he came back, he realized reality meant being chained to a bed in a slum on a nondescript street in Mexico, knowing he would die soon.

Maybe it's not such a bad way out. Maybe I can have her back that way. If it's soon...

No. She said it's not time.

He was coming apart now, viewing death as an escape.

It wouldn't be so bad just to let go. So easy...

As his mind drifted back toward the fog, voices penetrating the door pulled him into consciousness. They sounded far away at first, then louder and clearer. Grateful to be alert, he strained to hear anything except the voices in his head. When he heard Raul, he snapped fully awake.

Cathedra! You son of a bitch! It's you! You did this!

He pulled hard against the handcuff, pain searing through his raw wrist. Had he been free at that moment he would have charged unthinking into the room and fallen on Raul. Wild with rage, he felt alive for the first time since he'd been taken, but all he could do was twist in agony and pull against the cuff on his left arm. He fell back against the mattress and tried to calm himself. The jolt of emotion energized him, and he focused on whatever his ears could hear. If all he could do was listen, then, damn it, he'd listen as hard as he could. He'd find a way to make it matter.

"The message was delivered to Dwyer three days ago?" he heard Raul ask.

"Just as I said," Juan answered. "It may not be so easy to put the money together. I wonder if we gave him enough time, Raul. What if there's nothing at the drop in 10 days? What do we do then?"

"Don't worry about it. The money will be there. Dwyer loves him like a son. He'll find the money."

"The gringo has seen no one but Mario?" Raul asked.

"Mario and me. I had to make him write the letter to Dwyer," Juan replied.

Mario shifted in his chair. "Why doesn't he ever see the rest of you?" he asked, looking at the other two men standing in the background.

"We explained that. It's safer this way," Raul answered. "Don't worry. He won't be talking to anyone when we're finished with him. It's just a precaution. Someone had to keep him alive. I'll see that there's a little extra in it for you for taking care of our guest."

The conversation shifted as Raul discussed the details of the pick-up and delivery of cocaine shipments. The men talked about merchandise, delivery dates, and payment arrangements, as though they were running a retail store. When they'd finished, Raul sat back in his chair and lit a cigarette.

"The damned election," he said. "Maybe it was a bad investment."

"He lost badly. How much did you give him?" Juan asked.

"Hundreds of thousands of pesos. I made a damn big move for him." Raul laughed as he took a long drag on a cigarette. "But it isn't over for Oro. He explained it all to me, how this might play out, and it's exactly as he said. I may get to cash in yet. He told me he expected to lose this time but that he'd keep everyone worked up and raising hell. He said he needed money to pay for all of that. It looks like that part of it is working out."

"So you talked to him face to face, then?" Juan asked.

"Hell, yes," Raul replied, a self-satisfied look on his face. "He told me everything, the whole plan. God knows, I paid my way in with him. He felt obliged."

"Do you think he knows where all the money comes from?" Juan asked, lifting a bottle of beer and swigging almost half of it before wiping his face in his shirt sleeve.

"Oh, he knows it comes from the narcos," Raul answered, smirking. "And he told me he didn't care. He didn't care! He said he thinks the government actually ought to find a way to use the drug traffic against the norteamericanos, believe it or not. He hates them."

"No shit. So, Oro knows that drug money is going into his campaign and he doesn't fucking care?" Juan said.

"Exactamente," Raul replied.

Chapter Fifty-Two

Federico burst through the door of the jefe's office, shouting. "We found him! We goddamned found him!" Jimenez' eyes locked onto Federico.

"It's Flores?"

"Yes! Look at this!" Federico said as he fumbled with the cloth, spreading Scott's crude note out on the desk. "A boy brought it to the policía municipal. He told them it fell out of a window in an alley off of Calle Otilio Montaño in Jiutepec. They think Flores is being held in a second floor apartment there. Pedro, I think we have him!"

An incredulous Jimenez picked up the scrap of cloth. "I can't believe it. He got a message out? What the hell!"

"There's more." Federico beamed. "You were right about Cathedra. He's behind it."

"How do we know?" the inspector jefe asked.

"The tail I placed on him after Flores went through his office saw Cathedra park on a street not far from this place last week and disappear into the same alley where the note was found. We didn't know what to make of it at the time, but if Flores is in that block, Cathedra has to be involved."

"Excelente, Rico. Excelente. Have your man pick up Cathedra," the jefe ordered.

"Can't. The tail lost him a few hours ago. He won't be hard to pick up again, but it might not happen until tomorrow."

"Hell," Jimenez said.

Jimenez examined the note that Marco had taken to the first policeman he saw, a municipal officer. The note seemed authentic enough, and the circumstances left little doubt in the jefe's mind that Scott Flores had been located.

Jimenez thought for a moment before asking, "How long did the municipales have this note?"

"Day before yesterday," Federico replied. "They didn't take it seriously at first."

The smile disappeared from Jimenez' face.

"We need to move quickly," the jefe said. "We should go tonight. Depending on who in the policía municipal knows about this, we could be screwed. I don't want to lose him now, not after this break."

Jimenez had considered the harsh reality of police corruption. If the wrong person in the municipal police learned that the Policía Federal knew Scott's location, Scott's kidnappers could be tipped off, and the opportunity lost.

"This is going to be tricky, Rico. There's no time to bring the special operations group down here so we're going to have to do it ourselves or risk losing him. We have the personal attention of the president on this case, and if we just go charging in there it's going to go badly if Flores ends up being a casualty. We have to get him out alive. It has to be carefully done, and we don't have much time to figure out how. How quickly can you get someone good out there to scout the access routes?"

"He's already there," Federico answered.

As their eyes met in silence, Jimenez knew what worried Federico.

"I know, Rico. I'm worried about it, too. These people may not have enough sense to know when to quit. I don't like the feel of this. We don't want to lose anyone."

"Are you going to tell Dwyer and Señorita Mendes that we're going for Flores tonight?" Federico asked.

"It's Mendes' daughter. I have to."

***

Jerry and Ana listened to the details of how the Policía Federal had located Scott on the second floor of a tenement in the nearby town of Jiutepec, 30 minutes' drive from where he'd been abducted, and less than 40 minutes from where they sat.

The inspector jefe held nothing back.

"This is dangerous, and there's no easy or safe way to do it. The people holding Scott are vicious and when we move on them they'll feel trapped. Trapped people sometimes do crazy things. There's the possibility of gunfire in a situation like this."

Worry crossed their faces at the jefe's words.

"There's no way to avoid it," he continued. "We'll be as careful as we can, but we have the safety of our own officers to deal with as well."

"I understand, inspector jefe," Jerry said. "We understand. But I have to ask for something."

"Certainly." Jimenez replied.

"I want to be there when this happens. So does Ana."

Jimenez' reply was immediate, uncompromising.

"Out of the question. It's far too dangerous. You don't seem to understand, doctor. There may be a gun battle when we assault this building. These people are unpredictable, and certainly armed. It's no place for civilians, and if you're there, you become my responsibility. If something were to happen to you, it would be a disaster for us." He paused. "And for you," he added dryly.

"When are you going to try to get Scott out?" Ana asked.

"Tonight, in a few hours," Jimenez replied.

"So quickly?" Jerry asked, alarmed.

"We have to," Jimenez explained. "The walls have ears in some Mexican police stations. Unfortunately, the boy who retrieved the note took it to a municipal policeman, not a federale. Most of the locals are okay, but here and there some have friends we wish they didn't have. There's an opportunity to get your man right now, tonight, but if we wait, they may find out they've been compromised and move him. We can't take that chance."

"Inspector jefe," Jerry said, "you have to let us come, please. Keep us back from the danger as far as you have to, but at least let us be close after you free him. When it's done, we need to be there."

"Please, inspector."

The man is begging. If I keep them well back, there isn't any real danger.

Jimenez considered that Ana Mendes' father had the ear of the president of the republic, but that only complicated things. If he refused to allow her nearby, he might be asked why, if it could have been done safely. If he let her stay close enough to watch the operation, and something went wrong, what she reported to her father could cause problems. And she wouldn't have any real idea what she was seeing. It was a day for quick decisions.

"Alright. You can come along," he said, "but well back, and out of sight of the operation. We'll let you know when the danger has passed. If we can get him unharmed, you'll be able to see him straight away. But if not..."

Jimenez rubbed his temples, then his eyes. With no easy way to explain, he looked at them and saw two terrified people, sick over the prospect that someone they cared about might die in a few hours.

"Dr. Dwyer, Señorita Mendes. Let me explain this as plainly as I can. As soon as we can arrange it, we're going to assault that building. We're going to try our best to get him out of there safely, but men with guns may try to stop us. There might be shooting, maybe a lot of it, and someone may die. It's possible that Scott will be one of the casualties. The lives of my men are at risk as well, but we have no real choice. If we don't do this, he may be moved to where we'll never find him. Maybe he gets released when the ransom is paid, or maybe he doesn't. This may be his only chance to survive. So, you understand the decision we've made?"

After Jimenez' words registered, Jerry said, "I don't see that we have any choice. None of us do."

"Exactamente. Entonces, vayamos con Dios," Jimenez said. "And we go with Him tonight."

CHAPTER FIFTY-THREE

Raul had nowhere to park the beat up VW Beetle except in plain sight on the street that ran past the tenement block. He didn't think anyone had followed him, but his nerves had caused him to leave the flashy BMW behind in favor of the nondescript bug so common among Cuernavaca vehicles. Sure for the past several days that he'd had company on his travels through the city, he wondered what it meant. Is it the policía? The federales? And if it's them, how much do they know? Or maybe it's the Zetas? Raul hadn't felt fear like this in a long time, and he found it unnerving.

A quick turn down the narrow walk separating the tenement buildings brought him to the door and the narrow stairway leading to the apartment.

They'd better all be there.

He found his four men playing cards.

"Raul," Juan said, looking up. "You look worried."

"Someone's been following me for most of two days now, so, yes, I'm worried. I managed to lose him but it makes me nervous. It might be the Policía. We have to move Flores now to somewhere away from Cuernavaca. You can't tell what they might know."

"How the hell could they know he's here?" Juan protested. "Unless they followed you here, they can't have any idea."

"They can have any ideas they want. And the way you fools roughed up Mendes' daughter probably put this at the top of their list, so we have to assume the worst. I want Flores moved tonight."

"To where, exactly?" Juan asked.

"The cabin outside of Cuautla. That should do for a few days, anyway," Raul answered.

"I wanted to take him there in the first place," Juan said, disdain in his voice. "But you thought hiding him under their noses was such a great idea."

"Things change," Raul replied. "Do you have everything ready for the pick-up in Taxco?"

"It's all arranged," Juan explained. "My contact there will have a young boy pick up the package and run with it for about a block, then enter a building and exit by a different door on the next block. He'll toss it into the back seat of a car right outside of the door. The boy will know nothing except that he's been paid by a stranger to do this. The kid has already been picked and will be there, for sure. He'll do as he's been told. My contact will drive the car and deliver the package to me at a location well out of town. Even if the policía are watching the pick-up, they'll never be able to follow this, not in Taxco. It's too crowded. All they'll have is a picture of the boy, and when they catch him, he'll know nothing useful to them."

"Bueno. Wait until later tonight, after it's totally dark and no one's walking around outside, then move Flores to Cuautla."

"You still haven't told us what we're going to do with Flores after the money's paid," Juan said. "You've decided?"

The final decision had been surprisingly easy for Raul.

"We'll keep him until the money exchange is over. After we have the payment and it's clear the pick-up has come off clean, we'll get rid of him. At Cuautla. It will be easy enough to bury him in the hills where he'll never be found."

Raul pulled a chair up to the wooden table.

"Deal me in the next hand."

CHAPTER FIFTY-FOUR

Federico rested his fingertip on the picture of Roncito taped inside the door to his locker. He'd called Felicia to tell her he'd be on an assignment tonight, and that she shouldn't worry if he came home late. He knew she'd worry until he walked through the door, no matter. She knew what an assignment often meant. He looked out of the locker room window at the Cuernavaca sunset.

Such a beautiful evening for business like this. I should be sitting on the patio, drinking tequila, with Roncito close and Felicia looking at me with those eyes of hers, waiting for the little one to go to bed.

After he slipped his body armor over the combat fatigues and attached a web belt, he removed his M-4 carbine from the weapons locker and inspected it, turning it over, admiring the black rifle.

The norteameticanos, they make a nice piece.

Satisfied, he tapped a fully loaded banana clip of thirty 5.56 mm military grade rounds into the weapon, and racked the slide to chamber one. The loud, crisp, mechanical sound as the heavy spring closed the bolt on the cartridge reassured him. He set the safety and loaded three more magazines into his belt. He'd never needed the extras, in almost twenty years of work.

After he entered the squad room, Federico looked at each of the six grim faced men assembled there, all dressed, as he, for combat. The best in the sector, each man had faced danger before. The room fell silent when he entered.

"We have an opportunity tonight," he began.

Despite the poker faces, Federico could see the excitement in their eyes as they focused on him. He loved being here, in the front.

His men needed little encouragement. They'd been warring against the narcos for too long, and they'd lost too many friends. Federico was about to give them a precious chance to hit back. After he described the location and briefed them on the basics of the plan, he handed the closest man a set of two photographs. On top was a picture of Scott.

"The first photo is Dr. Flores. He's the objective. He must be brought back alive, if at all possible. We received a telephone call from the President about this mission," he continued, waiting for the words to register. "El Presidente de la República. He's personally asked our sector to find and rescue this Flores. You've been selected to do it." He paused. "We need to bring the doctor home alive if we can."

Federico waited as the first photograph passed around the room.

"The second man may be there tonight. His name is Raul Cathedra. Take a good look at him. If he's there, and there's shooting, try to take him alive. I don't want any of you risking your ass just to grab him, but if you can, we want him. He's the one responsible for this."

After he finished the rest of the tactical briefing, as the assault team started toward the door of the squad room, Federico held up his hand and raised his voice.

"One more thing," he said, the room falling silent again as the men turned toward him. "We want to make sure each of you comes home tonight as well."

***

Darkness had fallen on Cuernavaca as the darkened police vehicles slowly moved through narrow streets toward the barrio where the Policía Federal hoped to find and free Scott Flores. An open bed truck carried Federico, the six other officers of the assault team, and their equipment. Jimenez was in the second vehicle, a large box van, along with the commander of the local municipal police, a few municipal officers, and a medical team. Trailing a bit farther behind were two ambulances and another police vehicle with six more federal officers. Even farther behind, an SUV transported Ana Mendes and Jerry Dwyer, in the charge of an officer with orders to keep them far enough back that they couldn't see anything that happened.

As they rode toward the barrio, a knot in Federico's stomach tightened. There was no mistaking the excitement. His hand ran down the side of his carbine, caressing the cool, smooth metal of the black rifle, then to the pistol that hung rakishly from a combat holster strapped halfway down his thigh. The weapons felt like part of him, ready to do whatever he wanted. He felt strong.

Federico had been on dozens of raids and had made a hundred dangerous arrests. He'd drawn a weapon in the line of duty more often than he could remember, and had fired it on a dozen of those occasions. Although he'd never shot anyone, he hadn't the slightest doubt he would do it if he had to. He wondered if tonight would be different. Federico never felt fear at times like this, only anticipation and excitement.

Should I be afraid?

As the caravan rode on, Federico emptied his head of everything, turning his mind into a blank, onto which he could project the task ahead and focus on it. A simple technique, he'd been using it since his school days, when, before soccer games, he'd isolate himself to prepare.

The two lead vehicles stopped 100 yards from the tenement and quickly unloaded. The seven members of the assault team formed in a loose circle, tightening the chin straps on their ballistic helmets, and checking their weapons as Jimenez stepped in among them.

"I want you to be careful with yourselves," the jefe said. "We need to get this man out in one piece, but I don't want it to be at the price of any of you. Understood?"

He looked each in the eyes. Several of them nodded, the rest just stood quietly. One replied, "Sí, comandante. We'll get him."

Jimenez smiled.

"Good then."

He took care to look again at each for a moment before saying, "Good luck and God be with you."

He turned to Federico.

"Rico. Be careful. No heroics. Cut them down if you have to. Just get Flores out of there."

Federico nodded and turned toward the alleyway leading to the tenement. He noticed several children

317

standing back, away from the police vehicles, and an older woman with her arms resting on the shoulders of one of the niños. The operation had been rushed, with little consideration given to the presence of the uninvolved people who lived all around the place. Federico motioned for one of the reserve officers and instructed him to keep the onlookers from moving any closer.

The tenement could not have been a worse place for a forced entry. Rico's team would have to approach for 50 yards down a narrow pedestrian alleyway crowded between two buildings barely 10 feet apart. The apartment was on the second floor of a two story building with only a single, narrow flight of stairs for access. There were several windows, but none were practical as an entry point. The only way in was up the stairs and straight through the front door. There would be nothing subtle about it.

Federico had developed a simple, but dangerous, assault plan. The six man team would move up the stairs as a unit behind two men carrying a four foot long rod-shaped metal battering ram. The door of the apartment could probably be kicked in easily, but there hadn't been any way to confirm that, so Federico thought it best to make sure the door could be easily and immediately breached. Federico would follow the team, at the end of the line. Quiet was important, but difficult, with such a large force in such a small space. Once the ram broke through the door, a flash bang grenade would be thrown into the room by the third man in line and the entire assault team would rush the room, ordering anyone inside to raise his hands, and firing at anyone who showed a weapon. Once inside, two members of the team were to clear the room, two would clear any adjoining rooms, and two were tasked only with locating and securing Flores.

The seven helmeted officers moved in single file down the narrow walk leading to the entrance to the tenement's staircase. Federico directed them, in the proper order, through the doorway.

"Go slowly, as quietly as you can," he reminded each of them in a whisper as they entered, Federico last in line.

Before ducking into the stairwell, Federico looked up and took a deep breath. The full moon and the stars spread across the Mexican night sky like a tapestry. He made the sign of the cross, brought his fingers to his lips, and stepped inside.

Barely halfway up the stairs, things began to go wrong.

The old wooden stairs groaned under the weight of the seven heavily armed men, the sound echoing off of the walls of the narrow passageway, forcing them to choose between hurrying and creating more sound, or slowing and exposing themselves longer to discovery.

Goddamned noise. One man at the top of the stairs with an automatic weapon could kill us all in five seconds.

But Federico's orders had been to move as slowly as possible, and his disciplined officers did exactly as they'd been told. The march up the stairs seemed to take forever, Federico expecting at any moment that someone would appear to investigate the sound.

Five steps from the landing at the top, in the darkness, the first officer caught the toe of his boot against the riser and pitched forward. As his hands shot out reflexively to break his fall, he let go of the front grip on the steel rod battering ram, the sudden movement wrenching its rear grip from the grasp of his partner following close behind.

A loud thud reverberated off the walls of the staircase as the ram fell to the floor, then slid backward down the steep stairs, slamming into the ankle of the third officer in line who cried out as he toppled over in pain. The ram slid all the way to the bottom, banging off of each step and scattering the remaining officers. It gathered speed until it landed at the bottom with a crash that echoed through the confined space of the passage. Federico knew that in a few seconds someone in the apartment would come looking.

"Safeties off and up the stairs!" he shouted. "¡Ahora mismo! ¡Rapidamente! First man put a shoulder into the door and toss the grenade! ¡Adelante! ¡Adelante!"

With his men scattered all over the staircase and disoriented, four of them not even on their feet, Federico had little time to process the confusion in the dark stairway. Reflexively, he shot up the stairs past the downed officers and made it halfway to the top before he saw the door at the landing open and a tall man emerge with a pistol in his hand.

"'Policía Federal! Manos al aire!" he shouted.

In an instant he realized he should have opened fire the moment the man appeared.

The man pointed his pistol down the center of the staircase and fired into the confused tangle of officers at his feet. The blinding muzzle flashes of the pistol lit up the passageway as the sound of the firing thundered all around Federico, pounding his ears with echoing explosions. He felt a sharp, searing pain in his left arm as a pistol round sliced through soft tissue. Ignoring the pain and raising his carbine, he framed the man in his tactical sight and gently squeezed. The three shot burst of high velocity military rifle rounds caught the man full in the chest, shredding pieces of bone and tissue as it hurled him back into the room.

Federico charged forward, ignoring the wound in his arm and stepping over two downed officers as he reached for a flash bang grenade. He let the carbine fall from his hands and hang in its sling against his chest as he grasped the grenade and reached for the pin. It was his second mistake. Another armed man appeared, silhouetted in the doorway. Federico saw him turn back toward the room behind him. He heard the man shout something unintelligible. Dropping the grenade, Federico shouldered the carbine just as the second man turned back toward the stairway and started firing a pistol into the trapped officers. Federico squeezed the trigger three times, each pull automatically sending three rounds at the doorway. The rifle's muzzle flashes blinded him in the dark of the stairwell, the sound deafening. The man in the doorway spun around, then disappeared, stumbling back into the light of the room at the top of the stairs.

Federico saw one of the officers down just ahead of him struggle to his feet. He staggered forward and charged up the last few steps. He turned and looked down at the rest of the assault team, sprawled all over the stairs, several starting to get to their feet.

"If any of you can move, rush the room behind us. Now!" he shouted.

Federico struggled to reach the landing at the top of the stairs and charged into the room with his companion close behind.

The scene was chaos. Federico heard confused shouting and, adjusting to the light, quickly picked up three targets. At a quick glance, none of them looked like Flores. The three men stood well apart from one another, each holding a handgun. Federico saw them firing rounds wildly in the direction of the doorway.

"Fuego!" he shouted at the officer who'd followed him into the room. "At all of them!" he yelled as he raised his carbine.

He dropped the man closest to him with one burst that exploded the man's head in a shower of crimson. He saw the man to his left fall as the second officer's carbine fired. As he turned to face the final threat, Federico felt a blow to his chest as a pistol round thudded into the front of his body armor. He reeled and fell to the floor, landing on his back, the carbine falling from his hands.

The last thing he saw was the muzzle flash from the pistol pointing squarely at his face.

CHAPTER FIFTY-FIVE

Just before sunset, Scott made his final trip of the day to the baño. By now he had no idea how long it had been since he'd tossed his message through the window. He'd lost all track of time, caring less each day whether he lived, time melting into a meaningless jumble of memories and blank pages. As he unraveled, he was just aware enough to know it was happening. In a little while, even that would be gone, and nothing would matter. It seemed so easy to give up now.

As he staggered through the kitchen to the baño, and back, Scott saw three men sitting at the small table. He recognized, Juan, the man who'd shattered his cheek. They ignored him, as Mario shoved him through the room, and then back.

Three. Ten. Who cares? I'm going to die here.

He collapsed onto the bed, wandering back and forth between profound sadness and a foggy, semi-consciousness where he felt nothing, and nothing mattered. A familiar voice from the other room tugged him back to reality.

Cathedra? You son of a bitch. You're back. Where have I been? This is real.

He yanked his wrist hard against the bed frame, sending searing pain shooting through his wrist and forearm. He'd learned it was the only way to force awareness on himself, if even for a moment. He rolled his head to face the door, and stared, unable to do more.

Scott heard nothing but muffled voices, but Raul's was unmistakable. He tried to concentrate on what little he could make out, but after a few minutes, he found focusing impossible. He surrendered and let time drift past, his thoughts becoming a strange mix of images. He saw Lisa reaching to caress him, then Ana hovering over him. He saw Raul's face, laughing. He stared at the ceiling as if it were a blank piece of paper, then...

Gunfire!

Scott bolted upright, eyes wide open. His raw left wrist strained against the cuff as the sudden movement launched pain through his broken cheekbone. But the sound of the gunshots brought him to life as his mind suddenly focused on the sounds from the adjoining room.

They're coming to get me! Yes! They're coming!

All he could do was pull at the cuff and listen.

Please. Let it be this.

His head fell back hard onto the thin, filthy pillow, the impact sending more pain coursing through his broken face.

Am I crazy? No! I heard it!

He stared at the door.

Then more gunfire, much more, followed by an explosion, and then still more gunfire.

My God, it's a war! Please, God, let them win!

His eyes darted all around the room. The simple bed, the walls, the window, the door, the stark empty place, all suddenly came into sharp relief, no longer a world of fog and blur.

It's coming down. It really is. Kill them! Kill them all!

Helpless and chained, he waited. Energy that came from some reservoir he didn't know he had, deep inside, surged through him as he pulled his shackled wrist against the bed frame, again and again, rubbing the raw, bloodied skin against the hard metal cuff. He wanted to do something.

Then quiet, except for his pounding heart.

In a few moments he heard voices in the other room, too indistinct to make out. He let out a long, deep, breath. His hands trembling, he stared at the door, and waited.

If they win, even for a little while, I'm done. They'll just kill me right here and run.

He heard heavy footsteps, then men shouting. Then silence again for a moment before the door exploded inward, falling forward with a crash flat against the floor, its hinges still attached to the wall. Scott recoiled at the shock, turning his face away. A second later the concussion of a flash bang grenade simultaneously blinded him and pounded him with a shock wave. He screamed and covered his eyes with his free hand, pain piercing his ears and the sound of the grenade ringing in his head.

With the next words he heard, his heart soared.

"¡Policía Federal! ¡Manos al aire!"

Scott collapsed against the filthy mattress with his eyes tightly closed. When he opened them, he laughed and cried as he looked up into the helmeted face of a federal officer leaning over him. He lifted his head off of the pillow a few inches and reached for the officer with his free hand, trying to wrap his arm around the officer but lacking the strength to pull himself up off of the bed. He fell back onto the pillow. The man took his hand and held it tight, his grip comforting.

Thank God.

He wanted to talk but couldn't make any words come out.

"Are you Scott Flores?" the officer asked, kneeling by the side of the bed, still grasping Scott's hand.

Scott couldn't speak, only nod.

"Easy, doctor. Everything's alright now. Easy."

The officer motioned to another, who took a small cutting tool from his web belt and clipped the chain links of the handcuff that held Scott's left wrist to the metal bed frame. The two officers helped Scott sit up. One offered him a priceless gift of a drink of water from a small canteen.

Scott tried to stand, but collapsed back onto the bed.

"Don't try to move, Dr. Flores," one of the officers said, wrapping his arm around Scott. "Just stay right here a while. We have medical people down below who will look after you."

Scott looked at the officer, still unable to speak. He wanted to say so much.

"I know," the officer said. "Everything's alright now."

Scott sat on the side of the bed, the officer's arm holding him upright. When Scott finally found the words, he asked if any of the policemen had been injured in the shooting.

"Yes, some were wounded badly." The officer's face revealed the stress of the night as he answered. "The man who led the assault was killed. There are still men down back there on the stairs."

"My God," Scott said, barely loud enough to hear himself

"The men who were holding me?" he asked, his voice weak.

"There were five here. Four are dead, and the fifth will wish he was," the officer said, this time without emotion.

"The one who survived, do you know who?" Scott asked.

"I believe it's the jefe. Cathedra, I think, is his name," the officer replied. "They should have him down in the street in one of the vans."

They kept Scott in the bedroom for what seemed like a long time. He heard sirens in the distance. As he waited, he heard the crackling of electronic voices from radio communications, and the sound of heavy boots treading on the wooden floor in the adjoining room, then what sounded like something being dragged. Even though the door had been knocked off of its hinges, from his position on the bed he could see nothing of the inside of the next room. Finally, another officer entered and asked if Scott felt he could manage going down the stairs.

I want out of here.

The scene in the kitchen staggered him. An overturned table and chairs rested in the center of the room, one of the chairs shattered from gunfire. Walls riddled with bullet holes framed the room, and chunks of splintered wood and spent metal shell casings rested in thick pools of blood that covered the floor. Playing cards were scattered all over, stuck to the blood. The air, heavy with the smell of cordite from the gun battle, mixed with the sickening odor of fresh blood. He noticed what he took to be pieces of human tissue lying in the congealed, bloody mess at his feet. Scott had never seen anything like it.

God. This is awful.

The stairs were worse.

With no handrail, Scott's escort wrapped an arm around his back and under his armpit as they started down. The blood on the stairs made it hard to keep from slipping and tumbling to the bottom, and an overpowering, sickly sweet odor filled the confined space. The stairs were the only way in, and, as Scott realized that the blood lying at his feet and splattered on the wall belonged to the men who had saved him, his heart broke. By the time he reached the bottom, tears flowed over his cheeks and he was sobbing uncontrollably.

My God. I'm so sorry. I'm so sorry.

Stepping through the doorway at the bottom of the stairs, he let the fresh night air fill him as he looked up at the stars he hadn't seen in so long. He was alive, but the price of his freedom had been immense.

A crowd from the barrio had gathered after the gun battle but stayed a respectful distance from the police vehicles that lined the nearby street, their lights now flashing. After the assault began, additional units had been called, and eight vehicles now lined the nearest roadway. In one of several large box vans, as a medical technician tended to Scott, Pedro Jimenez introduced himself.

"Dr. Flores, we're going to see that you get cared for here, then you're going to the hospital. Is there anything we can do for you right now?"

Scott's mind burned with the thought of Raul close by. "I want to see Cathedra. He survived, didn't he?"

"You know this?" the inspector jefe asked, surprised.

"Your man told me up in the apartment."

"Yes, he survived, but I'm afraid that's not a very good idea, doctor. He's being questioned before we move him to headquarters."

"I need to see him."

"And to what purpose?" Jimenez replied. "Doctor, with the shape you're in, you really shouldn't do anything but look after yourself. Seeing Cathedra will just prolong an evening you should want to forget."

"Forget?" Scott said, his voice plaintive. "Forget? No, inspector, I don't want to forget anything about this. You asked me if you could do anything for me and I've answered you. Please, let me see Cathedra."

The expression on Jimenez' face told Scott that his request would be a tough sell. Scott lowered his gaze, let out a deep breath, and wiped his eyes and face with his filthy hands. He looked back at Jimenez.

"He's responsible for all of this. For what happened to your men back there, for everything."

Scott held his bloody left wrist, the lock of the cuff still dangling from his arm. The side of his face where Juan had smashed it with the pistol had turned black, and the swelling made his eye almost invisible.

"Please."

Jimenez looked at Scott with a victim's heart. He'd suffered his own loss tonight.

"Please, inspector."

"And if I take you to him, what will you say?"

"I want to see him in chains, the way I was in that room up there. For me, it's justice to see it."

***

A shot of adrenalin rushed through Scott when he saw Raul sitting on the bench inside the box van, handcuffed. The policía had not been gentle with Raul. Cuts and bruises covered his face, and an eye was starting to swell. But Raul's expression spoke defiance, as though he didn't believe the world as he knew it had ended.

Machismo, the asshole. Why does he look that way?

Scott stared at him, channeling hatred as their eyes met.

"How does it feel, you son of a bitch?" Scott spat the words at him.

Raul looked at him with a face full of contempt. "Arrogant gringo," he said, turning away.

"Don't look away from me, you murdering thug," Scott shot back. "You should have been killed with the rest of your fucking gangsters. You'll rot in a stinking jail for the rest of your life."

Jimenez took a step toward Scott.

As Raul turned to face Scott, a smile that sickened Scott spread across Raul's face.

"You norteamericanos. You think you know everything. You know nothing about how Mexico really works. The government will pay dearly for what I know, gringo. About important people. Political people. In a little while, the government will forget all about tonight and it will make a deal with me to get at its enemies. Just follow the story, gringo." He laughed. "You'll see."

At Raul's words, one of the federales moved toward him, and only stopped when Jimenez held up his hand.

What if he's right?

Scott recoiled at the possibility that Raul could find a way to evade justice, refusing to accept what his gut told him might very well be true.

No, that can't be. There can't be any deal. Not after this.

Scott was so close he only had to take one short step forward before he smashed his clenched fist into Raul's face.

CHAPTER FIFTY-SIX

As Jimenez sat next to Scott on the rear bumper of the police van, he reached into his shirt pocket, pulled out a pack of cigarettes, and offered one to Scott.

"No thanks," Scott said in a quiet voice.

"Bad habit," the jefe admitted. "Truth is, I don't smoke much. Hardly at all, really. Just times like this. I've probably had this pack for a couple of months."

"Maybe a little when I drink, too," he added as he lit the cigarette.

"I'm sorry about losing it," Scott said. "You were right. I shouldn't have gone there. Back in the states I'd probably be in a lot of trouble for that, and you probably would, too, for letting me at him."

"Likely so, doctor," Jimenez said, looking up at the clear night sky. "But this is Mexico. We're less polite with people like him. My men all wanted to do exactly what you did, so you're a hero at the moment."

Jimenez held the cigarette and looked at it for a few seconds, then tossed it to the ground. He'd barely smoked an inch of it.

"Perhaps we're the more sensible society. You know, these people would almost certainly have killed you," the jefe added in a matter-of-fact tone.

Killed me?

"These were amateurs," the jefe said.

"Amateurs?"

"Yes. The narco gangs that usually get involved in kidnappings as a sideline business understand that if they don't release the victims, eventually the business goes bad. But amateurs, they worry mostly about getting caught. And the easiest thing to do after they get their money is just to make sure they can't be identified. So they just dump the body somewhere. We're sure that these men were new at this."

As he looked at Jimenez, Scott noticed now the dim street lights reflecting off of the moisture glistening on the officer's cheeks. Scott hadn't seen that Jimenez was crying.

"You all right, inspector?" he asked.

"No," Jimenez answered, his eyes focused on the street at his feet. "No, I'm not all right."

"Inspector..." Scott tried to find the words. "I can't think what to say. Your men..."

"Dr. Flores," Jimenez said as they sat together, struggling with their emotions. "I understand. None of this was your fault. You've been through your own hell. What happened tonight was something that's always possible for us. But we lost the third man in a month. All of them with families. I'm sorry you had to see it, how it all was."

The jefe's words hit him like a punch in the gut.

My God. A family.

"The man you lost tonight. Tell me his name. I need to know."

The inspector took a deep breath.

"We lost Federico Salinas. The man who arrested you. He has a wife and a young son. And he was a son to me. Rico was my friend," the jefe said as he broke down, his voice now trembling and tears running down his face. "My right arm. Mexico can't afford to lose men like Rico...I can't...." His voice trailed off as he leaned forward and covered his face with his hands. No longer the tough police commander, Jimenez looked up at Scott, and said, "I have to tell Felicia. I don't know how... my God..."

As the jefe wept Scott sat with him in the dark, a privileged witness to the comandante's grief. He wanted to say something comforting, anything.

Damn you, Mr. Harvard Ph.D. Say something.

"I'm so sorry, inspector."

It felt pathetic. Not enough. Not close.

There's no way to deal with this. No words. No way.

They sat in silence for a long time until the jefe's radio crackled, its static tone cutting through the warm, night air.

"Yes, let them come now," the jefe said quietly into the mike attached to his shoulder. Jimenez forced a weak smile, the only one he'd have that night. "You have friends here who've been very worried about you, doctor."

At the sight of them, Scott's heart pounded against his chest. He stood and watched as they approached the van, then he turned toward Jimenez.

"Thank you," he said.

The jefe looked up at him and only nodded.

As Scott turned toward them, Ana and Jerry stopped short, silent, their eyes fixed on his.

They're afraid of me.

Scott's body shook as he took a halting step toward Ana. Arms, legs, all of it weak, he feared he would fall. His arms quivered as she stepped into them and pressed her head against his chest. He struggled to embrace her but had no strength to hold her.

"Ana," he said. "I..."

"No, no, Scottsito mío... no."

Her lips stopped his from saying more.

CHAPTER FIFTY-SEVEN

The prospect of meeting Felicia Salinas filled Scott with apprehension. He'd hidden in the background at Federico's funeral, unsure how she'd react to him, or what he'd say when she did. Worried that he'd be viewed by some as the cause of Federico's death, Scott had melted into the overflow of officers, friends and family, and had paid his respects from a distance.

Yet Scott knew he had to be alone with her before he left Mexico, to tell her...what, exactly, he wasn't sure. He only knew he had to do it. He owed it.

What the hell do you say? 'I'm so sorry?' What good does that do? I hated it when they told me that. I'd have rather they'd left me alone and said nothing.

With his return to New York only a few days away, Scott had arranged through the inspector jefe to meet her at the Salinas home. According to the jefe, Felicia was holding up as well as could be expected, and he surprised Scott when he said she welcomed a chance to talk.

Nervous and unsure, Scott hesitated before ringing the doorbell. He had little confidence in his ability to manage a meeting with the widow of a man who had died saving his life. His emotions were an uncontrollable jumble of gratitude and remorse, and not likely to lead to the impression he desperately wanted to make.

What if I make it worse for her?

Felicia's appearance when she opened the door surprised Scott. He saw no outward sign of the stress that he knew sudden loss and profound grief impose — no red, tear stained eyes, not a face that betrayed days without restful sleep — none of what he'd shown when it had been his turn. Scott took her reserve and composure as extraordinary grace.

"You must be Dr. Flores. I was expecting you. Please. Come in, doctor," she said in a soft voice.

"It's Scott, Señora Salinas," he said, taking her hand into both of his.

"And it's Felicia, please," she replied, managing the faintest trace of a polite smile. "Can I get you anything? A soft drink or some cold water?"

"Thank you, no."

"Come and sit, and we can talk for a while," she offered.

They sat across from each other in the living room in awkward silence for a moment, before she said, "I'm glad you came. I think it's good that we talk. Maybe for both of us."

After another moment of quiet, she added, "You probably feel responsible somehow for what happened. Please don't. There's enough pain already."

At her gesture, Scott felt his control beginning to slip away barely a minute into their conversation.

He stammered, "I know in my head that I shouldn't feel that way, but in my heart....I just... if I hadn't come here, maybe if I'd handled things differently... if I tried to fight when he let my hands loose...."

"I wanted to talk with you more for my sake than yours," she said before he could finish. "Forget all of that, please. Tell me about your life back home, and about what brought you here. I'd like to know about that."

Scott told her everything, and, when he'd finished, she asked, "You came here to try to forget, then. Has it helped?"

"Yes, but not the way I expected or wanted."

"I'm sure," she said. "Maybe I asked the question in the wrong way. Did coming here matter? For your heart, I mean?"

"She'll always be a part of my life. You can't ever change that. And I don't want to. But things happened here that took me so far from the past in such a small time...so, yes, it helped."

"Felicia," Scott said, his eyes filling with tears. "I thought for a long time about what to say to you. I know this means nothing. Oh damn, it sounds like what everyone kept saying to me. But I'm so sorry. It's so little, but I don't know what else to say to you. You go to these wonderful schools and collect fancy degrees and think you know so much, then something like this happens and you can't even say anything that helps. I just..."

"We're hermanos now, you and me," she interrupted. "Like brother and sister. You know what my burden is, and now I know yours. You don't have to explain how you feel. Not to me. I know that in your way you mourn my Rico, too. I knew that the moment you asked to come here."

As the conversation drew them closer to one another, Scott now began to see in her the pain he'd expected to see the moment she opened the door. She'd been holding it back, he realized. He wanted to hold her and tell her everything would be alright.

"I wanted to know about you for a selfish reason," she continued, in a voice that now betrayed the emotion Scott knew had to be tearing her world apart. "My Rico was a good man. No, he was better than that."

She turned her head aside for a moment and looked away from Scott, toward the window.

"He was the best man I ever knew. He believed that his work made a difference for people and when that meant risking his life to save yours, he freely took the risk, just as he'd done his whole life. I needed to know the person he saved. To see how it mattered."

Until that moment, Scott hadn't fully appreciated the cruel transaction that he'd been part of.

She needs to know that I'm worth it. That's why she wanted to talk to me. I have the burden of his life on me. She's telling me to use this, that I owe him.

"Maybe this will help," he said. "I came here barely alive. Nothing mattered much. But when they took me I wanted to live and I fought for the chance until the moment your husband came for me. But without him it all meant nothing. My life now is on him. On your Rico. Whatever I do is on his life. If knowing that I understand that helps..."

"It does," she said. "I don't know you, and I can't, in only a few moments that we have. But my Rico was so good...he was worth so much...."

Scott remembered how he'd reacted to Lisa's death, crawling into himself and shutting off everything but his own self-pity and sense of loss, refusing to move past it. He felt ashamed. Felicia had been noble and uplifting, when he'd surrendered. With the shame came a resolve such as he'd never felt. He didn't know yet what it meant, or where it would take him. He only knew his life would never be the same.

Scott reached into his pocket and pulled out the figure of the Aztec child that the jefe had returned. He handed it to Felicia.

"This is real. My wife gave it to me when she told me she was pregnant. It was her way of celebrating life. Please, take it."

"Real?" she asked.

"It's authentic. It's Aztec, not a reproduction."

"I can't accept this," she said.

"You must. Please. I don't need it now. I want you to have it. When I came here I didn't know what to say to you, what would be the right thing. But now I think passing this to you...and to your son...perhaps it will help us both.

Chapter Fifty-Eight

"Come in, doctor," the jefe said as he took Scott's hand. I was hoping I'd have a chance to see you again before you left for New York. To say goodbye properly. And I was wondering how your meeting with Felicia went. I imagine it was difficult for you."

"It helped. For both of us, I think."

"How is the cheek feeling?" the jefe asked. "It still hurts?"

The swollen side of Scott's face where Juan had smashed the butt of his pistol against it wore a dark, purplish color. His rebuilt cheek throbbed with pain, but he'd refused to take the pills the doctors had given him for it.

"Yes, but it's getting easier to deal with. Jefe, thank you again for what you and your men did. For the chance I have."

"It was our job. Thugs like those are an unfortunate part of our lives here these days. But we fight them and, God willing, we defeat them. And Mexico will survive them."

"I need you to do something else for me," Scott said.

"If I can," the jefe answered.

"You told me that your sector had lost two men before Federico died. So there were three then, all with families?"

"That's so."

"I need you to get me information on the other two — names, addresses, and I'll need the names of the children as well. And contact information for the widows."

"May I ask why?" the jefe asked.

"So some good can come of this. Cathedra didn't kidnap a poor man. He knew what he was doing when he made me a mark. I'm going to make sure that those families are taken care of and that the children have what they need."

"Doctor, so generous. I don't know what to say. The government helps in these situations, but it isn't enough. I can surely get you the information you need."

"And there's something else," Scott said. "Would it be all right if I called you once in a while? To see how Felicia Salinas is getting on. It would mean a lot to me. But please don't say anything to her about this."

"Of course. You can ask anytime and I'll leave it between us. I'll be checking on her."

"Thank you, jefe. There's so little I can do now. It all seems so pathetically small."

"There's nothing any of us can do, doctor, except continue with our lives and live them as best we know how. This sort of thing tests us all. It tests what kind of people we are. We, at least, are used to it — or as used to it as one can become. But you?"

Scott looked at Jimenez for a long moment.

"You're right about that, jefe. It tests us. It surely does."

CHAPTER FIFTY-NINE

As the waiter cleared the lunch dishes at La Universal, Scott pointed toward the front page of the day's copy of La Reforma, lying on the table. The headline shouted "Oro Aide Claims Candidate Took Drug Money; Government Vows Investigation."

"Your papá must be happy about this," Scott said. "He's no fan of Senor Oro."

Ana nodded. "No, he's not. He'll be pleased. He was terribly upset at all of the rioting and disturbance after the election, but things have settled now. Papá told me that there were rumors about narco money in Oro's campaign for a long time, but no one could prove anything. Until now, anyhow. This Felipe Bencivenga the paper talks about was close to Oro. His talking to the government could be the end of Oro."

"If he had anything to do with the narco traffic, I hope Oro ends up in prison," Scott said. "The inspector jefe told me yesterday that during the interrogation Cathedra said he'd had financial dealings with Oro that were drug related. Jimenez thinks Cathedra's going to try to make a deal to save his ass by turning on Oro, just like this Felipe is doing. The night I was freed Cathedra said something to me about having information the government would want about important people. I overheard him talking about delivering drug money to Oro when I was locked up in the tenement and I told Jimenez about it. He said he'd pass it on and that I might end up having to come back to testify."

"Not sure how credible I'd be as a witness, though," Scott added. "I was delusional most of the time."

I want you to come back. I don't care why.

"It probably won't do Raul much good to try to make a deal," Ana said. "A federal officer died and they aren't going to let him off easy. Raul should never get out of prison."

"If there's a God, no," Scott replied, lifting his hand to the side of his face where his cheekbone had been broken by Juan's pistol. "But I wouldn't bet against it. I don't have much faith in your legal system. I've been through it."

Ana had done her best to conceal the turmoil inside as they finished talking about Raul and Oro. She'd replaced one terror with another, with fear of losing Scott to his past and his career now replacing the fear of losing him to his kidnappers.

For a few moments they sat trapped in silence until Scott broke the tension.

"We have an afternoon to ourselves," Scott said.

"Let's not waste it then. Can we walk through the Jardín?" she asked.

A short walk from the sidewalk cafe along Avenida Miguel Hidalgo took them past the ancient cathedral near the entrance to the Jardin. As they walked, Scott slipped his hand into hers.

He's leaving.

"Scottsito, can we stop for just a minute here?" she asked, turning toward the cathedral. Scott's face told her he didn't understand.

"To me, it's important," she said. "It will only be a minute."

"Of course," Scott said, as they turned into the cathedral's courtyard, her hand still in his.

As Ana led them to the second row of pews, their footsteps echoed off ancient plaster walls that had listened to the prayers of Hernán Cortés over 500 years ago, as well as those of Anarosa Mendes each day of Scott's captivity. They shared the cathedral with only a few respectfully quiet tourists standing in the rear, and an elderly man praying the rosary six rows behind them, his mumbling chant barely audible even in the overpowering silence of the massive room.

The wooden kneeler creaked under Ana's weight as she crossed herself.

Thank you for sparing this man. Whatever your purpose is with him, he'll be worthy. I know it.

Ana closed her eyes and gathered her thoughts.

I never ask for gifts...

Resting her forehead on her folded hands for a moment, Ana tried to empty her mind of everything but her faith. After a few minutes, she made the sign of the cross again and turned to Scott, who had watched her as she prayed, curious, his eyes never leaving her.

"We can go now," she said in a voice barely audible, even in the quiet of the enormous church.

After the lush, green arms of the Jardín welcomed them, they walked deep into it and found an isolated bench. Sitting quietly for a few moments, Scott leaned forward, placed his elbows on his thighs, and ran his fingers through his hair.

"I know what you're thinking," Ana said, watching him struggle with his thoughts. "You're thinking, 'How am I going to tell her'?"

"Remember when you told me not to suppose that I knew what you were thinking? You said that once," he said.

"Tell me I'm wrong then, Scottsito. Just say what's in your heart."

"I can see what's in my heart clear enough. I would stay here, in Mexico, if I could. I belong here, crazy as that sounds after what's happened. It feels like I've been here all along, like this is home."

"Perhaps it is," Ana said. "Home is where you feel you belong, the place where you feel connected. New York hasn't been kind."

Ana could almost see the thoughts racing through Scott's mind, coming at him too fast.

"But you can't stay. If that's what you have to tell me, I already know," she said, suddenly wanting to get it over with.

"I have to go back."

It sounded stiff, unfeeling, and Ana knew there had to be more. She hated doing it, pressing him after all he'd been through, but she was running out of time with him.

"There's more, isn't there?" she said, as she saw the pain. It hurt to see him this way.

"Mi Scottsito. We don't have time for this. They took the time from us."

"Ana, I have to go back. I have a life there that isn't finished yet. I didn't choose this. We needed more time."

"It's hard to fill the cup that's already full, isn't it?" Ana asked, as she brushed her forearm across her face, wiping away the damp.

He's going to tell me this is it. This is how people sound when they end things.

Instead of answering, Scott caressed her face with his hands. Their eyes met, and a long moment later he leaned forward and kissed her. As their mouths opened to each other, the fear left her and the long, wordless embrace told Ana more than anything he could have said.

He can't kiss me like this and then just leave and never come back. Not this man. I know it.

She tried to make her words gentle and understanding, worried about demanding with no right to ask anything. Frightened that she'd never see him again, she had to search for a promise, something to hold on to.

"Scottsito mío, what happens now? You're getting on an airplane and going back to Albany, and what then?"

He can't just leave. He can't. No.

"When I was in that tenement I did things to stay alive. I had to give myself a reason to live, and you were always there. You were so damned real. I would have died if you hadn't been there. But there were ghosts there, too. This is so hard to explain."

She wanted to wrap her arms around him and capture him.

"I have to finish it, Ana. I have to make sure."

"Can you, Scottsito?"

"Puedo, amor mía. Sí puedo."

Perhaps he could. It would have to do, she thought, as she disappeared into his arms.

Chapter Sixty

As the passengers moved down the narrow aisle and struggled to put their bags into the overhead compartments, Scott sank back into the soft, welcoming leather of the well-worn first class seat, rested his head against the curve of the jet's cabin, and closed his eyes.

He'd asked for the window seat, wanting to watch the country slip by. He needed to know how he'd feel as it did. He felt still connected. He was heading home, he supposed, but unsure where home was anymore. An empty Albany apartment he'd barely lived in didn't seem to qualify. Lisa's death had turned his life inside out what seemed a lifetime ago, and Albany only meant a place to live while he looked for a job and tried to rebuild his career. It held memories he no longer wanted, and little more. Mexico had its hooks into him, but apart from the hard parting from Ana, he didn't fully understand why. He couldn't shake the feeling that he'd known it so much longer than a few months.

Comfort flowed from Jerry's touch, as Scott's only anchor reached over from the adjoining seat and rested a hand on Scott's bandaged wrist. Since the awful, bloody night at the tenement they'd talked for hours, replaying everything, with Scott getting all of it out, over and over again.

Scott closed his eyes again and saw a brave woman's tear streaked face as Felicia Salinas said goodbye to him at her door, her face distorted with a grief that he knew might never end. Scott remembered the cold December night when he'd heard a knock at the door that ended a life, just as Felicia had the night Jimenez visited her. Before he'd ever met her, he'd understood Felicia and exactly how her world had changed forever. He forced the melancholy image from his mind, as he had many times in the days since Federico's death, and as he would many times in the days to come.

Deciding to use his trust fund to insure that Roncito Salinas and the children of the other Federal officers received the best education money could buy was the easiest decision he'd ever made, but it was so terribly little. How could he ever pay that debt? How?

You repay it with every day you live, with everything you do. In an instant, one life is traded for another. It's so simple and so cruel. You survive and he doesn't. You try to deserve the chance he gave you, and it's all you can do.

The Aeromexico steward interrupted, offering the first class passengers the opportunity to place orders for drinks before the flight took off.

"We have a good selection of alcoholic beverages, if you'd like," the steward added, encouraging the sale as he looked at Scott.

Scott looked up with an odd, satisfied expression the steward must have thought curious.

"Thanks, no," Scott replied, before turning toward his friend.

"Jer, I'm not sure what I'm going back to. There's more for me, but it's not there. Not in Albany."

"More?"

Jerry smiled.

"Ah, yes, the charming Señorita Mendes. La encantadora. You're having a lot of trouble with it, aren't you?" he asked.

"Yeah," Scott answered.

"You're feeling guilty?"

"Something like that."

"Not something like that," Jerry said. "It's exactly like that, isn't it? First you felt guilty because you noticed her, now you feel guilty about leaving her. You need to be kinder to yourself."

"You're tough, dad," Scott replied.

The old Scott, from Albany and the university, had answered Jerry with a smile, the quip, and the compliment. It all felt good, and familiar.

He's right. He always is.

"Look, Scotty," Jerry said. "You've lived more in the last six weeks than most of us ever will. More than I have in a lifetime that's been a hell of a lot longer than yours. You're entitled to fast forward..."

Scott thought he saw his father's love in Jerry's eyes.

"...don't be afraid to turn the page. Not now. Not after this. God knows you've earned it. It's time to let go. To let all of it go."

A wry smile crossed the Jerry's face.

"Besides, you've left something behind, haven't you?"

Their eyes met, Jerry's telling Scott that he understood.

"Then do it. Don't worry about details. I'll tend to them," Jerry said.

"Thanks, Jer."

Scott stood and walked to the front of the cabin. He turned, looked back at Jerry for a long moment, and then walked down the jet way and back into the terminal.

Author's Note

The characters and events depicted in this work are, of course, fictional. Cuernavaca, however, is real. You can walk where almost all of the Mexican scenes are set — in places like the amazing mountaintop pyramid at Tepoztlán, the beautiful botanical garden at Jardín Borda, the zócalo in the center of Cuernavaca, the ex-hacienda de Cortés or the beautifully preserved ruins at Xochicalco. I've photographed many of the places where the story is set, and you can view the locations at www.richardperhacs.com.

The description of the excavation activity at Xochicalco is entirely fictional, the site having been extensively excavated and reconstructed in the conventional way some time ago. Still, there are areas adjacent to the restored ruins that have yet to be explored, as the story suggests. Although Mexico and Cuernavaca have suffered many earthquakes, the notion that an earthquake caused the sudden collapse of a pyramidal structure at Xochicalco, trapping a treasure of artifacts, is the author's fanciful invention, for the sake of his story.

The Mexican government is devoted to the preservation of the nation's patrimony, and I do not intend to show disrespect for that fervor by casting as a villain an official of the INAH. No nation, and certainly not mine, has done more to preserve the heritage of its indigenous people than has Mexico. I ask its indulgence, again, for the sake of the story.

The inspiration for this book came during my time in Cuernavaca where I've lived all too briefly. The combination of an exotic setting and contemporary political developments in Mexico seemed perfect for a story about personal renewal, set against the backdrop of a re-awakening nation and people I admire.

Now off of the beaten path for most travelers, Cuernavaca was once the preferred destination for American ex-patriots and long term vacationers. Although replaced by San Miguel de Allende in popularity among gringos, Cuerna still has an active ex-patriot population. Blessed with a near perfect climate, and warm, welcoming people, Cuerna is both romantic and historic, and I've tried to give it a role as a character in the story. I have affection for the city, and will be delighted if my reader senses that.

I offer a word of apology to my Mexican friends who may see cynicism about Mexican politics in the political background story. Certainly, that is not my view. At this writing, the Mexican political system appears stable and the Mexican republic vigorous, although suffering from a legacy of corruption. The spirit of representative democratic government is alive in Mexico, as anyone who has lived there during a political season can attest. Still, in some aspects of Mexico's political culture — most notably its three party division of power, which virtually guarantees a minority government — I see real risk of instability if Mexicans allow themselves to be distracted from the orderly, moderate, constitutional government of recent years. The political backdrop of this work simply suggests that the long suffering Mexican people need to be vigilant in the preservation of what they've waited so long to achieve.

Mexico is a rich and beautiful land, with enormous potential. Tragically, the American media has unfairly and inaccurately portrayed it as a lawless nation. I've found it

to be home to patriots like Rico, and to proud, hard-
working people, and not at all as my countrymen often
imagine it to be.

¡Viva la patria!

Richard Perhacs
Erie, Pennsylvania

ACKNOWLEDGEMENTS

Too many people helped with this work to mention them all by name. To everyone who encouraged and showed interest, I am so thankful.

First things are important. Here's mine.

Without the encouragement of my friend, mentor and relentless critic, Lenore Skomal, this book might never have been completed. Our long conversations over coffee, and late night exchanges of emails kept me focused and motivated. Lenore is accomplished in so many ways, and needs no praise from me. Each time I touch the keyboard I feel the burden of the confidence she's shown in me. Most importantly, she's convinced me that it gets better from here, and that means everything.

Living with someone with a demanding career who's also trying to write a novel can't be easy. Some type of award surely is due to my wife Grace, and sons Doug and Sean for putting up with a man who practices law all day, then closets himself in his study all night. No writer, or lawyer, ever had a more supportive family.

To Professor Susan Escobar, my friend in San Antonio, I owe such thanks for her support of my project. Her encouragement, before she ever read a word, meant so much. Muchísimas gracias, Sonrisa.

Licenciada y Abogado Birgid Mueller, my Mexican legal resource, provided valued insight into both Cuernavaca and the Mexican legal system, and, most importantly, became a treasured friend.

Ex-patriot Jeannie Anderson and her husband,

Rodolfo Tripp, welcomed me into both their home and the Encuentros language school in Cuerna. When they learned that I was writing a story about their city, they enthusiastically helped in any way they could.

My two adoptive Mexican families made me feel a part of Cuerna and its people. Marusa and Mario Quiñones, and Maria Henriquez and Machis Roberto Ramirez, graciously opened their homes to me during my many stays in Cuerna both as a language student and during my research as the book was written.

My Spanish teacher and friend, Isabel Flores, worked against great obstacles I placed in her path to teach me the beautiful, romantic, melodic language of her country. With so much pride, she shared with me her beloved Morelito. I've never met anyone who loves the place where she lives as much as Isa. What little I know of her language is the result of her endless patience and enthusiasm, and not any aptitude on my part. Te debo tan mucho, Isita mía. Mil gracias, amiguita, por tu apoyo, pero, especialmente por tu amistad.

A story has no value if it's never read. For my story's first readers, Karen Jez, Holly Myers, Susan Escobar, Steve Huefner, Rose Dwyer Fielding, Shannon Callahan and Craig Hartle, I'm so grateful for their gifts of time and insight. They've helped more than they know.

Last things are important, too, and I offer a final word of thanks to a teacher from a lifetime ago, who, in four intense months, taught my first lessons. Ron Tranquilla's only motivation was that I had asked for his help. The years have increased my debt monumentally. I knew that someday I would try to write something worthy, and he helped me to learn how. I hope I've had at least a measure of success. I know he would respect the effort. I doubt he remembers me, or that he'll ever read this, but I remember him.

RP

About the Author

Richard Perhacs is a native of Pittsburgh, Pennsylvania. He received an undergraduate degree in political science from Saint Vincent College, where he was educated by a Benedictine monastic community. He earned a law degree with honors from the Duquesne University School of Law, where he edited the law review. Although he'd much rather travel in Latin America, or write books, he holds down a day job practicing at a large law firm in Erie, Pennsylvania.

Rick has led an interesting and rewarding life, and intends to continue it at full throttle. A former commercial pilot, he's flown a world class aerobatic plane through maneuvers that put amusement park thrill rides to shame, coached a hockey team to a New York championship, tried cases before juries, climbed a real mountain, and crashed a Presidential State of the Union address without a ticket or a security clearance. For fun, he rides a Harley.

A published author of professional works, *Cuernavaca* is Rick's debut work of fiction. He's at work on his second novel.

Rick's devoted much of his free time during the past decade to traveling in the interior of Mexico. He's been a frequent visitor to Cuernavaca, Morelos, where he studied Spanish while living in the homes of middle class Mexican families. Rick feels a special connection with the city.

After retirement from the full time practice of law, in addition to writing, he plans to relocate to Mexico as a part-year resident and to immerse himself further in the language and culture. Back home, he devotes himself to volunteer work with the Latino immigrant community.

He lives with his wife Grace in Millcreek Township, Pennsylvania. They have two adult sons, one a college student and the other proudly defending freedom in the United States Army.

Comments, suggestions and inquiries are welcome, and can be submitted through the contact page of his website, **www.RichardPerhacs.com**. He'll respond to all of them.

Made in the USA
Middletown, DE
12 September 2015